Rob Parker is a married father of three, who lives in a village near Manchester, UK. The author of the Ben Bracken books *A Wanted Man, Morte Point, The Penny Black* and *Till Morning is Nigh,* and the standalone post-Brexit country-noir *Crook's Hollow,* he enjoys a rural life on an old pig farm (now minus pigs), writing horrible things between school runs.

He writes full time, as well as organising and attending various author events across the UK - while boxing regularly for charity. Passionate about inspiring a love of the written word in young people, Robert spends a lot of time in schools across the North West, encouraging literacy, story-telling, creative-writing and how good old fashioned hard work tends to help good things happen.

Also by Rob Parker

Ben Bracken Book Four

Till Morning is Nigh

Rob Parker

LUME BOOKS

LUME BOOKS

First published in 2019 by Lume Books
85-87 Borough High Street,
London, SE1 1NH

ISBN 978-1-83901-186-3

www.lumebooks.co.uk

For all readers everywhere.

And Becky, always.

'Be not afraid of sudden fear.'
Book of Proverbs, 3:25

'Any fool can make a baby,
But it takes a man to raise a child.'
Chris Young

Prologue

With all that gel bleeding off his skull, it's hard to keep his head under the surface - but I manage it. He's kicking, but the spirit has gone from the thrusts. They're now more like the hopeless spasms of the goldfish sitting down the toilet, waiting for the big flush.

I tilt his head so his ear clears the water, steam immediately licking off the lobe into the cold night air, and whisper:

'I want you to hear this, and I want you to know it's the last thing you'll ever hear. For all the awful things you have done with your life, I got you, you bastard. You understand me? I beat you. You took everything from me, like you did so many people, and I came back and *beat* you.'

He stills, and within seconds his body goes concrete-heavy. The weight of my words and his finality hits me hard.

It's over.

I've won.

It's done.

The adrenaline floods out of me so fiercely I can feel its vacuum. My veins, lungs, legs, body, all feel empty. I let his body go for no reason other than I seem not to be holding onto it any more. A reworked nursery rhyme starts looping in my head: *There's a hole in my body dear Liza, dear Liza, there's a hole in my body, dear Liza, a hole...*

My control seems to loosen and I can feel myself tilt back. The water is freezing, but somehow... it's OK. I look up, and float.

I keep drifting, think of her, and close my eyes.

Chapter One

I love Rocky, but he talks a lot of shit. I get the message. It's a positive one. It's not about how many times you get hit, but how many times you can keep getting up from it to make progress. Grand. But if it keeps happening, there's even less left to put you back together with. Every time chips more pieces off. You ain't the same as the time before, or the time before that. The jigsaw loses more pieces with every go around. Hence why Rocky is clearly talking out of his battered arse.

I wish someone would turn that fan off. I'm absolutely freezing, and I have enough nightmares about the cold already. It seeps under my skin at the best of times, without those bloody blades forcing iced air into my eyeballs every time I open them.

'A visitor for you,' a voice says. Another. Ever since I woke up and realised I was in some hospital, and that there was a plain clothes guard on the door full time without exception, I've been graced with a number of visitors, each one trying something new to get the story out of me. About how I got in this state, and who I am.

They come in here armed with certain facts, fragments which they think can build up the bigger picture and try to break me down with the weight of what they think they have on me.

But I know, in truth, they have near enough zero on me. Well, nothing remotely close to the truth.

'I wasn't sure I'd ever see you again,' says a different voice, but its gravity has me hooked. I look to the door, and the owner of the voice is miraculously, against all possible expectations, *there*.

'The feeling is more than mutual,' I say, finding myself struggling not to tag *sir* on the end. The man walking into my drab, too-cold hospital room demands authority, and he has done since the moment I met him. It's not an awe thing - it's a hangover from an earlier period of my life. He too was a man of service, although much higher up than me. He was never my actual superior, although I do find it hard not to act as if he was and still is.

'You have a habit of appearing and disappearing at the most surprising of moments,' he says, releasing the top jacket button of his navy three-piece suit and resting his hands on the footboard of the bed, either side of the charts. He looks just as I remember. Tall, gracefully aged at about seventy, steel eyes fixed in a gaze that implores you to *play it straight with me son.* William Grosvenor. Minister Without Portfolio.

'And every time I do either of those things, I end up regretting it...'

'I don't doubt that. They tell me you were in ribbons when you arrived here.'

'I haven't seen under the bandages yet but it feels that way.'

Grosvenor smiles. He looks at me as if there is more to say, and pokes his head out the door to address the guard. 'Can you grab us some coffees from downstairs, my friend? With one for yourself. White, no sugar's fine for us. An american, I think?' he says, passing the man a pound note.

'An americano?' the guard says.

'That'll probably be it.'

The guard, out of my eyesight, scoots off, before Grosvenor moves with poise to the end of the bed.

'I'll say this once, and once alone. Ben Bracken is dead. End of story. Now, near to where they pulled you out of the river, you stashed a bag of tricks - which contained a number of documents belonging to a Tom West, bearing your picture. So, from here on that's who you are.'

I'm listening, but I'm not sure it's going in. 'Whatever it is you found, I was using it to leave the country, William. I am done. I'm out, like I said.'

'We both know where you are supposed to be,' he says, cocking an eyebrow. I look to the window, at the frosty sunlight. It's late November, I think, and looks every bit of it.

'Yes. And I've accepted that I'm going back there.'

'HMP Manchester isn't how you left it. I don't know how you got out and I don't care, but the circumstances of your exit are long erased. As far as I'm concerned, Tom West was never there. Ben Bracken, the escaped convict, died on the River Bure after an incident at a local pub.'

I'm forced into a corner. 'Yes.'

'Well, from what I know of Tom West, he could be a useful man.'

'I'm out, William. End of story. If you are going to persist with this line, please let me go. You won't regret it. You'll never here from me again.'

'You are a skilled ex-soldier, with a, let's say, vivid moral compass. You've proven yourself adept in an anti-crime capacity, particularly of the organised variety. I know a place you can be of considerable assistance.'

I sigh. I don't want this. I want to leave, go where it's sunny, and hide away from it all. Maybe do some fishing. Maybe read the key texts from that English Literature degree I started before an elongated stint in the army stopped me from finishing. I don't want to owe anything to anybody anymore. 'I trust no authority in this country. Police, government, they've proven themselves to be as bad as each other. I'm not interested in assisting either.'

'Luckily for you, that's not what I'm suggesting,' Grosvenor says. 'Tom West is out of a job, and needs the work. The job opportunity I'm suggesting offers a competitive salary and a chance to completely start again - should you choose it. You have the opportunity of a complete restart, and it will be one that comes with the potential to do good. Men like us don't forget that. You've shown yourself to be capable of good, now this is a chance to do it the *right* way. My advice would be to consider it.'

'There was money in that bag. Enough for me to-'

Grosvenor shuts me down so I don't waste my breath. 'That was Ben Bracken's. And he's dead.'

The door opens again, and the officer enters with a couple of coffees and some change. Grosvenor thanks him, and puts one of the cups on my tray table. He tips his coffee to me. 'Say the word, and I make the arrangements,' he says, before leaving, as does the guard.

I feel paralysed. A chance to live? A job? But how long before my past comes knocking? But if Ben Bracken is dead, is that past dead too?

I reach for my coffee, feel a point prick my finger as I grip the cup. Poked between the paper sleeve and the styrofoam is a business card, with a solitary number on it. No name. No other identifier.

What option do I have but to call it?

Chapter Two

Babies. I mean… *babies*.

It's early days. This little blob of legs, arms and a gob is only two weeks old, but I'm big enough to admit I had no idea it was going to be like this. I mean this thing in my arms is helpless - like 'if I forgot about it for just a little while it'd be dead' helpless. That kind of thing is demanding and a bit overwhelming.

However, the bond I feel is granite. It's mine, this little one. I've waited all my life, and against the odds, I've got it. I'm a dad. And it means something.

I've got a little cheat going, that only I seem to be able to pull off. He gets hot especially when he sleeps. But he can't stand the dark, or the silence - neither helps him drift. So I added all those together, and now in the middle of the night when he won't sleep, I rock him in my arms by the open door of the fridge, the soft glow soothing him, the white noise hum of the light inside drowsing him. I sway, imitating a thousand mothers I've seen before, tapping into an innate paternity I always felt was there, but is now fully realised and larger than life.

I'm a father.

'The smell of that minging old lettuce not putting you boys off?' I turn to the source of the voice, knowing just who it is, and I feel the warmth swell in me already. It's love, that is. 'Or is this all a ploy to sneak chocolates off the tree again?'

'You're not supposed to be up,' I say. 'You need your rest, and you've got, you know, the stitches and all that. Plus, this is our time.' I nod at Jam Jr, who's little eyelids are closed serenely. Jam, as in the middle bit of Benjamin, as in my name. I'm holding Ben Bracken Jr.

'I can't really sleep without you both,' says Carolyn, crossing the small kitchen towards us. She wears a purple nighty which features Snoopy dead centre with a frazzled expression, a hundred little Woodstocks fluttering around his head. Underneath is only a slight trace of the bump that was so impressive just a short fortnight ago. Her hair is tousled Bournville, her sleepy features effortless in their unhurried fineness. She'll always be beautiful to me, how could she not? She gave me all this I hold, and on top of that, she's five foot seven and forty years old of everything I've ever wanted.

She comes to me, her pupils contracting a little as the fridge light hits her, and I kiss her on the cheek. 'You're under orders, ma'am,' I say.

'How is he?' she asks.

'He's mega. Look at him.'

She does. He's got blond tufts on either side of his head, and a little red mark on his fontanelle where he was pulled out from we all know where. His nose is incredible, like a perfect doll mould. He's got full eyelashes, now meshed together. And his cheeks carry echoes of my grandfather's jowls - a patriarch he'll never meet. His eyes are bluer than pools in a slate quarry. Damn right he's mega.

'I'll let you have that.' She strokes his thumb, wanting to touch him, but not wanting to wake him.

'You hear anything from the other two?' I ask. Carolyn has two kids from her former marriage, a boy and a girl, ages 8 and 7 respectively, asleep upstairs.

'Not a sound,' she says.

'That's good.' I'm slightly surprised. Six months of living here with Carolyn and her kids has been a little up and down, mainly because I've never lived with kids, and I'm not their dad. Their dad is dead, and to make matters worse, it was me that killed him. I remember the way his pupils also contracted when he realised the trigger had been pulled - either it was that, or his heart thumping its last meaningful pump.

'Come on, soldier,' she says. 'Let's go to bed.' It's talk like that that got us in this predicament, and I find myself following. I kick the fridge shut with my ankle, as my phone buzzes in my shorts pocket.

Carolyn and I look at each other, and before we can wonder if we misheard, it buzzes again, and this time, as I look down to the source of the sound, I can see the screen glow straight through the cotton of my pocket.

'I've got him,' she says, taking my son in her arms. 'Don't be long.'

'Ma'am,' I say.

They leave the kitchen, and once alone, I check the damn phone.

First message: NEED YOU IN. J.

Second message, a full eight seconds later. I KNOW YOU'RE AWAKE. YOU'VE GOT HALF AN HOUR BEFORE I TELL THEM YOU'RE A LIABILITY.

Best get moving. I know, as unofficial as my new role is, I'm still on probation, especially with the man in charge, Jeremiah. I'm still trying to get him to trust me again, so I head for the shower. A twenty-minute drive, nine minutes and counting to get out of the house and ready. I text a reply.

THAT'S A BIT LEISURELY BY YOUR STANDARDS, BUT I'LL BE THERE.

Chapter Three

Ben Bracken, lawman.

Sorry, no - Tom West, lawman.

Whoever the hell I am, this was not a career trajectory I was expecting. And yet, here I am, in a National Crime Agency meeting room at five in the morning.

When I started working here, it was made very clear that my role is advisory, not to get in any way dirty and definitely not to get involved - so to be called in like this? Consider my interest piqued.

The atmosphere in the small space is grave and tight. There's two on one side of a small interview table, and two on the other, one of whom is me. Next to me is our boss, who never changes. Wild dark hair, rumpled clothes, stubble and dark framed glasses. A wheelchair user for a decade, the only difference today is that his eyes, while usually bright with studious mischief, are this morning clouded with sadness. Jeremiah Salix. Our relationship is only a couple of years old, but we've crammed a lot into that time, and now I'm an advisory bystander on his team in the NCA Organised Crime Command, based in an unassuming office complex west of Manchester, in Birchwood. It's a ten-minute drive from Carolyn's house, so in a strange quirk of fortune, this *works*.

Our house, I keep reminding myself.

I've been on the periphery since I started working here, so much so that calling it work is very generous. But I'm earning a wage, and I chip in with the odd bit of info and ideas, all of which suits me perfectly. So, I'm flummoxed as to why I've been called into this urgent meeting, especially with the two opposite me, who are at the pointed end of the department hierarchy. In army parlance, I'm in with the brass here.

Blake is speaking, who's about thirty years of age, with dark mascara and brown hair held up by a genuine, honest-to-god office bulldog clip, wearing jeans, a white shirt and dark jacket. She has a pointed chin, a regal nose and eyes that tell of focus that takes the shape of empathy. Of the two units under Jeremiah's command, she is the head of one. She looks at us dead on in turn.

'I have a crime scene to get to ASAP, so I'm going to get right to the point,' she says, taking out a solitary sheet from a blue file resting lone on the table top. 'Quick catch up. For a couple of years, Manchester has been a landscape in flux, after one of the major players fell off the map.'

Ah.

'Obviously,' Blake continues, 'the sudden absence of the Berg left a gaping city-wide hole in the criminal underground, and the streets were largely cleaner for a time. The city centre is a patchwork of districts laid out as turfs. You step on someone else's turf, there's recompense. It could be a slap on the wrist, it could be a sawn-off tickling your tonsils.

'Now all these turfs, apart from one, were owned and operated by the Berg, give or take minor ups and downs throughout history. That one anomaly was operated by a group out near Spinningfields, who also disappeared around the same time as the Berg did.'

I know all the people and players she is talking about, because essentially, it was me who put them all out of business - and that's why Jeremiah has called me in here.

Catterall, a tall, blonde, angular man in blue jeans, a red t-shirt with a trendy band logo on it I've obviously never heard of, and a brown leather jacket that looks stomach-wateringly expensive, sits opposite her. He looks preened, sharp, and that kind of good-looking that must have ghosted hundreds on Tinder.

'I'm familiar with the lay of the land, Blake,' he says. I'd already pegged him for a bit of a dick, so his condescension comes as no surprise.

She replies without missing a beat. 'I'm offering some context for West.'

In a common feature throughout my short-ish tenure with them, I forget once again that West is me.

'The city was unoccupied in any real sense for the past year. The odd party has traveling-circused and pitched up and sold a bit, following the usual tropes of the demand and supply flow through. In this case, when the source went, the users didn't go with it. We viewed it as a perfect time to try to stamp out drugs in the city as thoroughly as we could, and tried to wipe out the last of it - as did the local police force and relevant authorities.'

I've never been at the grown-ups table in my time here yet, so this is fascinating.

'So, in a coordinated and one-of-a-kind undercover programme, called Operation Gaslamp, arranged in conjunction with the Greater Manchester Police, we installed a wave of fake addicts across the city, with a remit to buy in an environment that has short supply, seeing who comes out of the woodwork to offer solutions to the growing demand. This was twinned by a sharing of intel provided by existing informants, in an attempt to establish as full a picture of the narcotics networks of the city as we've ever had. This level of cooperation with GMP has never been attempted nor achieved before, so this has been a big deal for both parties.

'There have been a number of arrests made, but it's all been a bit small-time so far. On top of that, bad quality products seem to be the only thing on offer, and nobody but the truly desperate is biting. This has all changed however, thanks to a tip that has been corroborated by both our undercover junkies and regular on-the-street informants. There is a new source in Manchester, offering a real supply of quality product. In the last two weeks alone, we have seen a huge increase in sales but there's been a big problem. They won't sell to our undercovers. They know who they are. No collars, and no chance of tracking down the source. They stay well clear of us, it's like the dealers can smell us. And our worst nightmare has become a grim reality - one of our under covers has been found dead just north of the river. And it's far from pretty. That's where I'm headed after this with Catterall.'

Catterall nods, and his chest puffs up. God, he enjoys himself, this bloke.

'Both sub teams are on this?' I ask. I'd been doing some data handling as part of Catterall's team, a spare pair of eyes used for rooting through some phone data, looking for keywords pertaining to a cyber-crime investigation. Not really my area of expertise, but it was simple enough. If both sub teams were on this, that meant we were likely on to this as well.

'Both teams. Everything's dropped. We're all on this now.'

Blake presses on, leaning her knuckles on the table top - one of which cracks audibly. 'My assessment of the situation would be as follows. The Berg is gone, and there's a big hole left behind. Someone is coming to the city with power and reach, and they are taking it for their own. This could coincide with the return of a man who has history with this city, a man who used to operate here, although we could never prove it. Our airport alert systems caught him returning to the country, and facial recognition caught him. He must have used a fake passport, but since then he's gone to ground. Can't get eyes on him at all.'

She takes that sheet from the blue case file and spins it around so we can see what is on it. It's a photograph, and the image blows me away. I know who that is. He ran an organisation called the River that caused the Berg a literal boatload of problems, and they used me and a guy called Jack Brooker to run him out of town. I quickly make the horrible realization that, if he is behind it, he's not come to take over anything - logically, he's come to take back what he believes is rightfully his.

'This,' says Blake, 'is Sparkles Chu.'

I look at Jeremiah, who nods. He knows my past, and he wants me to share some of it. I have useful definitive, useful intel and to suddenly have a purpose again is invigorating.

'I've got the inside track on this guy,' I say. 'I know him.' *Know* is a loose word, but you learn a lot about a person in that moment you have them at the dangerous end of a pistol.

'Aha, so now we know why you're here,' says Catterall. I would look at him with disdain, but shits like him are ten-a-penny and I read you use more muscles when you frown.

'What's your area of expertise?' asks Blake. 'Your *real* area of expertise?'

I look at Jeremiah, who once again nods. This is dangerous. Details could give away my identity, and even though I'm now in-house and onside, I'm still not supposed to be here.

Blake almost smiles - almost. 'Come on, he's hardly the greatest candidate for data entry, is he?'

I keep my mouth shut, before Jeremiah intervenes.

'The people in this room know discretion, and if they didn't they do now. You share what you're about to hear, and you all go back to pushing pencils.'

I go for it. 'My area was primarily military, but my training incorporated counter-terrorism, demolition, combat - both hand to hand and weaponised - firearms, improvisation tactics, survivalism… and my recent experience has been mostly with organised crime.'

Jeremiah nods with appreciation, but Catterall and Blake look at me with two different expressions of surprise.

'I just thought you were an intern,' says Catterall. 'Maybe someone in one of those rehabilitation programmes when you've been inside.'

Blake glances a question at Jeremiah, who nods to her. However strange my relationship with him has been, I admire the hell out of him. He's a righteous sort who'll do anything for a result, including colouring outside the lines. If he knows there's a chance a case can be brought to a more satisfactory conclusion by embracing the grey areas, he's been known to grab the white and black crayons and go for it.

'And how do you know Chu?' asks Blake. Ever the investigator, Blake's interest is snared, etched unintentionally in the way her mouth hangs open a fraction after she's finished speaking.

'And it stays in this room,' says Jeremiah. The other faces look at me imploringly.

'The plot thickens,' says Catterall, barely disguising his contempt that he just might not be the alpha male in the room.

'I met Sparkles for the first time just before he disappeared - so about two years ago,' I say, turning slightly to her. 'He was running an operation out of a Chinese junk that had a restaurant front, which was moored on the Irwell in Spinningfields. His operation had been deemed big enough to warrant concern by the Berg, and the Berg was behind him being taken out. I was there at the finale - that's how I know.'

'And from that, you got a picture of what Chu's like?' Blake asks.

'I'd say I've got a good idea.'

'And how does what you've heard today fit with your assessment of him?'

'Sparkles' involvement here obviously has me interested, but the manner of what's happened has my attention even more. For a start, all I witnessed at the restaurant was a workshop for arms production - nothing to do with narcotics. So to see that there has been a groundswell of Class A sales coinciding with his return confuses me. Then there's the other thing. Sparkles told me, in no uncertain terms, that he is no killer and that is not how he operates. His hired help was all armed to the teeth, which stands somewhat to the contrary of that, but I feel that they were there for defence and protection. They were no executioners.'

'So this doesn't feel right to you?'

'No.'

Catterall snorts. 'How could you possibly tell? Did all your fancy training cover criminology? Because guess what my mate, *ours* did.'

'Have you ever looked into another bloke's eyes when you're deciding if you're going to kill him?' It's the first time I've challenged him. Friction cracks the air in the room. Catterall gives me the smuggest smile he can, and spreads his palms as if to say the floor is yours.

'I looked into a murder, and I thought it was him. I was wrong, and he emerged true to his claims. So this whole thing, despite the coincidence of his return, feels off. To suddenly be dealing in Class As, and murder someone in the fashion that's been suggested, would seem a major departure from his… What do you call someone's usual way of doing things? You lot have got a fancy name for it, haven't you?'

'His modus operendi - his MO,' Blake replies.

'That's the one. Now, he may have seen a gap in the market and ramped things up accordingly, acknowledging that to be the big fish you have to act like a big fish, but I don't know. Anyway, that's what I know.'

'Let's see if you're right. He needs to come to the crime scene.' She's pointing at me, but looking at Jeremiah.

'Woah, woah, hang on,' spurts Catterall.

'He needs to be there,' she reaffirms.

All turn to Jeremiah. He has final say.

'Give me a couple of minutes with West.'

Catterall gives an OTT eye roll, but finds it within his ego to rise. Blake has already gone by the time he gets out.

'Finally, something,' I say.

'The ID hasn't been confirmed yet, but if the whispers through the ranks are to be believed, this was one very good copper and a serious asset – this is no celebration.' He slumps forward, steeples his fingers, and strangely puts his lips to his knuckles.

'I mean no disrespect. I just haven't had much to do around here since I arrived.'

'This is why you were brought here - to offer your particular line of local expertise where possible. I'd say this is one of those times, wouldn't you?'

I move swiftly away. 'You knew the guy?'

'Yep. All the undercovers were handpicked from around the country by us here at the NCA - by Blake especially, with my say-so on top - and sent through to work with GMP. So personally I *do* feel a little bit like I've sent this man to his death.'

'I'm sure he knew what he was getting himself in for.'

'Spoken like a true soldier.'

'What do you need me for?'

'If I let you go, as Blake has asked, this'll be your first time in the field, won't it? Representing the NCA I mean.'

'Yes.'

He looks over his fingertips at me. 'I don't need to remind you of your obligations, do I? Your responsibilities?'

Being a man whose sense of duty has always been somewhat fully formed, I find it quite hard not to bristle. 'You don't.'

'You're merely an advisor to the NCA. Got it?'

'Got it.'

'When you get to the scene, you follow Blake's lead. She's your superior on this.'

'Not Catterall?'

'Not Catterall. I'm not sure you've noticed it, but you respond much better to female authority. I don't want any manhood measuring at such a sensitive scenario.'

I nod, chastened, but can begrudgingly see what he's saying. History says if I don't get on with you, I can be a bit of a git.

'You'll be there at the discretion of Greater Manchester Police, and it's taken a lot of cajoling to get the wheels as greased as they are. If they say it's OK, then you're in. Usually we get a report a week or so later, and we base our lines of enquiry on that, so to have direct crime scene access in this instance is a huge step forward in terms of our collaboration. So please don't step on any toes.'

'Consider any and all toes free from being stepped on.'

'OK, go to it. You and me, we'll have a little chat when you get back.'

I nod, and get up to leave, buzzing about getting to actually do something outside of the confines of the office, but Jeremiah's voice stops me.

'Nobody here except for me knows what you're really like. Knows what really brought you here. Please don't do anything that might make them ask questions.'

I mock salute. 'Aye, sir. And consider my manhood out of the picture when it comes to the aforementioned measuring.'

Chapter Four

We're in an NCA pool mini-van, and I'm in the passenger seat up front. Blake drives, her eyes never wavering from the grey streets flushing by in front of her. The high-rise towers of Salford Precinct stand bold against the heavens, somehow aged even more by the frosted grey sky. Salford had been needing some tender love and care back when I was a student in Manchester, and I can see that the area still suffers from the regeneration cold shoulder. All that investment in the city centre, the relocation of some of the country's most prosperous companies to the city's guts, yet here just a mile or two down the road, the rough touch of neglect is all too apparent. Even the occasional cheery glow of fairy lights beyond tired window panes doesn't help. It looks freezing, a suburban tundra of the forgotten.

'We will be there shortly, and the deceased is still in situ. How are you with that?' Blake asks, while stripping three slices of chewing gum from their wrappers into her lap. I could give a long, detailed answer, but opt for the simplicity of brevity.

'Shouldn't be a problem,' I say.

'Well, good,' she says, although, judging from the frequent side-eye mirror glances, I can tell she wants to ask more. The quick rundown of the shinier bits of my background back at HQ seems to have given the appetite for the wider story. She changes lane very carefully, into the slower outside lane on the East Lancs dual carriageway. 'What else can you tell me about Chu, from your experience?'

'I found him to be a straight shooter, with a case of genuine, honest-to-heritage honour. He was involved in some shady stuff, yeah, but I got the impression it was more out of necessity than anything else. He seemed to have a good relationship with the people who worked for him, and it looked to be reciprocated. Which is just another reason why the straight-up murder of an undercover policeman doesn't sit right with me.'

Catterall pipes up from the back seat. 'There he is, the expert on criminal psychology…' I'd almost forgotten he was there, if it weren't for the incessant clicking on his smart phone. 'They give you lunch time lessons on that back on Bastion?'

Mental reminder - don't measure manhood with this guy.

'Nope, but they do give you lessons on how to twat up pretty boy dickheads who've had their teeth whitened passed the point of nuclear, that any good?' Alright, we can measure a bit.

Catterall laughs. 'Point I'm trying to make is that this is our realm, our work. Our turf. Leave the case speculations to the professionals.'

I catch Blake rolling her eyes. 'This the standard spiel?' I ask her.

'Give or take. We've not had anyone give it back before.'

'Nice to be part of history.'

Suddenly, the buildings get bigger, the car gets slower, and we're in the city. Manchester.

After being waved through the roadblock by a couple of uniforms in high-vis winter jackets, the mini-van parks up outside a small office building cut tight into the shadow of a rail bridge arc. The street is full of police cars, both marked and unmarked, and the glass front of the building is shrouded by a white tent. The traffic is locked at both ends of the street, and a steady abundance of footprints leads through the soft frost from the parked vehicles into the office entrance, while the roiling sky above looms just as moody and portentous as the faces of the officers marshalling the scene.

It strikes me immediately as a bit over the top for the solitary murder, but then again, what do I know about this sort of thing aside from what I have seen on the silver screen? I also mustn't forget that this is not just any murder, not just any junkie who wound up paying for his life choices in the harshest of terms - this was a policeman, an undercover doing his bit for the city. When I tramped these streets, my goal was exactly the same. Shit prevention. How our fates and journeys have forked in the road of life, and churned us out in different jumbles.

We pass through the doorway, having given our names to the two guarding officers as Blake and West from the NCA. I have a basic badge which I use to get in and out of the NCA office building, and I flash it, but they barely look at it and defer to Blake's authority. We are instructed to put paper socks on our shoes from a box just by the door. On looking, the entrance opens into the higher of the two floors in the office let, and we stand at the start of a mezzanine platform, at the far end of which is an unmanned reception desk, overlooking the floor below. High, tinted, floor to ceiling windows line the upstairs area, sending light down onto the lower space. As we cross the mezzanine, I glance down, and see that the floor below is empty of workstations and the machines of modern business, but far from sparse. My breath catches in the bear trap of my throat.

Lying against the once-bare whitewashed walls, sits a man framed by crimson. He is slumped, but still somehow upright, his hands and ankles bound by thin plastic cable ties. A rude arterial spray arrows across the wall diagonally up from his left shoulder, as far as eight feet or so, and fans gradually lower down the wall, painting behind him one single butterfly wing of deep red, composed in Jackson Pollock splatter.

We take the stairs down to the grim scene. If I hadn't seen the things I have seen, this might trouble me. There is indeed more than a few things that are extremely horrible about the way that the man has been quite clearly executed, but too many times I have witnessed human life reduced to nothing but tissue and pulp, the romance of the miracle of life lain exposed for what it really is. Each time I have seen someone split asunder, their contents revealed, what comes out of the person is always the same as the last. Blood and organs arranged artfully on bone. No myth, no mysticism. We are made of soft material that splits and spills, nothing more.

As we arrive on the lower floor, I see that bright crime scene lights have been erected just below the hanging platform above, and waiting around them is a number of people, watching a photographer blink his camera flash through every possible angle of the grotesquery by the wall. It could be a grisly art installation - life imitating art in the most subhuman of ways - and the sombreness of the atmosphere bolsters the illusion.

'Follow me,' says Blake, as she strides to the group assembled at the feet of the cadaver. I do as she says, as a tall black man in a navy suit notices us. He steps away from the throng, and extends a hand to Blake, his eyes deep, earnest and spelling compassion. 'Thanks so much for the call,' Blake says to him, before gesturing to me. 'This is West, he's acting in an advisory role for the NCA. West, this is DCI Okpara.'

I shake Okpara's hand, and he gives me a cursory glance. His heart is clearly elsewhere, and he seems troubled very close to the surface. Blake fills me in. 'Okpara is in charge of the GMP side of Operation Gaslamp,' she says, before turning to Okpara. 'Who's leading the murder investigation?'

'DCI Mitchum,' he replies. 'Murder and narcotics are two separate entities although we all know the truth.' His voice is a deep reservoir with an obvious African inflection, and his manner of speaking is precise, efficient and composed - yet this has clearly got to him. I can tell from his posture more than anything.

'And the ID of the deceased?' she responds breathlessly, barely ready to look over to the horrible scene to our right.

'It hasn't been officially confirmed, but we all know the guy well - did know him well. DC Mark Kyle. A young lad, jovial guy, bought good vibes to the nick since joining us. Everyone here is very cut up. Fiancée and a child left behind.' Okpara turns to the brightly lit wall, as if inviting us to do the same.

The look in Kyle's eyes is one I have seen many times before. I don't dwell on it, especially when I note that when Okpara said he was young, he wasn't kidding. Kyle must only be in his early twenties, still showing the odd pocks of teenage acne in the corners of his forehead. This must be his first year on the force, surely. Brave lad, to put his hand up to go undercover. He obviously had a bit about him. So much promise, all cut so damningly short.

Cut is also an appropriate word to describe what has happened to him. It looks like somebody has tried to give him a second mouth in his neck with a very sharp implement, and the depth of the wound has been given morbid display by the way his body has slumped since death, gaping the wound apart as his head has sunk lower to his side. Blood has exited in a wide powerful arc up the wall, each spray a touch lower as the pressure has reduced, until it eventually pooled in his lap, giving the impression he spilled tomato soup all over himself. His clothes are of the downtrodden, or an approximation thereof - beat up combats and scuffed Reeboks, below a faded parka, the lined fur of its hood moth-eaten and sparse. His hands and feet are bound with thick, industrial-looking cable ties, so much so that the skin around the wrists is taught and bloody. His eyes are still wide with shock, as if he's just learned a truth, the reality of which wasn't what he thought or hoped. Like he appeared at the gates of Heaven, and God revealed he was not benevolent after all.

There is indeed a frightening hopelessness, panic and despair about what is left of Kyle.

'Cause of death, if other than the glaringly obvious?' asks Blake, her hands finding her hips. The photographer is now on his hands and knees, taking extreme close-ups of the wrist binds.

'Coroner's preliminary is exactly as suggested,' Okpara replies. 'Throat was slashed open, he was left to bleed out. The height of the... pattern suggests he was certainly alive at the time of the injury.'

'Time of death?'

'Between twelve and eighteen hours, at an early approximation. Post-mortem will confirm it.'

'And the poor bastard who found the body?'

'Every Monday morning the landlord comes and gives it a once over in case there are any prospective tenants or buyers requiring viewings. It's just lucky it happened last night or he'd have been here all week like this.'

'Any significance to the location that you know of?'

'None. It's been empty for four years. It was once a prime piece of commercial real estate, but its position north of the river and Spinningfields has left it fairly unfashionable, and that, twinned with the customary economic frailties of the era in which we seem to be stuck in, have seen no tenants for some time. No CCTV nor signs of forced entry.'

'The landlord has been checked out?'

'At the station giving a statement as we speak. But we already know he has a watertight alibi.'

'Prints?' she says.

'Too many at this stage to wade through. It seems this place has had quite a few viewings since its last tenants. It will take ages to work through.'

'It looks like a performance,' I say, fixated on the people watching. 'It looks like the final scene of a stage play, under the lights like this.'

Okpara looks blankly at me, then swings a curious gaze to Blake, who attempts some kind of explanation.

'West has experience of both Mancunian organised crime and of our principal person of interest,' she says.

'Chu?' Okpara asks.

'Yeah. What do you mean, West?'

'It looks like a stage, the way he is positioned there, facing outwards at the space beyond,' I say. 'And the spray, the blood. It's very striking. Almost too striking. You can kill someone in many different ways but this seems almost too deliberately showy.'

Okpara turns to look at the scene.

'I think this was a demonstration,' I say. 'It was a show. There must have been more people here, who watched this.'

'As in a macabre sort of snuff show? People getting off on this?' says Blake.

'No - more like, *you mess with us, this is what will happen to you*,' I say. 'You checked in with all your informants and undercovers? All the gangs round here operate under that stiff banner of enforcement.'

'Not yet,' says Okpara.

'I bet one of them was here, and is probably bricking it, maybe even on the run. I would too if I was made to watch this, knowing that I was set for the same fate if my true identity was discovered.'

We stand silently for a moment, while they digest that, but before long, I have more I want to add.

'And seeing this hasn't changed my opinion at all. This would be even more of a departure for Sparkles Chu than I previously imagined. For my money, you are looking at a whole new personality, a far more dangerous entity. If this is him, well... let's say I can't picture it.'

'Are you sure?' Okpara asks, his eyes more questioning than ever.

'Sure as I can be,' I say with grim conviction.

Chapter Five

We step back out into the frost, the sudden chill sticking to us in an instant, our breath preceding our every step. I've never been at a large crime scene before, moreover I've usually been part of their creation and have high-tailed it before the flashing lights showed up. Consequently, this is interesting. It's a hub of activity, of urgency, of constant footsteps and the cold crackle of static.

I take a moment, and feel it.

This street corner. An intersection.

It's busy now, the traffic backed up beyond the roadblock as the bobbies send the queues in different directions out onto the city's ring road.

You don't just pick a spot like this. Not for a performance like what you've got in that office building.

What do I do when I'm planning something? What did I do in Iraq, then Afghanistan, when I had an objective?

I amassed intel, and the best intel was always surveillance.

I have a look around. Where's the best spot to watch the front door? You could always use the street, surveil on foot. But, that's always best-suited to following a moving target, as you can keep changing position.

Up high. Building opposite - the corner of the roof has a chimney stack.

'Hey, Blake,' I call out, who turns. 'My NCA advisor badge give me any scope for a snoop about?'

She narrows her eyes, raises her chin and gives the faintest ghost of a smile. 'Talk to me.'

Moments later, we're round the back, the din of the street much quieter round here, looking up at a rusty fire escape. The building's only a couple of stories high, a Victorian terrace that's been kept well enough, and seems lived in. The alley behind features a small parking area, and a skip that's been there so long the dirt up the sides matches the dirt on the floor around it. A grimy old Renault sits marooned by the back wall, with a bumper sticker which reads charmingly 'So Fast I'm Touching Cloth'. The ladder is directly above it, so I clamber onto its bonnet, confident the old banger won't have an alarm, and use it to pull myself onto the roof.

Catterall appears at the end of the alley. 'Nobody home. I tried both doors - oh, for God's sake, what is he doing now?'

Flirting with tetanus, I dislodge the ladder catch, which screeches down to a couple of feet above the roof of the Renault. 'I'm going up here, are you coming?'

Catterall looks at Blake, who starts to climb up onto the car roof. 'For Christ's sake...' he mutters, stepping up onto the bonnet with the reluctant care of someone who feels he might contract a venereal issue from mere contact with it. I test the ladder's stability, and all three of us ascend, the air getting colder with every step. A snappy breeze greets us at the top, which is a pitched affair of old slate. When this building was first erected, I bet you could see the whole city from up here - but now, such is the changing shape of the metropolis around us, there's barely any difference between here and the ground below.

We tread carefully in a steady incline, before we crawl up to the apex. Before long I can see, directly in the centre of the roof, between two ceramic chimney pots, we are in the right place.

'There,' I say, pointing at the patch of slate just below the peak, facing the rear side. The entire roof is flecked by nuggets of moss, but there is an area a couple of feet wide here where the moss has been disturbed, with chunks of it overturned and brushed aside. On the rounded tip of the roof, before it slopes down to the front, is a conspicuous-looking shape, made of three dark spots in a triangle. Tripod feet. A lens of some description had been poking between the chimney pots, looking straight down at the front door of the target building. 'This is where you say bingo, right?'

'You can definitely say something,' says Blake, taking a couple of pictures on her phone.

'When was the last time we had rain?' I ask Catterall, who is scanning the area, his petulance gradually being replaced by the buzz of pursuit.

'I think we last had a proper rain middle of last week, so four or five days ago, why?' he replies.

'Then we have a time frame for when this surveillance took place,' I say, pointing at the slate further down the roof on the rear side, by the disturbed moss. A dark patch starts a little further back on the tiles, before getting thinner as it recedes back down the roof until eventually meeting the guttering. 'The watcher needed a piss, sometime in the last four or five days, before the rain could wash it away.'

'A urine stain,' he says, with a curious lilt in his voice.

'Can you get DNA from urine?' I ask.

'I think so,' he replies.

'Well I don't think they'll miss this too much,' I say, prising my fingers under the piece of tile that has the largest concentration of dark staining. 'Should be enough to go on.'

'This isn't exactly protocol,' Catterall says, as I hand him the piece of slate.

'You want the evidence or not?' He looks at the roof tile in his grip. 'Oh, just blame me, I'll say you were off down there knocking on doors, frosting your tips or some rubbish.'

Catterall nods unhappily.

'Let's get down before we have to add the embarrassment of slipping to our deaths to the list of *faux-pas* this morning,' says Blake, scooting back down the roof on her backside. When we're all back on terra firma, and emerge from the alley, a shout rings out from the back of one of the SOCO vans.

'There you are!' It's Okpara, waving us over. We join him, and his eyes are drawn to the slate Catterall is carrying. 'What's that?'

'Don't ask,' I say.

'OK.' He looks to Blake. 'Do you remember the informant we set up last year?'

'The one in Ancoats?' she replies.

'That's the one. I'd like to check in on her. When was the last time she was in touch with the NCA?'

'I don't know the exact date, but I know it's not recent,' she says, taking out her phone. 'You think she might have something worth knowing?'

'I think we set her up for a day like today. Let's go to her.' Okpara loosens his tie and his eyes take on a different intent.

I find myself piping up. 'Can I ride along?'

Okpara looks at Blake. 'He might have a different perspective.'

Blake looks at me. 'You're a bystander, get it?'

'Scouts honour,' I say.

'I'll come too,' says Catterall. 'If he's going, I'm going.'

'Why don't you get that crucial evidence back to base, and get the gaffer filled in,' suggests Blake. I can tell that for all her professionalism, she doesn't like the guy either - a trait that I find more than understandable, as he looks at me like I've just given his girlfriend a panda pop at the school dance. 'We need to get it to the lab ASAP, you're the best man for the job. Take the pool car. We can sort ourselves from here.'

Catterall blows air from his nose, and stomps off.

'We need subtlety where we're going,' Blake explains in a low voice as we watch him huff away, 'and he's never fit that profile.'

'Let's get going,' Okpara says, his tie and jacket over his crooked elbow, now in his shirtsleeves. This guy, however… now *this* guy is interesting.

Chapter Six

There we have us, a curious three. The NCA agent, the beat cop from shores abroad, and the last-minute trouble shooter, too valuable to discard.

Okpara is revealing himself to be a man far more driven by the rush of blood in his ears than a man chained to a desk. He's positively electrified at the prospect of going out into the murk of the city to upturn the nasty bits and see what tumbles loose to his feet. He marches us to a white Range Rover, which, while an odd choice, is clearly an unmarked police vehicle – I see the glinting boxes of the pursuit lights recessed behind the grille below the bonnet.

I sit in the back, watching the city as it grows bigger on approach, and trepidation fills my stomach. It has been a good while since I have been here, swaddled in its grey embrace, and last time I raised so much hell it's a miracle I can even return. There's a prison not far from here, HMP Manchester, Strangeways to you and me, which I'm supposed to be in. How long have I got left of my sentence? Should be about 13 years by now. I blackmailed my way out, and I haven't a clue how things stand in there now I'm working with the authorities. Did they square it away with the scum that run it? Who knows.

Back in the car, it's obvious that Blake and Okpara have worked together before. Their patter is easy, yet charged and driven. In the official setting of the crime scene they had clearly defined roles and jurisdictions to conform to, yet now they're a pair of boundless go-getters. I like them both, and I feel a little as if there could be a merry hint of romance between the pair. I feel a lone butterfly of my own, as Carolyn springs to mind.

In the years since I'd last seen Carolyn, I thought about her often, so much so that I employed Busby the East Anglian master-forger to track her down. She's from as broken a history as I am, but there's so much more to her than bad choices way back. She is beautiful, and I felt downright ill when I first laid eyes on her. She has a resilience, honesty and poise that I can't help but admire. In a way, she brought the best out of me when I bought down the Berg. I was drawn somehow to her then, and I still am now.

I drop back into the present and tune into Blake and Okpara, but before I know it, the car has stopped and they are both piling out.

'We're here?' I ask, as I follow suit.

'We're somewhere,' says Okpara, glancing up and down the quiet city backstreet. He seems satisfied.

'Going in front? March in?' Blake asks.

'With respect and care. Ruffle no feathers. You can do that West?' asks Okpara, as he walks round to the back of the Range, and pops the trunk. 'I'm not expecting trouble, but just pop this in your jacket pocket in case.'

It's a telescopic baton, in matte black. Heavy enough to leave a crinkle in anyone's outlook. They are far from standard issue, and he gives another to Blake. The sensation that this is an off-the-books matter grows.

'Hold the button, swish it away from you, out it pops. Hold the button, push the end right back in, and it's back to *oh look my torch is broken*,' says Okpara.

'Where are we and what are we doing?' I ask. I'm quite keen not to get in trouble so soon after being granted freedom, and I want to earn Jeremiah's trust back. I'm damn sure his toes would be curling into pretzels at the thought of me being handed a telescopic baton and instructions to use it if necessary.

'That building on the far corner, opposite side of the street to the little newsagents – you see it?' Okpara doesn't take his eyes from his preparations in the trunk.

I myself see a rather rustic three story town house, and by rustic I mean looking like it has survived both world wars then ten more. It looks quietly residential. I see nothing of any note, save for someone seems to be home – there's a desk light on the top floor window sill, quietly glowing behind a pair of net curtains, faded grimly by a film of mold. It looks like the Pixar logo lamp has gone off the rails. When I think of why it might have been left on during daytime, the penny drops.

'A knocking shop?' I ask.

'Kind of – you'll see,' Okpara replies. I'd like more than that – I hate going in anywhere cold and half-cocked. Info keeps you alive, however modest the threat here seems to be. Still, Okpara did give me the baton in case of trouble…

'Who's in there?' I ask.

'The owner of this place is a bit of everything, finger in all sorts of pies. She's a fixer, among other things, but a bookie as well. Keeps the place clean enough, and runs it tight – no drugs, no money, no nothing on site. The police have her down in their informant register as Maud Smithills, but round here she goes by Young Tilda.'

'She'll like you,' interjects Blake. I don't take her on.

'She's a snitch?' I ask, as we start walking down towards the house.

'One of the best there is, and most reliable. Has been for years,' Blake replies.

'How does she get her information? If she's been a snitch for years then why has nobody worked her out?'

'She's got good ears, a good customer base, and sex tends to cloud things like that, not to mention that her service is good,' Okpara says. Blake looks at him with an arched eyebrow. 'Or so I've been told.'

We are near the front door now and I really don't know what to expect, the scant information provided a scattering of juxtapositions. I feel the weight of the baton in my pocket. 'So why the big bats?'

'She's been known to have enthusiastic security.'

The windows on approach are dotted green in the corners, and the idea of consummating anything in there other than a rigorous disinfectant job is a grim one. I'm expecting a welcome of some kind, but considering I've never frequented such an establishment before, I've no idea how it works. Okpara buttons his jacket, and marches straight through the front door. I bring up the rear, with Blake ahead of me.

Suddenly, we are in a reception area to what could be a vaudevillian theatre. There is red felt upholstery everywhere, on the cushions, the sofas, even up the curtains and stairs. A leather reception desk stands at one end beside an indoor water feature, which is a six-foot rock wall with a trickling cascade down it, into a small box pool which house a terrified cluster of goldfish. The room smells warm and green, if such things had an odour.

'Tildy in?' asks Okpara, as he wanders to the desk confidently. I hadn't seen her as we entered, but sat behind the high dark leather desk counter is a young woman on a spinning desk chair. Her hair is loosely piled on top of her head with a couple of black chopsticks holding the creation in place, and is of a glossy natural blond. Her features are glamorously made up, thick foundation creating the kind of tan you should really see a doctor about, yet she is clad in a bright pink hoody and ripped jeans. With a shudder, I realise she must be on shift break.

'Nah, she's gone the Tesco metro for tea bags,' she replies in a surprising black country accent. Her manner of speaking betrays that beneath all the professional slap, she's in truth no more than a girl.

'Come on, Tildy's always in.'

'I can obviously keep you occupied while you're waiting, officer. Your friends too, but it'll cost more - but we can do a deal, maybe a three for two sort of thing.'

'Does that ever work? With police, I mean - do you get coppers in here?'

'We get all sorts in here.'

'I bet. You've had your fun, now go in the back and get Tildy, before we have a little chat about solicitation.'

'Who said anything about sex? I was talking tarot readings. You get me wrong officer, you really do.' She smiles sweetness and turns to pass under the stairs, but as she does so, a stout woman passes the other way, in a long red summer dress at odds with both the setting and the season. She drops a box of tea bags on the counter.

'Phew, just got back, and, happy days, they had my favourite brand.'

'What a relief,' says Okpara.

'Who's that?' she says, and I see she's looking over Okpara's shoulder to me.

'Told you,' murmurs Blake.

'A friend of mine,' says Okpara. 'And you know that means he's off limits.'

'It's a shame, because I'd come out of retirement to look after that one personally.'

'I appreciate the compliment,' I say.

'Careful, careful,' says Blake under her breath.

'Oh, he's lovely, isn't he?' says the woman I assume is Young Tildy, who is, as it happens, anything but young. She's in her eighties, her hair in fifties curlers, her eyes engulfed by the biggest prosthetic eyelashes I've seen since I caught a student production of Rocky Horror in my university days not far from here.

'Now Tildy, let's keep it professional,' Okpara interjects.

'Oh, but I am.'

'Be that as it may… We've got a couple of questions, if you don't mind.'

'I thought you might. It's never a social call, is it Mr Okpara?'

'Sadly not - curse of the job.'

'Sandy, go and make four cuppas please. Use the old mugs from the back kitchen. Keep the fine china for the customers and all that.' She turns to her guests. 'You understand.' It's a statement, not a question.

'Shall I let Vincent know?' replies Sandy.

Okpara stiffens, but it's Tildy who answers. 'No, leave the big oaf where he is. But best take him a cuppa of his own to keep him sweet.'

The girl took the box and shuffled off, but before she's even gone, Tildy is speaking again. 'The big murder?'

'What makes you say that?' It's Blake's turn to butt in. 'We haven't even made a press release yet.'

'The town's agog. Every man and his dog is talking.'

'What's the story?' asks Okpara.

'There'll be a few busier trains out of town today.'

'Why?'

'Nobody's sticking round to see where this ends up.'

'So you've got a big player sending a message?'

'And the message has been received loud and clear.'

'Do you have a name?'

'I always have names. Some of the names I could tell you who've popped through that very same door would make your toenails drop out.'

39

'You know what I'm talking about.'

'I know what you're talking about. But there's some people I'm even more scared of than you.'

'You want to tell me who?'

'Nope.'

'Then what can you give me? Remember, there is a lenience towards your enterprise that might not extend indefinitely should its usefulness expire.'

'I love it when he uses big words,' says Tildy, looking at me directly. 'Sends me all aquiver.'

'I'd rather not have to do anything.'

'Maybe we need Vincent after all.'

'Now we don't want that either. Just give me something to go on.'

Tildy takes a moment, cogs whirring, before replying in a voice stripped of all the playful flirtatiousness. 'I'm sorry officer, I really can't. Please be on your way.'

The fun has departed Okpara's voice too. 'Tildy, if you know something that can help us, you must. You should have seen what we saw this morning. It was appalling. This was a horrific, sick killing.'

'Then you'll know exactly why I can't talk. Now please go.'

'I can't. I wouldn't be doing my duty as a policeman if I did.'

'I'm sorry Mr Okpara.' She turns to the space beneath the stairs and yells, 'Vincent!'

I hear an immediate thumping, as if hell itself was marching up the stairs, and before anything else can happen the doorway is filled with a man built like Mr Universe with an extra tyre round the middle, sporting a buzzcut and a t-shirt so big and loose it would do the three of us on this side of the desk as a tent. 'We need to ask them to leave, love,' says Tildy leaning towards him. She steps aside to let him pass, which he manages in the space - just.

'You heard the lady,' he says in a Manc growl, spreading his arms out wide like Atlas. 'On your bikes.'

'She's got valuable information pertaining to a murder enquiry, Vincent. We're just trying to get some answers.' Okpara widens his own arms and pleads with the big man.

'Go, now,' says the giant, as he takes one step to Okpara and places a hand like a baseball mitt on his shoulder. Before he can do anything else, I've whizzed the cosh out of my jacket, down to splay it, then up - right through the crook of Vincent's elbow, which bends backwards horribly with a snap.

Keeping the momentum going, I bring it straight back down onto the top of his knee, chopping him down. With a howl, he's on one knee nursing a limp arm like a freshly dead pet. With my left hand, I grab his jaw, digging my fingers up under his mouth into the sensitive pressure point, and hold his entire head like a frisbee. I raise the cosh high over my head, ready to crash it down on his skull. Held in place by my control of his pressure point, he's a sitting, static target.

'Get nattering,' I say to Tildy.

She looks at me wild eyed, then turns to Okpara. 'Where in the blue hell did you find him?'

'I'd do as he says,' says Okpara.

Tildy speaks with concern. 'There was a lot of witnesses, made to watch it. They were told that the same would happen to them if they were found out to be coppers or informants. Word is, everyone's skipping town.'

'There must be something else.'

'That's all.'

I squeeze the pressure point, pushing my fingers up into his mouth from underneath. The big man screams.

Tildy caves.

'Those responsible, they've hired some outside help. Some really horrible help. A proper sicko.'

'Do you have a name?'

'You'd know him as the Dog of The Moors.'

My cohorts appear stunned into silence, but I say, 'Who?'

'Ask around. Not too loudly though, you don't want him coming after you. Which is why I can say no more.'

Okpara looks at me. I squeeze the pressure point again, and raise the cosh higher.

'It's political. It's a politics thing!' gushes Tildy. 'But that really is all I know.'

Suddenly, in my hand, the entire weight of the man goes floppy, and I can't keep him up anymore. Vincent falls forward, and lands on his face.

'He passed out,' I say. 'He'll come round again in a couple of minutes.'

'I think I might have to skip town too,' says Tildy, looking at Vincent. 'Poor lamb.'

'This obviously wasn't what we wanted today,' says Okpara, stepping over Vincent's mass. 'We'll see you soon Tildy.'

'Jog on,' she replies, folding her arms. 'But I won't forget you.' She's pointing at me. 'I won't forget you at all. And the offer still stands by the way.'

'Good day, Ma'am,' I say, and follow Okpara and Blake out of the knocking shop.

'Bloody hell,' says Tildy as we go, before shouting, 'Sandy, cancel three of those teas!'

Chapter Seven

Judging by her focused reticence on the drive back to base, I'm beginning to think the sight of Kyle and the fraughtness of our visit to Young Tildy's has affected Blake. As an NCA officer, I'm not sure how many crime scenes she's seen in the flesh. The NCA is a base of more cerebral operations - a place where you plan to get hands dirty, but rarely actually do so yourself, passing that moment on to someone with specialist training in the hand-dirtying department. And that may dictate that the actual blood, guts and thunder of the field may have passed the likes of Blake and Catterall by. It could be that, or maybe she's processing what Jeremiah alluded to earlier this morning - that their roles in Operation Gaslamp denote a contribution to Kyle's demise. Blood on your hands, however convolutedly you put it there, is always hard to get off.

All the way in we embrace the silence and the horror of what we saw earlier. I feel the phantasm of what I'm supposed to feel, too desensitised down to bluntness and the matter-of-fact. On top of that, I'm feeling an excitement I can't deny.

Okpara too seems focused and comfortable. A man built for the street and the heat of confrontation, and he drops us back off at the front of the NCA complex with, 'That was good. See you soon.'

I find the guy fascinating, so in the lift up to three where the Organised Crime Command is situated, I ask Blake, who smiles at my inquiry. 'Interesting isn't he?' she says.

'You can say that again.'

'He's a Maasai warrior.'

'Excuse me?' In my head I can see the formal attire of the indigenous fighting tribe of Kenya, but can't quite key it in to the man I just visited a brothel with.

'Yeah, came over here in his late teens to make money for his family. Started as a taxi driver, learned the city, learned the lingo, sent all his money back to his home village. Decided to enroll in the police, where he's been for twenty years, steadily climbing the ladder.'

'Holy crap,' I say, while admiring how the guy's got a better backstory than I have.

'Never went home. In his forties now, and shows no signs of slowing down either.'

The lift pings and we hit a turquoise corridor, before taking a quick right hand turn. We are suddenly funneled out into a wide central octagon with glass walls, and on each wall is an office. The centre is a communal area, with a large table and other smaller tables dotted around. A bank of computers line the furthest three walls, and to the right of the door I just entered is a kitchenette. One of the walls by the conference table, in the middle of the room, is a huge magnetised panel, on which is placed all manner of notes, scraps of paper, and photographs. In a supposedly festive concession to the season, a sparse, drab, desperately unfestive, five-foot Christmas tree stands lone and confused in a corner like the guy at a party you didn't really want to invite. This is the nerve centre of the OCC.

I'm gasping for caffeine, so I slide immediately over to the kitchen, while Blake heads to her office as unit head. There's a pot on constantly, never spectacular but always hot, and I grab a mug from the stack on the draining board, fill her up and take it black. In the time it takes me to come out, Catterall and Salix are emerging from one of the off-shoot meeting rooms, locked in conversation, their body language agitated and expressions urgent. Catterall is holding that roof tile like a wedding cake, while Jeremiah rolls his eyes when he sees me.

'Was it really too much to ask not to go and do anything stupid?'

'I thought I was helping?' I reply. 'You get a match?'

'On what? The piss-stain retrieved out of the bounds of protocol? And how quickly do you think this sort of thing works?' replies Jeremiah. There's the sarcasm.

'It takes a while?' I am surprised. 'So what's the hold up?'

Salix pushes himself back, and lets himself roll a couple of feet, sighing as he goes. 'Is this you being willfully dense? This slate and the manner in which we got it would be inadmissible in court.'

'You're serious?' I ask, shocked. 'We didn't break into anywhere, it was out in the fresh air, it was –'

'Private property, affixed to a dwelling' Salix interrupts. 'Ordinarily we would need a court order to do what you went ahead and did.'

'So, we go ahead and find the guy, and pull him up on something else. Or I'll make him talk – I always do.'

Catterall coughs involuntarily, like his throat was squeezed tight for a second. He keeps his eyes on the table, having obviously taken a rocket.

'That's if we have any DNA for this guy on file. Do I have to remind you again, Tom West, that you are not a field man? You're a desk jockey, plain and simple.' Salix looks cold with reprimanding.

'But you're doing the test, aren't you…' I venture.

Salix is mid-theatrical sigh when Blake appears, and fills Jeremiah in on everything from the murder scene itself and what was gleaned from Young Tildy, tactfully missing out the bit where I maimed Big Vincent. I'll have to thank her for that later.

Jeremiah takes it all in with quiet, troubled acceptance. I offer my opinions, reiterating what I told Blake and Okpara at the scene, and he listens with intent. He knows my pedigree, if you can call it that, and the purity of my intentions. He knows me too well to know that I'm not deliberately rattling any cages for any design other than justice.

'I'm going to check in with the other under-covers and informants, see if any of our guys were actually there,' says Blake, snap-cracking her ring binder shut.

'And I'm going to lean on Big Brother to give us some angle on Chapel Street,' says Jeremiah.

'Big Brother?' I ask.

'The surveillance networks liaison. Basically the department that gives us access to CCTV recordings and feeds we want to investigate. We are going to want more facial recognition outfits on the scope for Sparkles to

45

either rule him in or out of the murder scene, and then there's anything we can get out of the location itself.'

'GMP will be all over that already,' Blake interjects.

'Then let's keep the relationship greased like a pig at a hog roast,' Jeremiah replies. 'We want everything they've got. And hopefully we spot a bloke going for a piss on the roof and we can use this slate for real. If we catch someone, we can use it to get a Judge's order.' I do love how he's always willing to bend the rules just that little bit.

'What can I do?' I ask. I want to help, the competitive edge in me urging me to justify my own position here. 'Who is he then? The owner of the piss?' I ask.

'I truly don't know how long it's going to take. I mean, *if* we do it, I have to find some budget to squeeze off to fund the test, considering it wasn't exactly obtained in a way we might be able to use.'

'When we find out who it is, let me go to it.'

'Don't scare me, for God's sake. We have more than enough paperwork for one day. Go home, squeeze that baby of yours, and let us do the forms. Come back in normal time tomorrow, OK. And don't, *please*, do anything stupid. I'll ring you later to check you haven't.'

Blake speaks quietly, folding the folder under her arm. 'You've had a baby?'

'Yeah. A boy, two weeks old.' I feel my face split in a wide grin.

'Congratulations,' she says with a kind smile of her own.

Catterall can't help himself. 'Shit, if that ever happens to me, shoot me,' he says, before moping off with his roof tile in tow.

Chapter Eight

It's our first trip out as a family of five. The woman, her two kids, the man who killed her husband who was also their father, and the new fruit of that highly improbable set up. We've gone to Nando's, a seemingly super-popular chicken house, and we sit at a table which faces the door, as per my silent wishes. Jam is cradled in my arms, and I'm feeding him a bottle of expressed breast milk - something Carolyn prepared earlier. She sits opposite, radiant and at ease, helping her kids decipher the menu. It's a domesticity I'm getting gradually used to, and surprisingly very much enjoying.

'So, can I just get this right in my head. We pick a piece of chicken, say how spicy we want it, then what we want it to come with?' Jake looks up at his mother under a tangle of hair that's so blonde it's nearly white. He's nine, is no slouch, and is fiercely protective of his mum. He thinks his dad walked out on them, so for another man to appear - that would be me – it has taken him some time to adjust to. That said, he's probably been more grown up about it than I would have. We have a relationship that works, and that's fine for me.

'I think that's right, sweetheart. And go carefully with the spiciness you pick - hot will be *hot* hot. Mild will be fine I think.'

'Medium.'

'You're sure?'

'Final offer,' the boy confirms with a smile.

Carolyn turns to her daughter, while flashing me an amused look as her eyes switch child. She's a natural at this, and it's something I find almost hopelessly attractive in her. I smile softly, swishing Jam onto his front so I

47

can burp him. I rub his back across my knee, my palm rolling his incredible little spine.

'What about you, Gracie?' she asks, nudging the girl conspiratorially shoulder to shoulder.

'I want sausages.' She's eight, her hair having darkened sooner than Jake's, having gone a mucky blond since I first met her. She's as stubborn as I am, and when we're not at odds, we're firmly on the same page.

'This is a chicken restaurant, darling. The clue's in the description.'

'But I don't want chicken.'

'I'm sure you can find something.'

'What kind of restaurant only has one meat? What if there's twenty people coming for a party, but one doesn't want chicken. Would it kill them to do one sausage?'

'I can ask I suppose?'

'If they'll do one, push them for two.'

'I won't push my luck.'

'Tell them if it makes them feel any better, they can make it spicy. But not too spicy. Spicy sausage trumps are not very ladylike.'

I can't help but laugh. Carolyn admonishes me playfully. 'Now, Ben, we don't encourage that kind of talk do we.'

'We certainly do not,' I say through a smile, throwing a wink at Gracie. She giggles and slides round the booth next to me.

'Can I?' she asks.

'Sure can,' I say, and she replaces my hand on Jam's back with her own. She rubs tight little circles between his shoulders for a few seconds. 'Gentle,' I say, placing my hand over hers, and I guide wider rings with more pressure. Within two seconds, Jam rips a throaty burp that would have *me* proudly embarrassed.

'What did you do to him!?' I say to Grace, laughing.

'You did that!' she says, and before we know it, all four of us over two feet tall are in stitches.

My phone goes, the buzz on silent. Carolyn looks at it on the table, then at me. This drop of happiness is something I don't want to evaporate, but I know the rules. I know just how easily I can become expendable if I don't play by them.

It's a number I recognise as being from the main NCA switchboard, so I answer. 'Hello?'

It's Blake on the line. Her voice is urgent and breathless, as if she's just run up a flight of stairs only to call me at the top. 'Post mortem on the Blackfriars victim is complete,' she says. 'They've got some anomalies they want to run by you.'

'Me?' I ask confused. Carolyn cocks her head slightly, as if the gesture will allow her audio of the call.

'You were talking yesterday about Sparkles' MO, about how you weren't convinced? Okpara's asked for you personally. They're at the mortuary now.'

I look at Carolyn, and spread my free arm in a weak *I'm sorry*, before speaking again. 'What does Jeremiah have to say about it?'

Jeremiah's voice cuts in, evidently listening in on a different handset. 'He says, don't let me down.'

'Yes, sir,' I say.

'Do you need a ride?' Blake asks.

'No, I've got it sorted.'

'OK, I'll wait at HQ for you.'

I hang up, then turn to the kids.

'We'll have to get your spicy sausages to go I'm afraid, Gracie.'

Chapter Nine

The first thing that strikes me is the cold. It's bloody freezing in here, and I would be wondering what ridiculous government cutbacks had caused it if I hadn't remembered why it was essential. I'm used to the actual moment of death and its mechanics, not what happens afterwards.

The body, here in a mortuary at St Mary's Hospital near Manchester's university district, shorn of clothes, posture, or anything that would indicate that there was once life in it, looks pathetic. A mottled white sack of nothingness topped with a sad little walnut that used to be his manhood. It's depressing.

'Initial thoughts?' asks Okpara, standing by the back wall, his hands buried deep in the pockets of a woolen overcoat. He studiously makes no attempt to look at the body, preferring to focus on me.

'It's a nasty way to go,' I say, taking a step closer to the body under the ice-cold tungsten overheads. With all the mess of viscera scrubbed away, the neck wound is clinically apparent in all its glory. Aside from the obvious mortal injury, the body is almost untouched. No bruising, no cuts, no nothing. The only obvious anomaly is the ligature marks from the cable ties that bound him. The man was clearly no bottom-feeding addict, nor was he roughed around prior to nearly having has head cleaved off.

'Seeing him like this,' I say, 'makes me even more convinced that Sparkles had nothing to do with this. You may have seen him in the vicinity with the fancy facial recognition software, but this is as far from the work of Sparkles as you can get.'

Sparkles is a man that exists in a world with a strict code of honour, albeit in a very illegal sense. He was offended when I suggested that he was just another gangster with blood on his hands. No, he is not driven by wanton killing without reason, and whenever I saw him motion to defend himself, it was always with a firearm, none of which I ever saw him actually use – he had protection. He is a man who knows that violence exists, and sure has a place in the world he has chosen to dwell in, but this… this is far removed from that. This is gratuitous. This is over the top. This is not Sparkles.

Unless my putting him out of business scrambled both his brain and his MO.

'This wound isn't typical, is it?' I say.

'You can say that again,' says the coroner, Dr. Marian Grealish, who I was introduced to when we arrived. She is tall, angular and carries herself with the same measured precision as the instruments she wields. 'This would be a first for me, and anyone else in this building. Believe me, I had them all in to take a look, and by the time word got round, I could have made a mint selling tickets.'

I approach the cadaver and peer in closely at the wound. The tissue is, for want of a better word, ripped – and dried to a soft crinkle where it is at its thinnest. The blood that gushed is now all gone, and only yellow and pink rags remain around the wound. The edges of the wound oddly seem to angle away from the body, making the deep cut look like a second sneering mouth. It looks like something hatched in there and burst out.

'What am I looking at?' I ask.

'The work of a complete paid-up member of the psychopath union,' says Grealish. 'For a start, the wound was created from the inside, with the move to sever the jugular, carotid and windpipe coming from within the neck outwards. Not the kind of strike you usually find when someone's throat has been cut.'

That explains that. She continues with a latex-clad finger.

'There is one traditional entry point here on the right side of the neck, where we can determine a narrow and extremely sharp blade was inserted laterally across the neck, and from following the angle of the wound, you can see that the blade was inserted directly through the soft tissue between the oesophagus and spinal cord, and out the other side.'

'Just… can you give me that in layman's terms?'

'A thin sword, or something similar, was pushed through this person's neck, initially avoiding anything major.'

'An accident surely,' I say.

'No. It will have hurt like bloody murder, but nowhere near fatal. Initially.'

'How can you tell?'

'There are nicks and grazes up and down the back of the trachea where the blade was pressed up to.'

'And that's because?'

'He was talking. With a sword right through his neck.'

Jesus Christ. The ring of people around the resting place of the body. The delivery of a message. He was interrogated and tortured in front of them, then executed in the most graphic of ways.

I glance over the body at Okpara, who has finally looked over. He nods slowly. He knows it too.

'After they'd had a little chat, the killer sliced towards the victim's chin, cutting his throat from the inside out,' I whisper.

'Hence the curious direction of the wound,' Grealish confirms. She leans against a rattling radiator in the corner, and it struggles before holding.

'So you are positive this isn't Sparkles?' asks Okpara.

'No way,' I say. 'You're wasting your time in that direction.'

Blake evidently sees no point dwelling on that revelation, so she pushes on with momentum.

'The territory we are talking about here is pretty distinct, so we've been trying to call in our undercovers who covered it since yesterday. Nobody is talking yet, which doesn't surprise me if they saw this happen in person.'

'They're probably scared for their lives,' says Okpara.

'There'll be more bodies, you think?' I ask. I look at Blake, who glances at Okpara.

'Most likely, yes,' he says firmly. 'A homicide of this nature would never usually be a single incident. This took deliberation. Practice. This wasn't a heat of the moment thing. This guy was cold and precise.'

'A card-carrying psychopath,' says Grealish, her voice echoing from the corner.

'Right,' agrees Okpara. He finally lets his eyes rest on the body, and the concern I see in them is very real.

Blake clears her throat. 'Jurisdiction is yours, DCI Okpara. How do you want to play it from here?'

'I agree with Mr West,' he says, nodding to me. 'The scene did look like it was for the benefit of viewers. And the fact that our undercovers have gone quiet would back up the theory that it was them made to watch this fiasco. This problem straddles both our institutions so I think it's best we look into it together, even though this has become much less a question of drug trade investigation and more a manhunt for a murderer. Does that sound OK to you?'

Blake looks downbeat. 'I appreciate the professional courtesy, but I'm afraid my department's expertise won't be any good to you with such a direction change. We are essentially number crunchers – when the pace changes we farm it out.'

She's right, of course. I've learned throughout my tenure, the NCA Organised Crime Command's North West Office is exactly that – a think tank that points others in the right direction.

'Fair enough,' says Okpara. 'But *he's* no number cruncher.' It takes me a second to realise he is pointing at me.

'I don't know what I can offer you,' I say. I'd love to help track this maniac down and find out who's now pushing drugs into Manchester, but I have a strict deal with even stricter terms. I don't want to lose my freedom now I have it. Not now… Carolyn, Jake, Gracie and Jam.

'If I can square it with your higher-ups, would you care to give me a hand?'

'Of course.' I've said it before I've thought about it. I'm bursting to get out there, and I didn't even know. The thrill and pull of the field is magnetic.

'If he's going, then so am I,' says Blake with a tone of finality. 'This is as much your problem as mine – we both put these people in the field, it's on us both.'

'Alright then. I'll speak to Salix. Do you think he'll be OK with that?' Okpara asks.

'He'll have to be,' Blake replies.

'I'll put a bit of a lean on him. 9am, I'll pick you up at your base. And wear some comfortable walking shoes. We're going out into the city to see what we can find.'

I almost smile, but then I remember that there's a mutilated naked corpse between us, and surely that would be classed as poor form.

Chapter Ten

I'm at the office at 8.30, heading straight up to the centre of operations on three. Christmas is a few days away, but this feels like it.

I'm in jeans, a blue down coat, and a pair of trail running shoes that grip so fierce I could walk up a wall. Jeremiah is already working in his office, so I keep my head down and head into the kitchen to top up one of the travel mugs saved in the top cupboard.

Black stuff in the cup with a dash of milk because I missed breakfast, my eyes are suddenly drawn through the kitchen door to the display wall on one side of the hexagon. It's no longer a mess of various disconnected strands of different individual cases. Now, I see as I get closer, the wall has been cleaned and re-covered with a very different singular purpose and a crystal clear objective - namely, the murder of DC Kyle, the possible reasons for it, the potential players involved, and all the key info. It's comprehensive. It's *good*.

'Catterall was here all night, until I got in at four and sent him home,' said Jeremiah, having quietly rolled up next to me. He looks exhausted.

'He's a dab hand with blu-tack, I'll give him that.' Strangely, I feel a tang of admiration, which I quickly brush way.

'He's the kid that always goes for extra credit. You should have seen some of his powerpoint presentations when he first started. One had a self-composed soundtrack, him on a keyboard, then him wandering the fretboard on a twelve string.'

'Can't fault his confidence. I thought this wasn't going to be an NCA matter?'

'It wasn't,' he says, as he guides himself back towards the central conference table. 'But we've had a good old chat, Okpara and me. We think it'd be in the best interests of ongoing cooperation, if we pooled resources. After speaking with his informant yesterday, he suggests there's an organised crime connection under the surface, and that's certainly within our remit. So yep, looks like we're putting the band back together.'

'And as for me?'

'Okpara's taken a shine to you, which, knowing him in the abbreviated way I do, scares me a shit-tonne. You two let loose knocking on doors in the city gives me the straight-up heebie-jeebies. However… he's a persuasive bugger.' He shakes his head at himself.

'I'm not looking for any trouble, but I can't say I wouldn't enjoy getting out from behind the desk.'

Jeremiah swigs from his own cup of something hot, which smells a lot more fragrant than mine. 'I don't need to make any threats do I? You cause the department trouble, you'll have to go back where you came from - you're aware of that aren't you?'

'I am.'

'OK. At the end of the day, you're under my command, so it's me you answer to. If I'm not there, it's Blake.'

'Not Okpara?'

'Not Okpara. Blake's about the most sensible head we've got between the three of you. If she says jump, you ask which cloud you're aiming for.'

'OK.'

'There's some cereal in a tub under the sink. Get some of that down you before you go. Back here for 4.00 pm please, unless circumstances prohibit.'

'Aye aye, sir.' I mock salute and wander back to the kitchen for some chow before the day truly begins.

Chapter Eleven

Okpara picks us up in that absurd white Range Rover again, and we sit in its plush embrace as we fly along the outside lane of the M60, the ring road of Greater Manchester encircling all and sundry. Blake is in front of me, in jeans, a black hoody and some eye-catching red DM boots, while Okpara drives next to her. He's hunched over the wheel, focused as a tweaker, in a leather jacket and cream chinos with, and, this is no joke, velcro sandals on his feet, bare toes and all. I suppose we all have our own definition of comfort.

'Slight change of plan. Tildy will have shut up completely, so we'll need to try somebody else,' he says.

'One we set up?' asks Blake, as she furiously types on her smartphone with the swish of a thumb in a loose sweep.

'Not a CI, but an ex-copper. You remember that name yesterday - the Dog Of The Moors?'

'Yeah,' I say, as we cruise off one motorway onto another. 'What was that all about?'

'It's a name I've not heard in an active case context for ten years or so, maybe longer. He's the suspect in a series of murders in the mid-2000s, but nobody was ever identified or arrested.'

'What happened?' I ask, as we pass a car driven by a man shaking his head at us, I'm guessing at the big brash vehicle going much quicker than his is. I can't help but smile - this car doesn't fit its driver in any way.

'A series of bodies were found on the moors up over Rossendale, towards Holcombe Hill. Six of them, each one buried three feet deep, all forensics indicating a killing spree across a five year period.'

'Shit, I don't remember that,' I say.

'You don't?' asked Blake, turning to face me. 'What planet were you on in the mid-2000s?'

'I was in Iraq, I think.'

'A military man?' Okpara asks. He looks at me in the mirror.

'Used to be. Now I'm a pencil pusher on a day trip out.'

'West here only just got interesting,' Blake says, turning back to face front. 'We thought he was a low-level admin assistant until yesterday morning, when it was revealed he's a highly-trained action man.' I say nothing.

'Aha. Explains what happened to Big Vincent,' Okpara says. 'And also explains why you never heard of the Dog of the Moors.'

'Why was he called that?' I ask.

'Journalists gave him the nickname to sell more papers. Two of the bodies had bite marks in their flesh. Human. I always found the nickname quite lazy myself.'

'There weren't any bite-marks on Kyle yesterday, at least none that I saw.'

'No, but we are talking sharp blades and precision, which is what the moor murders and Kyle's have in common.'

'What about evidence of torture? Kyle was put through the ringer, were the moors bodies too?'

'Yes, if I remember rightly. But that didn't necessarily mean torture. Old bodies, old wounds.'

'If the bodies were there for ages, can the time frame of yesterday's crime still play out right? Can they be the same person?'

'There's about fifteen years minimum between yesterday and the original spree. I'd say so.'

I look through the windshield ahead, and see a broad, humped hill in the distance, with a pointed stone monument standing proud and heavenward on the top. 'That where we're going?'

'That?' Okpara points at the dark tower. 'That's Peel Monument. It stands on Holcombe Hill. The bodies were found pretty much in its shadow. So we're going to head up the hill from Rawtenstall.'

As he says this the motorway dwindles to two lanes, and grey cottages begin to appear on the hills and along their slopes. There's a quiet, working-class pride to them.

'Real textile country, this,' says Okpara, clearly having noticed my interest. 'Textile mills all over the area played significant roles in the industrial revolution.'

'Cool.' I mean it. I love history, especially of our country's better moments. Stuff that we can be proud of, rather than looking back through a modern prism of shameful cringe.

'Ah, interesting,' says Blake, and it takes me a second to realise she's not also preoccupied with the vagaries and lessons of our country's story.

'What have you got?' asks Okpara.

'I'm responding to an email from Daughtry back at base. I had him do a cross-reference check for notable social media growth in political posts and groups on social media, geo-targeted to Manchester. Tildy said there was a new political slant to things, I'm just seeing if anything jumps up on social media.'

'Great thinking,' says Okpara.

'Facebook always amazes me when it comes to just how much information people are willing to share on there. Your brother got your auntie pregnant? Bang, best Facebook it. It's a library of info that's better than any database we have - a dirty laundry, naughty secret treasure trove. Long story short, we do have a serious spike here in Manchester on something that has a political angle.'

'It's not the Green Party is it?' I say.

'Nope, the markers are right of far right. As in the extreme right.'

'That's the case for the whole country isn't it? Broadly speaking?'

'It is, but not when you factor in that it's those with a certain criminal history who are suddenly pushing a far right agenda. We're talking known pushers.'

'How do you know this?'

'Once they're in our system, we find them on Facebook, and match the two. It's resulted in a resource of our own, which includes the info on PND and PNC databases together with whatever they've chosen to share on Facebook and Twitter. It creates a more in-depth, personal picture of the one-time offenders. We take that info, and pass it through known associates too, both on social media and off it. After the death of Kyle the undercover drug user yesterday, I added the keyword marker for drug offences into the search, or I should say, I got Daughtry to do it, and bingo, a clear picture emerges that the drug friendly underworld of Manchester are suddenly pushing a militant, extreme far-right agenda.'

'Why would they do that? From an ideology standpoint, I don't get it?'

'Yes,' ponders Okpara. 'Why would drug pushers and users suddenly be so pro-right wing? Drugs have a far more liberal connotation.'

'That's the question. But it gives us a start point.' Blake sends the email with an audible swoosh I can hear from the backseat.

'I have to ask...' I say. 'The car?'

'Mine,' he replies.

I smile. 'And now?'

'The extreme right can wait,' says the Maasai. 'We need to have a chat to a good old boy of the service.'

On the side of a potholed track, half-way up yet another hill that Okpara's Range is making mincemeat of, the improbable shape of a giant ice cream cone looms out of the green. As we approach, a red and white awning emerges just further up from it on the roadside, replete with the uneven holes of age and wear, hanging withered off the gable end of a stone cottage.

'We're going for a Mr Whippy?' I ask, as I'm upended for my insolence by a pothole that must have been deep enough to break a leg in.

'Bartoni's is the best ice cream shop for five miles,' replied Okpara, swerving between further roadside blemishes, which suggests to me he aimed for the one that caught me out. 'Not that there's much competition round here.'

'Nobody comes up here, surely,' said Blake, holding her own thermos with two hands like a Fabergé egg.

'You'd be surprised,' he replied.

We are. No sooner have we parked up, can we see through the front windows that it's jam-packed in there. It's not big, the decor is tired, the furniture even more exhausted, but there's people at every table, most of whom are in thick jackets with panting dogs at their feet. A sign over the door reads in a calligraphic swirl, 'Bartoni's'.

Inside, the atmosphere is chilly with two freezer chests next to a counter.

A small TV hangs in the corner playing BBC News 24, a flat screen that may have been ahead of its time when first bought, but whichever time it was predating has long since passed. A man about sixty is serving a customer beyond the colourful rows of tubs, moving with a grace and patter of such composure, he makes the serving of ice cream look damn-near operatic. He's a bit hypnotising, with shoulder-length grey hair beneath a white chef's hat, and an easy smile across his face.

Okpara whispers to us, 'Meet Ricardo Bartoni, proprietor of Bartoni's Gelataria of Rossendale. Or as I know him, Richard Barton, ex-head of Lancashire Murder Squad.'

As he says this, Barton breaks no stride at all while offering a wink to Okpara, and proceeds to pop two cones in a small prep stand, and load them up with bright blue spheres from one of the tubs. Blake checks the menu, while I take it in. I love it. A dog-friendly ice-cream shop half way up a hill on the middle of pretty much nowhere. Life is full of surprises.

Blake sidles up to me. 'He offers his own home brew as well,' she whispers.

'Moonshine?' I ask.

'God knows.'

Bartoni's voice lands above everyone. 'Everybody served for the time being?', which is followed by slurping murmurs of acquiescence. 'Shout if you need me.' He exits the counter via a flipping counter-top, and shakes Okpara firmly by the hand.

'Olly,' he says, his accent more Merseyside than I expected.

'Dick,' the Maasai replies. 'Can we chat?'

'Can you handle the smell of hops?'

'I drink now, Dick. I relented.'

'Did you now! Please, this way.'

He leads us outside and round the building to a green door so old and battered it looks like it may have caught the last moments of the Jacobite rising.

'Step into my boudoir,' he says, pulling a dangling light switch. A room is revealed congested by a mad disarray of tubing snaking atop steel kegs. Lots of them. Some of them have instruments embedded in the top.

'You've been busy,' says Okpara. 'Real ale?'

'I've got eleven different beers going in here. One of them has to go right.'

'You have a drop to try?' I find myself asking.

'Good man,' says Barton, approaching the barrels. He pulls a plastic pink tumbler from an overhead beam, and surveys his stock.

'I think this one could be approaching alright,' he says, before squeezing off a half into the cup. 'Might be a little hoppy,' he says, passing it to me.

'Chin chin,' I say, bringing it to my mouth. It's like drinking beer that's not quite beer. He's almost got it, but there's an earthen taste that makes me think of hamster food more than crisp booze.

'For the lady?' asks Bartoni, turning to Blake. I expect her to decline given the professionalism she's exhibited in clear spades these last couple of days, but she nods. 'You got something with any fruit?'

Bartoni, Barton, whoever this guy is, his eyes light up, and he bounces like Willy fuckin' Wonka over to some kegs at the back. 'I had a go with kiwi in this one?'

Blake frowns with a touch of trepidation. 'Go for it.'

A hiss and a gurgle, and she's furnished too. Before we know it, he's poured two more and given one to Okpara, and one for himself. 'The sun is always over the yard arm somewhere,' he says before taking a sip. 'Might need more time, that one.' Blake's cough on tasting suggests he's not wrong.

'We heard a name yesterday that you might be interested in,' says Okpara, swinging down to business sharply.

'*The* name?' asks Bartoni, suddenly still.

'*The* name.'

Bartoni takes a moment to finish his beer, and dusts a cobweb from the mantel over his head, raining specks of lint across the bare bulb light. 'Active?'

'That's the word.'

'You saw the work?'

Okpara looks across at Blake and I. 'We all did.'

'And was it him?' Bartoni is suddenly very still.

'I really don't know. Some obvious similarities, however. But something new.'

Bartoni's eyes fix on a distant point behind the door, as if a thousand graphic crime scene photos have blown past his eyes in one go. 'Go on.'

'Did you ever picture him being a knife for hire?'

'What do you mean?' He turns to look at us, confused.

'Did you ever feel that his services had been paid for? In the original killings?'

Bartoni looks at us one at a time, his eyes staying on me for a moment. I feel the urge to speak. 'Word is, the Dog of the Moors is doing a bit of contract stuff for some big narcotics players in town - at least that's what we were told.'

He pours himself another, and midway through pauses to check if any of us would like a top up. We all decline politely. 'I lived on Merseyside, St Helens way, commuting to Lancashire every day for work. I wanted the sensation of going home, that I wasn't just bedding down in the filth we so often had to wade through. I could always leave cases in Greater Manchester, go home, and pick them up when I came back in the next day. But not this.

'I bought this place on retirement, for reasons I couldn't originally work out. Needed something to put my head into, felt like trying a little business. An ice cream shop on a popular dog walking route seemed a great idea. I didn't know quite what I was doing, telling myself that Holcombe Hill was where I wanted to settle down and give it a try. I could have picked anywhere.

'I thought if I was near where the bodies were found, I might come across some inspiration, something jarred loose by proximity to that godawful place. I then thought maybe I'd get lucky, and he'd be one of those offenders who returns to the crime scene to relive it all, and I might end up serving him an ice cream on his way back down and I'd just know it was him. But… there's been nothing. Years have gone by, and nothing. This bastard committed the most appalling crimes, then disappeared. And he's never once come up for air - until now, with you lot.'

'Were you on the original case?' I ask.

'I was. Lead investigator. When the case went cold I kept the file open, not that I was able to add anything to it.'

'What can you tell us about him?'

'Nutshell… all victims were under the age of twenty, his preferred weapon being very deliberate stab wounds. The bites are still something we can't establish the methodology for, apart from him being a fair indication that he's an above bog-standard nutter.'

'Any giveaways of background?' asks Blake, taking another swig - which she actually appears to be enjoying.

'I imagine he was close to the area, in that he had knowledge of where he could bury those bodies with maximum secrecy. The statistics of such crimes usually indicate that we're talking about a male between the ages of twenty-five and forty, and that there would be others to go with the ones we found. He was killing them somewhere else at a location no police has ever had any knowledge of, and bringing them out here one at a time. As I mentioned, there's no other obvious wounds on the victims, like ligature marks, signs of struggle, or any other associated bruising. This suggested to me he was a talker, and therefore charismatic.'

Everything is fitting for me here. 'The victim on this one was killed with a single blade thrust, out from inside the body - where it had been placed with, as you say, precision.'

'Explain,' he says.

'The blade was inserted crossways through the neck, and pulled out through the front, right under the chin.'

'Messy. That'd be a new one for him, and wouldn't necessarily fit with what we dug up. However, if he was in his twenties when he started, he'd now be in his mid-late thirties, maybe even forties. Killers have been known to evolve across a central ethos. That could be the case here. He's handing a new tune to his old favourites. And besides, if he's essentially a contract killer now, the usual modes and methods won't apply so stringently. He'll have a client to appease.'

'Did you have any ideas as to range?'

'The victims were all across Greater Manchester and never the same place. You've got Oldham, Salford, Wythenshaw, Irlam and Trafford. Dotted all around the map of Manchester, with the only obvious central point being Manchester city centre. It's only because he was putting them up here did I think he might be from round this way.' Rossendale indeed sits north-east of Manchester by some twenty miles, and you wouldn't really go there unless you were familiar with it. It's not like a tourist attraction or major traffic thoroughfare. In short, you tended to go there for a reason. 'Where's your victim from?'

I look at Okpara, who's voice takes a grave timorousness. 'He's one of ours, Dick. He was an undercover.'

'Jesus.'

We stand there in silence moment, when a muffled jangle of a bell rings out - Dick abruptly starts walking to the door. 'Close up when you've finished please. And please, keep me posted. I live upstairs, so just ring the shop. And if you get any more information on him, bring me in. I don't care where you're up to, or what's happening - you have to bring me in.'

Okpara nods, while Blake and I watch him go. 'Just do the door and light when you go,' he says, before departing.

We stand in the dim room for a moment, our respective thought settling.

'This consumed him, didn't it?' I say.

Okpara sighs. 'He's extremely decorated and revered. But his last years on the force were dominated by the Dog of the Moors, and the fact they couldn't catch him.'

'We best try to catch him then,' says Blake. 'Maybe then he can concentrate on his brewery prowess.'

'I can't disagree,' I say, eyeing the remains of the murky liquid in my cup with an unexpected mix of suspicion and appreciation.

Chapter Twelve

After a quick respectful snoop at the top of the hill, which offered incredible vistas over Manchester, its vicinity and very little else, we pile back into the Range, which by now is streaked with dreck up its flanks. We retrace our steps, until Okpara takes a more direct route into Manchester, taking the A-roads and stop-start traffic of Bury, then through Prestwich. Okpara has a charity shop he wants to check in at, but it's only around Piccadilly and the northern outskirts of town that I realise I have a possible source myself.

We sweep past Piccadilly station, with its curved glass frontage which seemed so futuristic at the time but now looks a tad tired, and I shout up, 'Can you pull up and give me half an hour?'

Silence from the front.

'Hello?' I call. Okpara slows the car, and Blake turns in her seat.

'I'm not supposed to let you go off on your own,' she says, earnestly.

'Before you ask, I'm keeping out of it,' says Okpara, holding his hands up.

'Come on,' I say. 'You've got places to go, and people to see. So have I - only the people I want to see won't say a dickie-bird if you two are within a hundred yards of the place.'

Blake looks at Okpara. 'I told you, I'm staying out of it,' he says.

Blake sighs, and pushes a lock that's escaped her ponytail back behind her ear. 'Who is it?'

'Ask me afterwards, OK?' I say. 'It might not pan out and I don't want to look like an idiot.'

'You're asking a lot of me here, West. We've both been briefed with the same instruction. You're on my watch and I can't watch you out there.'

'Look if it goes wrong I'll square it with *him*. Say I jumped out of the car or something. But I'm sure if I get the goods here, you won't be disappointed.'

Blake rolls her eyes. 'Thirty minutes, and you're at the taxi rank at the station there.' She points out of the window. 'You let me down, I'm sure your career, or whatever it is you're doing, will go with it.'

'Loud and clear.' Wasting no time, I slip out of the door, and I'm on the streets - the streets I called home once. The streets I'm buzzing to stomp again.

Turns out in the past few months of pushing pencils, I've managed to gain an appreciation for data collection. I'm now much better at looking for patterns, organising the results into ways that are easier to digest, and learned how powerful it can be. So, I did a bit of number crunching last night when I got in.

When I blew up Sparkles Chu's restaurant, The Floating Far East, it went up in proper smoke. But I'd researched the target all afternoon before heading down there - I'm talking everything I could find on the web. A lot of company records are freely accessible to the public, so I managed to take a gander at who owned the restaurant itself. It was a holding company with the name Guangzhou 22 Ltd. So, with that in mind, now aware that Sparkles is back in town, I had a look for any other businesses under that same banner.

If my hunch about Sparkles being a man of principle is right, which is certainly the impression I got at our first meeting, I think business is his core motivation. In that case, the logical progression to the thought process would be that he's come back and opened a new one. Only problem was, I didn't find any other businesses owned by Guangzhou 22 Ltd. But I kept my search going, using the theme of the name as a guide.

A Chinese city, followed by a number that must carry some resonance to the incorporating parties. Of all the companies based in Manchester, not one carried that same characteristic. I then looked even wider, to look for any name that carried any hint of an eastern origin. There were a few, and all were based in Manchester's Chinatown district. They just all looked too obvious however, and Sparkles is no mug.

And then I got thinking about Sparkles name. Sparkles Chu. That in turn led me to remember how a lot of Chinese westernise their first names, so I then applied that not to Guangzhou as a place, but to the name of the city itself - which literally translated, means *wide city*.

And that's why I'm stood out front of Splitter's Axe Throwing Bar and Grill, owned by the holding company, Wide City Ltd. It popped out on the list bright as a brain injury. And I used my head to find it for a change.

Just round the corner from Piccadilly station, the front of the establishment is made up of shipping pallets affixed in rows to the brickwork like a half-finished fascia, although there is a frankly excellent neon sign in the middle of it proclaiming *Splitter's* in red neon swirls, with *Axe Throwing Bar and Grill* a blue neon mouthful in a ring around it. Windows sit embedded in the planks, and it looks dark inside. No surprise for eleven in the morning, I suppose.

I enter to dim lights and my own rising nerves. If this is the right place, I don't know how this'll go - I've not seen Sparkles since I pitched us both into the Irwell, and I'm hoping the fact that I let him live just before doing so will grant me some leniency. There's a counter to my left, also constructed with rough pallets, with a quaffed hipster sat behind it. Thick frames, a beard and lumberjack shirt are the tip off, but then I notice someone else in back towards the bar wearing the same thing. Over the receptionist's head are banks of flatscreens, this year's as opposed to the one in Bartoni's earlier, and they show different CCTV feeds of the establishment. You can see the bar area, which is empty, and four wood-lined booths of some kind, empty aside for that omnipresent bare wood up the walls and a set of three evenly spaced targets at the back. One of the booths is occupied, and a blond woman is, as suggested by the very name of the place, fixing to hurl an axe across it.

'How you doing?' says the man behind the counter, less like Joey from Friends, more like an extra from Coronation Street. As I get closer, I see he's not too old, and could well be a member of the abundant student population that dwells right across the city - one of whom was myself, many moons back.

'Yeah, I'm just dropping by. Wondered if I could have mooch?' I play off like I've got legitimate business on my mind.

'OK, like a liquid brunch mooch, or an active slinging steel mooch?'

'Like an *is your manager about* kind of mooch.'

The guys face changes. 'You want my boss? Have I done something?'

Poor bloke. 'No, no, no, I don't mean like that, I mean… How do I put this… Give me a booth and some axes, and ask your superior to come down for a natter. I'll give you a glowing report, and we can get to business, OK?'

'Oh are you like from the authorities?' His eyes are wild. I can imagine the fusion of booze and airborne axes might give the relevant authorities a *health'n'safety* unease.

'Something like that. Bit of a mystery shopper, but you've caught me out. Tell him Mr Bracken is here.' I give him a wink.

'OK, booth two is free, there's a crate of axes already in place, no silly business, don't go over the line while an axe is in flight, hit the red button on the left wall if you need any help.'

'That's great, thank you.'

'I'm Sandor, by the way. For your glowing report.'

Good God… 'Thanks, Sandor.'

'I'll go grab him, go right through.'

I nod, smile, and walk. The bar and tables are all empty, save for an identikit barman busying himself with some cocktail-tossing practice, who looks like he could well be Sandor's twin. The liquor bottle he twirls through the air is wrapped in masking tape, and empty, but he still gives me a nod proudly as I pass through to the well-lit area through the bar. Here, there are four booths as specified, as a loud *thunk* rings out from the far end, I'm guessing in the one labelled by the large red paint-splattered *four*. Two is just to my right, and a box of axes sits in front of a red streaked line across the floor some twenty feet from the target wall. The ground is green astro-turf, and overhead sit harsh strip lights with a bug-eyed camera in the corner. I wave a *toodle-oo*, take off my jacket, and go to the box.

Hatchets, all the same size. I lift one. About a foot long with a weighted blade of five inches in length. Maybe three pounds in weight, possibly four. I've not thrown an axe before, but I've thrown lots of stuff at lots of people. The competitor in me murmurs in its sleep. I take a step back, overarm throw, pick the bullseye and let fly.

It hits the board side-on and clatters to the floor. I frown and grab another. *Slower this time, Ben.*

It goes with that satisfying release you get when you know you've got something right, and this time the arrow hits home. Not on the bullseye, not even in the target, but on the board at least, lower down.

It suddenly strikes me that myself and Sparkles having a chat surrounded by axes is perhaps not the most sensible idea I've ever had. I shrug to the camera, and keep throwing. Five more throws, and I'm getting there, and it's then that a voice I haven't heard in ages speaks up from behind me.

'I knew you had bollocks, but showing up here?' It's Sparkles. I'd know that deep Manc vibe anywhere. 'You gonna burn this place down too?'

Holding an axe, I turn. He's the same as before, only his hair is a bit longer, and he has as thick a beard as the Sandor brothers back there, and he now sports thick-framed glasses too. But it's the same man I threw into the river, no question. Barrel-broad across the chest, in a fitted t-shirt that would still be an XL regardless, under which I know sit over twenty star-shaped tattoos right across the skin of his torso. He's Anglo-Chinese, the genetic traits of both he carries in his features, and his black hair is held fast in a neat side-parting with some kind of cement-like pomade.

'I'd like to offer you my hand,' I say, 'but I'm not sure you'd take it.'

'Just stay where you are, soldier boy.'

I put the axe down and hold my hands up.

'How did you find me?' he asks.

'You really thought the name of your holding company was that clever?'

He takes off his glasses carefully and sets them down on the drinks counter with deliberation. I hold my hands up again.

'I mean it,' I say. 'I'm not here for trouble.'

'You drown my business in a very literal sense, force me to go underground for a couple of years, before I can rebuild and get back to where we were, and you say you're not here for trouble?' He's seething inside and out, teeth bared.

'Hey, hey, come on, I need to speak to you, and last time we spoke, I thought you were telling the truth - so much so that I didn't kill you when I was supposed to. You're here because of me, Sparkles.'

He steps forward, fists clenched.

'You're prime suspect in a cop murder,' I say when he's halfway to me, which stops him cold.

69

'What?' His anger dissipates like a steam cloud caught by breeze.

'I work for the authorities now, I'm legit. And they asked me to come look at a murder scene, and they were trying to fit you for it. Caught you on facial recognition back in Manchester.'

He subconsciously touches his beard and I point at it. 'You thought *that* was going to save you?' I say. 'I told them it wasn't you. I told them you were a man of honour, and it didn't fit you at all.'

Sparkles answers with silence.

'They believed me, but it took some convincing,' I appeal.

'You tell them I'm here?' If looks could kill, my funeral would be next Thursday.

'They're not interested in you.'

'Good. Because this is all clean, all legit, they'd find nothing here.'

'They're not bothered about you Sparkles, seriously. Not anymore. But I figured you can properly put this to bed if you tell me what you know.'

Sparkles is unmoved, and clearly suspicious. 'I'm not in that place anymore.'

'Fine, be that as it may, but you clearly have a knowledge base that we don't.'

'I'm not helping the police. They've taken the piss for years. A man with my heritage, you're not even second place in this city. You're part of the undesirable element. You might as well be a termite infestation.'

'Don't think of it as helping the police - think of it as making sure your nose is clean. You tell me what you know, and I can tell them for sure it wasn't you.'

'You said they believed you.'

'I think they do, but let's leave nothing to doubt, hey?'

Sparkles takes a moment, before, 'Make it quick.'

'Murder of an undercover policeman, posing as an addict, two days ago over on Castle Street. Theatrical, looked like there were witnesses, nobody talking.'

Sparkles says nothing.

'We've heard there's a political slant to it.'

The big man frowns just a touch, but I caught it.

'Come on, Sparkles.'

'I don't know anything about politics. All self-serving shits who couldn't care less about the people, as long as they get their golden pension handshakes.'

'I don't disagree with you. What have you heard?'

'I'm not active in narcotics. Never have been.'

'But you know the lay of the land around here, don't you? The Berg - I took them out. Who filled in?'

Out of the blue, Sparkles smiles, and it's something I've never seen before. 'Now that - *that* - was something I did enjoy.' The Berg were trying to force Sparkles out of business, since he was their nearest and most threatening competition. His face returns to its more comfortable scowl. 'Shame I wasn't there to enjoy it.'

'We all do misguided stuff, Sparkles. Let's not get into weighing each other's regrets.'

He actually nods. 'Alright. Yeah, I heard about the killing. I heard they got some rats together, then your copper was pulled from the crowd, and killed bad. They knew it was him, like. I only heard yesterday. I wasn't part of it, before you ask.'

'I don't care what you're into now.'

'I told you, this is all legit.' His eyes beg me to take him seriously, which I suppose, as an ex-crim of his caliber, is a regular plea.

'How'd you find out?'

'People always talk. I've got another business that's all legit but less clean cut, but if you think I'm naming any names, you can forget that shit.'

'Don't care about names, I just want the details.'

'Strip clubs. You'd be amazed at who goes there, and who says what.'

'Trust me, I wouldn't.'

'Drugs aren't this city's main line of business any more - now it's all protection-extortion. The market is still there, but spice has been the biggest player for ages. Changing public sentiment towards drugs, even a lean towards legalisation, means that the industry doesn't have that same appeal anymore for prospective vendors.'

'Is that why nobody properly filled the void after the Berg disappeared?'

'I think so. Why break your back trying to fill it in if there's risk your investment won't mean as much. Not everywhere is the same though. Down the road, Liverpool's drug scene is doing just fine. But things have changed recently here with a big old push into heroin. Someone has been trying to heave us back into the days of yore.'

I'll have to check that with Blake and Okpara, see if that tallies up with what their undercovers are telling them. 'Any idea who?'

'Not concrete, but there's an all new grid of faces out there, getting to it. This ain't the same old town you and I would know, not anymore.'

'This is stupid of me to ask -'

'But you're going to ask it.'

'Damn right I am. Give me someone at your strip club I can talk to. On the quiet. I'm not a cop or anything, just man to man. If I show him some faces, could he match them up to pushers?'

'I can't believe you're asking me that.' Sparkles has gone all burnt vitriol again.

'Think about it, you don't want that shite on the street as much as I do. Help me get it off, clear your name properly, and you go your way, and I'll go mine. Or it won't be long before whoever's getting bigger comes knocking on your door for a bit of protection juice too.'

He bristles. 'Nobody would fuckin' dare.'

'You said yourself. This ain't the old town anymore.'

He sighs and thinks it over, even interlacing his hands behind his head. I grab an axe, and chuck it at the board. I actually get it in the first ring of the target this time.

'There's a strip club in Chinatown called The Obsession Rooms, he says. 'Be there at 2.00 pm. I'll have someone meet you, and you alone.'

'Can I get a guest pass for a number cruncher and a Maasai warrior too? They'll have the faces and the tech to go through it, and get these guys off the streets.'

Sparkles rolls his eyes. 'Who are you lot recruiting these days… Alright. But you owe me big.'

'You're right, I do.'

I offer my hand again, and this time, he takes it.

I walk straight, waving to Sandor Two on the bar, then Sandor One on the counter. As I go, I catch the bank of screens over his head. One is just a blank screen of static, the feed cut. It should be the picture for booth two.

I smile. *Legit my arse.*

Chapter Thirteen

Okpara and Blake pick me up, no words, and the Maasai drives all of fifteen yards further up the taxi rank, bangs his hazards on, bounces a curb, and says 'lunch time' in a voice I'd never argue with. Within minutes, we're in the train station, up the escalator, and ensconced in a booth overlooking the platforms.

I can tell Blake is bursting to ask what I've been up to, and I'll have to tell them that the day will most likely go past any reliably relaxed pre-Christmas five o'clock finish. We've got a strip club to get to. Okpara, full of surprises, orders a Guinness and looks across at us for guidance. I go for a lager, then Blake goes for the same, adding, 'I don't know about you guys, but that half before at Bartoni's definitely gave me the taste.' And we all know *the taste*.

While the beers are poured, I call Carolyn. 'Just gonna check in,' I say. The phone is answered on ring five.

'Hello love, how are you doing?' I say.

'We're good,' she answers, and the sound of her voice hasn't got old on me. 'Your boy is eating us out of house and home - and by *us* I mean *me*. I've been sat feeding him all morning.'

'My boy. Gracie and Jake good?'

'Yeah, they went off to school grand. I think we're experiencing thaw where Jake is concerned.'

'With regards to me?'

'Looks that way.'

I smile. 'Let's never tell him how we met, OK? We might find it romantic, but holy hell, he won't.'

'I think that's for the best.' I can hear her shifting position.

'I'm gonna be late home tonight I think. They've got me out doing stuff, and there's all sorts going on.'

'No worries, Captain.' I read from that, that my novelty hasn't worn off either. Long may it never do so. We say goodbye and hang up.

'The soldier has been domesticated, bless him,' says Blake with a smile and a swig of lager. I grab my pint and do the same, as she asks, 'Go on, where have you been?'

I tell them, and they laugh in disbelief.

'You went and had a chat with Sparkles Chu?' says Blake, pulling out a pack of nicorette, a tab of which she snaps out and chews with a slug of fizzy gold.

'It wasn't as hard as you might think,' I reply. 'You need to call Daughtry and get some of his far right faces off Facebook so we can see if his man recognises them.'

'Leave it with me.' She wastes no time, and her phone is at her ear in a second.

'What about you lot?'

Okpara takes over, still fixated on the tracks below. 'Hopped down to the Oxfam shop on John Dalton Street. Word there was similar to Tildy's. Exodus in process. If you're not playing straight in the underworld, you're on a train out of here.'

Now I know why he chose this place for a lunch date. 'Have you spotted anyone bunking off?'

He slowly shakes his head. 'Nothing yet, but between the three of us, I'm sure we'd spot a narc doing a runner.'

'So what's the play?'

'I think we take it easy here for a bit, then go see your contact at the naughty bar.'

Blake's off the phone and pulls a small tablet from her jacket pocket. 'Daughtry's preparing us a line-up, going to email it through ASAP.'

Okpara places his palms on the table top. 'Then let's order a burger or something, crack our heads together, and call this our office for the next couple of hours.'

I'm not going to argue with that, and grab the menu.

As we get closer to the strip club, winding further into the centre of town along streets lined with twinkling strip lights, moving in what feels like ever decreasing concentric circles into the middle of the morass, I realise I've been there before.

There was a time, some years back, immediately after my dismissal from the army, when I was far from happy. I was going from bar to bar, then back to the bin in my hotel room to chuck up, only to rinse and repeat (very literally) the next day. Far from my finest hour, but it passed the time of day. During that period, I built upon the knowledge-base forged during my days as a student here. I'm originally from Rawmarsh, South Yorkshire, but from the moment I attended a university open day in the city, I knew this was my home. When the army let me go, I found Rawmarsh had nothing for me, so it was to here I fell - and learned a lot more about the city on the descent.

The Obsession Rooms is in Chinatown, a small handful of blocks deep in the city's gut that features an ornamental welcome (now with cheap seasonal string lighting), some traditional restaurants and this particular pocket of good ol' fashioned sleaze. Its neon sign flickers dully in the daylight, which has come to adopt a crisp blue throughout the day. A bloke sits out front against a chipped black doorway, and his eyebrows ask questions as we approach. We aren't the usual clientele for an early visit to a strip club.

I expect Okpara to step forward and take the lead, but he seems uncharacteristically reticent, and unsure of himself. I can feel his gait has taken a soft tremor, as Blake steps forward.

'We have an appointment,' she says with authority.

'The girls don't take appointments,' the bouncer, whose world weariness is clear despite an obvious recent shower that's reddened his skin to volcanism.

'What's the name?' she asks me.

'Wasn't given one,' I reply.

'Then it's a tenner each.'

'We're police,' she says, lying quite a bit but keeping it simple.

'We get a lot of police, and they all pay a tenner.'

'But it's police business.'

'They all say that too. Surprising how much *police business* involves a pair of boobs in your face.'

We pool tenners reluctantly, and we're in. As we descend into a long thin basement, neon lilac and darkness taking place of the daylight, we are faced with an empty elongated shoebox. On the right rests an anaemic dance floor, with a couple of obligatory poles. Bar opposite on the left, with nary room to swing a cat between the two. A small flock of girls sit on a sofa in the back, half in lingerie, the other half in sweats, two shifts chewing the cud. The less-clothed members of the group stand to attention and start walking over. One spits gum out as she approaches, and her face adopts a businesslike seduction.

Okpara breathes out deeply next to me, and I turn to look at him. His eyes are on stalks. 'You married mate?' I ask him.

'Never,' he replies breathily.

I can't keep from smiling. 'You distract the locals, and we'll handle the enquiry.' He looks at me, nods, and steps forward. I grab Blake and guide her to the bar. 'We'll leave him to it.'

'I wouldn't mind watching that,' she says through a smile of her own.

The barman asks what we'd like, and I enquire, 'What do we do with these?' On our way downstairs, we'd been given Obsession Dollars, and I hold them up to him. They look like slutty Monopoly money.

'You can exchange them for a drink. Your pick,' he tells us. We take a couple of diet cokes and tell him we're here to see someone.

'I know, I've buzzed through. She'll be down in a minute.'

We wait, and watch Okpara, who's guided all three women back to a sofa, and is chatting expressively in such a way that suggests he's found his groove. Beside me, Blake seems comfortable and confident, and is proving a brilliant ally. And this place hasn't changed one bit. The sofas might have been updated, but the overall vibe of wallowing in a neon body orifice is still the same. I can't say I'm not enjoying this trip down memory lane, especially because the state of my life on this revisit is much less hopeless.

Within a couple of moments, we are approached by a Chinese woman in her mid-forties, who, in a knitted olive cardigan (hard to tell in this light), glasses and jeans, looks like she's just done a particularly trying school run. We shake hands, as she introduces herself as Anne, the owner.

'My nephew said you'd be stopping by, and that you are looking for some cooperation,' she says, as she guides us to a small table on a platform raised by a couple of steps. I look at Okpara, who's caught our movements, and he nods once before going back to his congregation.

'That would be great, thank you Anne,' says Blake. 'We are West and Blake from the NCA.'

'He said there would be three of you.'

'Our third member is otherwise occupied,' I say, nodding to the mismatched group, as laughter breaks out. He's actually showing them his sandals and frostbitten toes - and they're lapping it up. Anne doesn't see the funny side, and turns back immediately.

'You have some pictures to show me?'

Blake takes out her tablet and lays it on the table, followed by a small notepad.

'And this is off the record? This meeting never happened?' says Anne. She's firm, an all-business vacuum of nonsense, with eyes you wouldn't dare lie directly into. I look at Blake, who spreads her palms.

'It would be great if we could use what you tell us in an official sense.'

Anne gives no ground. 'Then I can easily walk into the back and erase the tapes. You never came in here. You went somewhere else and we never met. It won't be the first nor last time the tapes have gone missing.'

I don't know what she just admitted, but it doesn't sound particularly wholesome, nor legal - and I can imagine Okpara as a cop on the ground here taking a huge interest.

'OK, but don't hold anything back,' says Blake to my surprise. Salix's charges have all taken on a touch of his devilment, it seems.

I leave them to it for a moment, as those faces won't mean a thing to me, and watch Okpara, who's grinning from ear to ear, with a girl in a turquoise negligé sat on his knee, laughing and joking with the other two as he spins whatever yarn he's in the middle of. A few minutes pass, during which time I've heard Anne say *no* a number of times, but *yes* quite a lot too, when the quiet is punctured by a thump from up the stairs behind us.

I turn just in time to see the bouncer from before tumble down the steps into the strip club, his head bouncing so much that if he wasn't unconscious when he started the trip, he will be when he finishes it. Boots pound down the stairs, and the opening is suddenly filled by four men - the first of whom is the giant form of Vincent. Big Vincent. Young Tildy's bodyguard, his arm in a sling, and bruising on his chin from where my fingers went digging. His eyes don't take long to find me.

'There,' he says, pointing a finger big and curled as a Cumberland.

I stand, while whispering to Anne, 'Is there a back way out of here?'

She looks up herself and it's the first time I've seen any emotion in her eyes. It's fear. 'No trouble. He said there'd be no trouble.'

'And we don't want any.'

I stand and turn to Vincent. The three guys with him walk towards me, and they're *big*. Retired rugby player big. Thick across every part. 'Can we talk?' I ask. 'Does it need to go uncivilised so quickly?'

'You owe me an arm,' says Vincent, stepping forward.

'Think about what you're doing before you lay a finger on any one of us. There are cameras everywhere.'

'The cameras are off, aren't they Anne,' he says, directly to the owner. She shrugs her shoulders and nods.

'Oh, cheers Anne,' I say. The men march towards me, and just as their arms come up to grab me, a bellow blasts from over my right shoulder, and Okpara appears airborne, having dived off the bar onto them. He must have snuck behind there when he saw them enter, and as soon as he hits home, I'm moving too.

I don't strike to play games or send messages. I don't hit anybody for fun. I strike to maim, because that's how you win. Combat is survival, plain and simple. Go for the sensitive bits. If you aim to debilitate, you'll win. From the writhing bodies now on the floor, I grab the first foot I see that's got a shoe on it, and rip it up and backwards. A wet snap that echoes through my palms lets me know I got it right, the howl that follows underlining the point. One down.

'Get out, Blake!' I shout, but she's not listening. Instead, she takes two steps to the edge of the raised platform she was on and hurls a glass table at one of the men who's getting up. The table effectively pops on impact with the goon's shoulder, and gummy glass chips spray over everyone like cheap crystals at a rich kid's sweet sixteenth.

'Watch your feet!' I shout to Okpara, who is straddling one of the men on the floor. Vincent, who had been staying back, wades forward and goes for

Okpara with his one good arm. He's wide open. I reach over the Maasai and land a big left to Vincent's nose, which I felt move on impact. Two down.

Hold that thought a second - the broken ankle guy is trying to pull himself up. A boot to the kidney's settles him right back down, and the ringing in my foot suggests he'll be up ten times a night pissing blood for the next fortnight. I'm suddenly grabbed by the last guy, who's trying to grind broken glass into my face, with one hand on the back of my neck while I manage to hold the other, full of shards, just inches away from my eyes. Too close. Time for a dirty shot. I jump slightly to knock his balance off, then unleash a sterilising left foot volley right up his bollocks. That's two guys in need of adult diapers for the near future. Three down.

'Are we arresting any?' I ask Okpara, as he starts punching the remaining guy with overhand rights, who's now curled up into a ball.

'No - do we have what we need?' he asks between swings.

'Yeah, I think so,' shouts Blake as she hops the railing to the platform and heads for the stairs.

I turn to Anne. 'Thanks for the help.'

'Get out,' she snaps, before abruptly pointing at Blake. 'And tell that one she can have a job if it doesn't work out with the pigs.'

Okpara appears next to me, and hands Anne a handful of notes. 'Is this how it works?'

She snatches them from him and points to the stairs. 'Get out or I'll send the tapes to the papers.'

I'm confused as to whether the tapes were ever running at all, but start to go. Okpara does the same, while sending a cheery wave to the women at the back - who beam back with smiles.

All three of us are up the stairs, when Vincent bellows from the bottom, and like, the boulder in Indiana Jones in reverse, starts to give climbing chase. We start sprinting down the street, and take an immediate left. I look back over my shoulder. Vincent is back there, puffed up and reddened, with twin streams of blood leaking from each nostril, and he's got one of his friends with him, having pulled himself together. We keep running, twisting this way and that in the back streets of Chinatown, until the only echoing footsteps we can hear are our own.

Chapter Fourteen

We head right across town, leaving Oxford Road, Princess Street and Chinatown well behind us, as the mid-afternoon sun begins to set on the city and everything begins to twinkle as the light fails. Okpara tells us he knows a spot to regroup and catch up, so we follow his lead. Say what I like about the warmth of those sandals, they don't compromise his speed - we've gone at such a pace that, yet again, I can tell that domesticity is blunting me a little.

We hit the main thoroughfare of Deansgate, the city suddenly opening like a split piece of fruit, and waste no time in crossing between the stop-start traffic, the city buzzing and ever-brighter with the holiday season. Seconds later, we are past a Sainsbury's, down another street and at the threshold of a real back street boozer called Mulligan's, a sign over which promises Manchester's finest pint of Guinness.

'We'll lay low in here for a while,' says Okpara on opening the door, as the melodies and rhythms of the Emerald Isle tumble out onto the street. A band is playing on a short stage to our left, a four piece with traditional instruments who make a very good go of 'Brown Eyes' by The Pogues, beneath a projector screen showing what looks to be the 2.50 at Kempton.

Okpara heads for the bar with the stride that suggests he's been here before - in fact, come to think of it, I know he's a Guinness man, so I'm sure he has.

Blake and I follow.

'She offered you a job you know,' I say to Blake, as we squeeze between the day drinkers.

'Who?'

'Anne, at the last place.'

'Fuck off.'

By the time we reach Okpara, he's ordering three pints of the black stuff. 'I don't drink it,' states Blake, but Okpara simply says with a smile, 'Trust me, this isn't the Guinness you're used to.'

The barman pours and sets them to one side while the pints settle. I've seen this before, but as a lager drinker, it feels strange to let the fizz slow before handing it to the customer. While the foam races down the velvet noir, Okpara pays and Blake talks.

'I'll write it up later, but, providing Anne has no axe to grind, the correlation is clear. Overwhelmingly, there is now a number of drug vendors in the city who have recently adopted a far-right agenda. For me, there's no doubt.'

'When you say far right, what do you mean?' I ask. I'm no politico, so I want to get my facts right.

'I'm talking right on the cusp of a modern day nazism. Every immigrant is worthless, and has taken our jobs, and needs forcing back out of the country, dead or alive. These guys exhibit a hatred to what is normally known as the right. Tories, Lib Dems, Labour, right across to Green – anything to the left of their position is all as bad as each other in the eyes of this lot. A lot of the rhetoric brands the regular political base as traitors. This is white supremacy, dressed up as the greater good, Queen and country.'

'So not the normal rise of the right we've seen in recent years after Brexit and the EU referendum?'

'No, this is best described as a steroidal version of that movement. That's nothing compared to this lot – although it has grown exponentially by the recent growth of nationalism in the country, because if you were that way inclined and were suckered in by any of their online propaganda, you'd probably end up all in. And Facebook, again, has a lot of such propaganda on it, being shared unchecked.'

The Guinnesses are poured and passed round, and we take a seat around a small round table at the back where 'Dirty Old Town' won't disturb us.

'You catch all that, Okpara?' Blake asks, as she takes off her jacket.

'Sadly, I did,' he says, subconsciously mirroring her gesture. They sit next to each other, easy in each other's company. 'We'd never notice it normally on the streets, because you'd be committing a public order offence if you were shouting that kind of stuff, but it's amazing what people offer to the echo-chamber of Facebook.'

'Used to be that trolls used pseudonyms in chat rooms to spout this tosh - now, they're proudly posting it on Facebook on their profiles alongside their full education history, employment history, raft of ID pictures to choose from, even their middle names and pictures of their kids.'

'Times, they are a-changing,' says Okpara.

'You got that right,' I concur.

It's something that I've struggled with, balancing what the political sentiment of this country has become, against what I've done for this same nation. As a soldier, I've given everything in the name of a patriotism that I thought was right. I've always felt there's nothing wrong with being proud of your nation, moreover it should be traditionally encouraged, but it has latterly become something viewed with scorn. For me however, the more worrying characteristic is to adopt that pride in your nation while forgetting the core aspects of what made the nation what it was in the first place.

In Britain's case, inclusivity, multiculturalism, hard-work and forward free-thinking are cornerstones. Yet, in the political split of the decade encompassing the 2010s, those characteristics seem to have been forgotten. The nation is divided, left and right, with so little in between, that the actual positives of a free-minded, forward-thinking Britain as we know it through history (albeit with a number of mistakes), has long since been forgotten.

It was simpler when I was faced with my decision to serve - we were all broadly on the same page, and political extremism was something reserved for people and places far removed from the shores of the UK. Now, it's rife. Left and right. And I know that, if faced the same question, if I would go and risk everything to protect this country, the answer now would be a resounding *no*. What would I be fighting for exactly? A bickering populace on the precipice of ideological combustion. That wouldn't galvanise me to take up arms.

So now, as far as politics go, I stay out of it, disillusioned with it all and sick to the back teeth of hearing about it.

'We've got to share this with Jeremiah,' I say.

Blake nods, a Guinness moustache on her top lip. 'Let's take an Uber. I want to get all this down, try to make a clearer picture.'

'I'll leave it to you lot to type it up,' says Okpara. 'I'll check in on the murder investigation, see if any undercovers have come up for air.'

We sit for a moment, knowing our next move but the adrenaline of the day is pouring out to the point that we can't follow up just yet. We pause and sup for a couple of minutes, like we have nowhere else to be.

'You got on well with the ladies at Anne's gaff, then?' I ask Okpara, he smiles bashfully.

'They hadn't met a man like me, it's fair to say. They asked for my name, and I explained it to them.'

'Olly?'

He nods and shuffles in his seat. 'It's short for Olamayian. A given Maasai name if you happened to kill a lion on your first hunt.'

'You're right,' says Blake with surprise. 'They won't have heard that before.'

I can't help but smile myself, and I've got a question of my own. 'I've got to ask you, mate. The White Range Rover. I can't work it out, at all.'

'That always gets people talking. It's very simple really. I've been forced time and time again to adapt the man I used to be, to the environment I have become accustomed to. Obviously, there are not many fellow Maasai warriors here in Manchester. In fact, I've never come across another. But I'm proud, and in a sense, devout.

'My parents are still alive. In Segera, back home in Kenya. I came here to support them and my village, in a way that was more productive than the well-meaning but misjudged handouts we are so often given. It was a time of drought when I left, and clean water was what we needed. We were getting sent clothes, toys and seeds - all of which we were grateful for, but weren't easing the immediate problems facing my people.

'As I looked more into it, I came to realise just how cheap it was, in comparative economic terms, to save us. A well, digging down to where there is known clean water, can be built for under a hundred pounds. As soon as I found that out, I knew that if I travelled north into Europe and get work, I could make a huge impact at home. My village was full of all living generations of my family. This could save them all.'

He takes a swig of Guinness, and I'm spellbound. Our journeys are all different, granted. But his? My *God*.

'When I'd sent enough money home to build a series of wells, which didn't take as long as you might think, I thought about what next. I wasn't sure what to do, because I'd done what I set out to achieve. But the potential for so much more good was right there. So, I knew the city quite well by this point, and became a taxi driver.

'I lived carefully and before long we'd built a school with the money I sent back. Again, it didn't cost what you'd think. We were then able to improve everyone's homes. And I still send a bit home every month. The police give me a percentage of my take home in dollars cash, which is immediately put in an envelope, and sent back to my mother. This year, we're working on shelter for young women who are at risk.'

'At risk from what?' asks Blake.

'I'm afraid it's as sad and simple an answer as rape and murder. Certain ways are hard to stamp out, and the roll of generations isn't stamping it out quick enough. Sadly, women in our culture can often be the ones on the receiving end of the choicest abuses. I'm aiming to change that, to give these girls a safe place to stay and sleep instead of having to do so outdoors where they are in harm's way.'

'That's incredible,' I find myself saying. 'Full respect.'

'Thank you. Ah, it was the Range Rover you were asking about. Well, I've had to make many compromises in my journey, especially in terms of adapting to this culture, and it involved me incorporating my beliefs and heritage into my day to day. My belt is one.'

I look down, to his waistline. His belt is a brightly beaded loop of leather around his midsection. 'Traditional and from home,' he says. 'I had a spirit guide growing up. An elder, who had been reincarnated many times over as different animals. He was a source of light and inspiration right from my birth. But when I moved here, his guidance was lost. I always felt him with me, however, and I heard of his pride from afar. But then he died.

'Before he passed, he told me he thought his next reincarnation would be as a white rhino - a species indigenous to our part of Africa. At the time

I felt lost, full of questions over what I was really doing over here, and I felt his sudden loss very much. This was soon after I made detective, and the day after I heard the news of his death, I was involved in the arrest of a small-time drug pusher, during which event, his car was confiscated. I remember it in the impound lot, staring at it. This huge, broad car, all in white. The Range Rover - and I couldn't stop looking at it. I was reunited with my spirit guide.'

'The car?' I asked.

'How many white rhinos do you see wandering around Deansgate? I had to go for the next best thing, and I felt this instant feeling that it was right. So, I kept an eye on the car, and bought it at auction. It was meant to be.'

'I'll drink to that.' I raise my glass, as do Blake and Okpara.

'I have succumbed to a few British compromises, I must admit,' he says, as he gives himself a foam moustache of his own.

The place begins to get busier, the band picks up tempo, and our time here, however pleasant, has grown short. And they weren't lying when they said the Guinness was the best either - it's an epiphany as pure and revelatory as finding Jesus and Elvis, all at once, in the same tall glass.

Chapter Fifteen

The white rhino drops us off outside HQ, just as the last of the nine to fivers are heading out. We fight the tide, and make it up to the OCC hexagon. When we get there, Jeremiah is sat at the central table, while Catterall flits around him like a coiffured, six-foot hummingbird, papers riffling as he collects them from the copier in the corner, spreading them on the table in an order only he must be aware of, and sticking the occasional one on the magnetic wall board.

As Blake and I walk into the space, it's impossible for our gait not to betray a little tail between our legs.

'I don't know what you've been up to, but I'm hoping it's good,' he says. He looks a little wilder than usual, his hair out an inch or so more since I last saw him this morning. His tie is loose, and in his left hand sits a can of some garishly-clad caffeine drink.

'It's been a busy one, gaffer,' says Blake, as she heads to the kitchen. 'Any coffee on?'

'As always.'

'You want one, West?'

'Sure,' I say, before leaning on the table next to Jeremiah.

'You behave yourself?' he asks me, his voice lowering a touch as he does so. I can almost feel Catterall crane his perfect neck to listen in.

'I always do. Lots to tell.'

'Same here. Have a seat.'

I do as he says, and Blake kindly furnishes me with caffeine.

'You lot start,' says Jeremiah.

'After you,' I say, nodding to Blake, who starts talking and doesn't stop for ten full minutes. She tells Jeremiah and Catterall everything, from Ricardo Bartoni, to Sparkles Chu, to our run in at the strip club - and all the findings in between.

'So there's an extreme right group suddenly pushing hard drugs in Manchester?' summarises Jeremiah.

'From what we've learned, I'd say that's 100% certain,' says Blake, picking up her mug for the first time, which is no longer steaming.

'You think this is the group the informant Young Tildy was warning about?'

'Yes.'

'And she said they'd hired the Dog of the Moors - any more on that today?'

'After Bartoni, it didn't come up again.'

'Good. Because we've got something here.'

Interesting. He continues.

'I pushed the urine sample from the scene through, expedited, and would you know it, we have a match.'

I can't hide my excitement and from the looks of it, neither can Blake. I look at Catterall who cracks a smile.

'Brett Scarborough,' says Catterall, evidently keen to share. We seem on much better terms than yesterday, any thoughts of manhood comparison long since passed.

'And where can we find him?' I ask.

'You'll have a genuine hard time doing that. He's off the grid.'

Too vague for me, that. 'Forgive me, but cut the crap. *Off the grid* is a telly phrase that might wash with some folks, but I know how you lot work. There's no end to the grid you've got your eye on.'

Catterall looks at me with a touché, and glances to Salix, who glances back with a hint of resignation. He spreads his palms and sighs.

'It's always a bugger when one of your old boys comes back to haunt you,' says the boss.

'He's one of yours?' I ask.

'In a fashion. We worked with him a couple of times in an interagency capacity. We are wizards with paper and pens, and general investigative procedures, but when it comes to shit hitting the fan in the field we often outsource to the best we can find.'

'And this guy was the best, I take it?'

'He was good for sure. Ex-military, ex-CIA, ex-a lot of other stuff we aren't supposed to know about. He's a black-ops spook who the Ministry of Defence had us working with.'

'Ex-military, can you elaborate?'

'I believe he cut his teeth in the Middle East.'

'The first Gulf War,' Catterall adds. 'That was when he was infantry, then when he left the army, he headed straight over to the states. He has an American mother, which got him into the CIA. Fast forward another fifteen years of god-knows what for god-knows whom, and he shows up back here being farmed out for the MOD.'

'Christ alive,' I whisper. The MOD are on my all-time shit-list. A rogue element of theirs tried to bankroll the acquisition of modified botulism until I stopped them, but that in turn didn't deter them from sending a pair of hitmen out into the Norfolk backwaters to take me out. 'So what did he do for you?' I ask.

'Three years ago, we had to dismantle a meth lab over in Swinton, not too far from Manchester. It was a haulage firm with a dirty little side-earner, operating out of a rusty industrial park. Because there were some heavy-duty chemicals over there, we needed a guy with experience of operations with a chemically hazardous risk. The MOD sent us Scarborough, amongst a few others, but he was the point man.'

'If he's so *off the grid*, as you put it, how do you have his DNA? If he's black-ops that stuff will be gold dust,' I ask.

Both men look back at me silently. A phone rings somewhere in the hub, but none of us move to answer it.

'You're not supposed to have it, are you?' I say. Jeremiah makes that sigh again.

'The lab we use for DNA comparison is not on site here, but we have a good relationship with them.' He rocks his chair back and forward again with agitation. 'When nothing showed on their official database, we suggested they try ours. And by ours, I mean this sole department.'

'How did you get a sample from him?'

'Everyone that passes through here gets added.'

'That isn't legal, is it?'

'Is it bollocks. But we live in an industry of backstabbing and subterfuge – it all adds to our own little safety net in our operations when we use outsiders. The more info we have, the better I tend to feel about carrying on this ridiculous juggling act.'

I hold up my coffee cup. 'I'm in there, aren't I?'

'One of our more recent additions,' Salix replies stone-faced.

'Cheeky buggers. But if you can't use it, isn't it pointless?' I ask.

'It got you a name, didn't it?' Salix replies with a raised eyebrow and I can't argue with that.

I take a moment to dwell on what I've just learned. The mistrust between agencies, for Salix to even think of collecting such an informal database which has blossomed from his own hysteria, is staggering. It's the lawlessness again – even amongst our lawmen, trust, commitment and doing the right thing are blurred ideals awash in the tide of bureaucracy.

'Do you think he could be the Dog of the Moors?' I ask.

'A man who's done the things Brett Scarborough has done… I'd hate to look in the dark corners of his head. In that sense, anything is possible. I'd have to say *yes*.'

We are silent just for a moment.

'And to think… he was here,' muses Blake, almost to herself. She takes in the hexagon, lost in thought.

'You've got to follow the evidence,' Salix reasons, his manners taking on the guise of private, internal reasoning much like Blake seconds earlier. 'And the evidence suggests that if the Dog of the Moors did this crime, then the Dog of the Moors might well be Brett Scarborough.'

'The first named suspect that case has ever had,' Blake says.

This story could blow national.

'So what are you going to do about this? You have the info – where do you take it?' I ask.

'Gaffer isn't sure we can do anything,' Catterall says, deferring to his boss but dumping him in it at the same time. 'I'd rather go after him hell for leather.'

'Where, Catterall?' Salix exclaims. 'Where? Hmm? Where do you suppose we go hunting for the black ops ghost? He's MOD property, which is, as we've learned many *many* times first hand, not our jurisdiction. We are specks of lint on the MOD's lapel, that's all. We have no way of going after Scarborough and you know it.'

'We forget him for now,' I say, my brain clicking into gear. They both turn to look at me as if I've started spilling my marbles on the cheap carpet. That phone rings again, jangling softly somewhere.

'He's our lead!' Catterall says. 'Our first concrete lead since the very beginning. And you want to forget it?'

Salix looks at me, knowingly. He knows I'd never let something go unless there was a reason.

'Guns for hire don't come cheap,' I say. 'Ever. The better the experience, the more expensive the gun. This guy has a shitload of experience, so he'll have cost a few quid, no danger. Whether he's still on the MOD books or not makes no difference to what we are trying to find out here. Scarborough is just the tool chosen for the job. Tracking him down may get somewhere in the long run but it won't get you any closer to finding out who used him, which is the real issue.'

'Agreed, I suppose,' says Catterall.

'So, we need to work out who hired him.'

'Bloody hell, this is grim…' mutters Blake. In the midst our discussion, she has obviously followed a train of thought and drifted to one of the communal computers, and from the blue strip at the top of the screen she's glued to, I can see she's on Facebook. I'm no user, but even I know what that is.

'What is it?' asks Catterall.

'Just skimming across the surface of the pond life Anne at the strip club says is pushing hard stuff in the city.'

Catterall grabs a remote and points it at the seventy-inch wall-mounted LED screen next to the display wall. He clicks a couple of buttons, and Blake's computer screen is replicated on it in eye-searing HD.

She's switching between profiles, and lines a handful up for comparison. The correlation between the feeds is glaring in its obviousness.

'They keep sharing videos of this woman, who is she?' I ask, as I look at all the accounts on the big screen. Many feature the same shaky video of a blonde woman with a loudspeaker, wearing a politician's trouser-suit with heavy eye makeup.

'Who, Helen Broadshott? Christ, where have you been?'

'I don't use Facebook.'

'You don't need to use Facebook. She's an independent candidate lobbying to become an MEP. Desperately trying to gain traction by travelling around the country spouting off pro-right propaganda, but all she gets is a lot of milkshake thrown at her.'

'What's her core message?'

'Racism. Take out her catchphrases, and it's pure racism. England for the English, a death to multiculturalism, revert back to a crusades mentality.'

'That sounds nice.'

'I don't know her education background, but I'd go so far as to suggest much of it wasn't great. But she's a fabulous public speaker, and she's easy on the eye. It's not hard to see why she's caused quite the stir amongst those that don't feel they have a political voice or spokesperson.'

Again, I'm thinking of what I've given just so that the country can descend to *this*. Hitler was a master orator, look where it got him - and Broadshott's blonde hair, blue eyes and statuesque frame could barely be anymore Aryan nation.

'Our pushers, the one's Anne identified. They all follow her?'

'Universally. Their videos are all over their pages. Every single pusher identified has some Broadshott propaganda somewhere on their timeline.'

'There's no way we can ignore that. It cannot be coincidence.'

'I would agree.'

'Our White Christmas,' says Catterall. 'Not a very subtle message.'

'What?' asks Blake.

'Look,' he says, up and pointing at the screen. A number of Facebook feeds are emblazoned with a graphic that promises *Our White Christmas 2019*.

'Looks like this movement's really up for the festive season.'

'Do we have a name for this movement?' I ask.

'They're an offshoot and there's a few of them with support bases dotted around the country. She calls hers the SGP - the St George Patriots.'

'Sounds deeply charming,' says Catterall through a frown. He's being facetious, but ten years ago a name like that would seem deeply charming for real, without any need for sarcasm. Take into account the present political sentiment of the country, it merely comes across as nationalistic and right wing.

'So what is motivating all these pro-military guys to push drugs and follow her? What do they want to happen? Surely, they've not just had a sudden career change and are trying something new? What is the connection?'

That is the connection. What has suddenly gone rotten for these guys, and *why*? And what the hell is *Our White Christmas*?

Chapter Sixteen

Finally, with the sun long since gone and the ground adopting a quick frost, I make it home at about nine in the evening. We live in a village about a ten-minute drive from the NCA offices, in a place called Croft. It's where Carolyn was placed when she was ushered into the Protected Persons Program, the stiff upper Brit version of witness protection, after she testified against a lot of people who I'd killed. She was an accessory held in place by fear and abuse, but her cooperation saw her receive favourable treatment.

She brought her two children here, of all the options, because it appeared quiet and was in the catchment area of a highly-rated village primary school. She got a nondescript admin job in a local office firm, and enjoyed living a normal life for a while. Then I showed up a year ago. I hope she's still happy I did.

The house is a detached red brick, two up two down, on a sixties estate, each identical to the one next to it. She's decorated hers with silver solar lights in the front garden borders, and a potted fern on either side of the door. The house is dark, but soft flickering light creeps round the edges of the curtains. She's up watching telly.

I use my key, so as not to wake the kids, and slip inside. The house is warm, the pull of comfort beguiling, and I kick my trail shoes off by the door. God, that feels *good*. I cast a glance up my stairs on the left, and see the ambient flicker of the children's nightlight on the landing, on all the time to guide them on midnight toilet trips. All seems quiet up there, so I head down the hall following the muffled laughter of the TV.

At the same time as entering the room and clocking *Fraser* is on, I see

Carolyn sat on the L-shaped sofa beneath the window, opposite the fattest Christmas tree we could buy at the local farmer's yard. Jam is in her arms, asleep, but she herself is silently crying, the tears on her cheeks flickering green and red in the glow of the fairy lights.

'Darling, what's the matter?!' I ask, as I go to her. Her tears cut my heart to ribbons, as they've conspired with her mascara to make a shoddy burglar mask of her eyes. She doesn't say anything as I take her and pull her to me. I don't think it's anger she's feeling, more of a sadness.

I turn her to face me. 'Carolyn, you've got to talk to me - what's going on?'

She looks at me, with poignant resignation in her eyes. 'It was what you said… I've been thinking about it ever since.'

I'm no expert in relationships, and this is all new territory for me, but I quickly peel back through my memory for anything I said that could have upset her. 'I'm so sorry if I've said something. Whatever it is, I promise I didn't mean to upset you like this. Can you give me a hint so I can fix it?'

'It can't be fixed, I don't think.'

Well, that's me stumped. She told me that, after her first two pregnancies, she'd suffered from an acute drop in hormones after the birth, which resulted in mood swings and a touch of post-natal depression. This may well be attributed to that, so soon after Jam's birth, but I'll be damned if I'm bringing *that* up.

'Baby, talk to me. I'm sure between us we can sort anything like this out.' She doesn't answer and it has me second guessing my own assertion.

Can we sort anything out? We've not known each other very long, not really, and dove straight into playing happy families, the sealant for which being the bundle that lies between us right this second - our baby. I can't think negatively about her, about us, so I won't. I saw childbirth - having gone through *that*, she can do whatever the hell she likes.

I grab the remote and mute Kelsey Grammar, then pick up Jam and cuddle him. I have a strange innate feeling to show her I can be her protector, not just for her, but for our child and her children. I *can* look after them all as an understanding parent, in the face of all I've done, and despite how new this all is. It seems to work. Her body language unravels a notch.

'You said we'd have to keep certain things from the kids. My kids. How

94

are we going to do that? I don't know how.' She adopts a coolness despite the tears.

'You mean about how we met?'

'They know you're not their dad. Jake is always asking questions about his real dad anyway when you're not there, and he remembers he wasn't the best guy in the world. I don't know how we keep it all a secret that it was you that killed him.'

She hushes those last words in case either Jake or Gracie have come down the stairs, while I feel warm at the thought of Jake keeping questions about his father from me so as to spare my feelings.

'I don't know legally what I can tell them,' I say. 'It's not a straightforward conversation, I'll give you that. But we're talking a long way in the future.'

'I'm not sure we are, Ben.'

Ben. So much of the time, I go as *Tom* or *West*, at least at work - but here at home, I'm *Ben.* It's a juggle, and a constant reminder of my poor choices.

But... if I hadn't made those choices, good, bad and supremely fucking ugly, I'd never have met this amazing woman, her lovely kids, nor had the chance to be a father to this little bundle that's my be-all and end-all.

'I don't care about any of that stuff,' I say. 'I just want to be with you all. Any hurdles we can tackle at the time.'

She softens a little. I think I might have stumbled on what she wanted to hear. *Phew.* The thing is, I love her. And I would do anything to be with her.

'They are getting really fond of you, you know.' Her words make me feel a new kind of warmth, one I'd never encountered before. My brief tenure in parenthood has shown me that the words and joys of children can be the most precious thing you'll ever receive. I'm humbled to hear I'm earning their approval.

'You've done an amazing job with them,' I say.

'Even if you're not their dad, you're shaping up to be more of a father than he ever was.'

'I'm not trying to be their father... but if circumstances allow, I'll be their best friend, protect them and love them as my own. I promise you.'

She snuggles closer, and feeling her next to me ignites the light in me that stays on all day, waiting to be near her again. 'Speaking of your own,' she says, sending her smile south to the boy in my lap. 'He's got his jabs tomorrow.'

'Oh yes, of course.' It's been on the calendar since his birth. I was determined to be there, but now, with all that's going on at work... I can't.

'You can't make it, can you?' Her voice is hopeful. *Dammit*.

'I can't, baby. This case, it's something else. It's taken a whole new direction, and finally after a year of being stuck on a desk, I'm doing something good. I mean, I know I've done a lot of bad stuff in my life, but this is my chance to do some proper good.'

'It's OK. I know how much that means to you.'

I look at Jam, torn. 'They're gonna put a needle in him?' I ask.

'Just quickly, yeah. He'll cry a bit, but that's all. Might have a slight temperature tomorrow evening. It's a big thing for a baby.'

Now I'm *really* unhappy about missing it. I want to be there for my boy's every requirement. I want to do what's right for him.

But what's right for him can also be helping keep the streets safe for him, and his older half-siblings. Surely that's the greater good, and his mum can look after him on this occasion?

I'm about to voice that, when I have an idea. It's come in from nowhere, born out of the sudden realisation of the depths I'd go to in order to keep these children safe. It's an idea that might not work, but if there's a slight chance it could, I'm there. It's one that only *I* could take, too. I'll sleep on it, and put it to Jeremiah in the morning.

'They're all asleep you know,' she says, and I look at her. She's looking up at me, her chin lowered slightly in a mock coyness.

'But...'

'Don't worry. I know *me*. It'll be fine.'

'You're sure?'

'Where you're concerned, yes, I'm sure.'

I put Jam in his moses basket, while she turns the lights off.

Hours later, and I'm lying awake, my baby boy on my chest, snoozing. It would be perfect. It's so close to it. But all I can think of is *Our White Christmas 2019*. I run it through in my mind, over and over, second guessing myself on repeat.

What is that?

You put a date to something, you give it a time.

96

Why a time?

To establish when something is to be done.

And what is that?

A deadline.

Something is coming.

The SGP is planning something for Christmas. I'm sure of it. And if their warmup act was the blood-soaked show-murder of a cop, I'd hate to see the main event.

Chapter Seventeen

'No, no - *no way.*' Jeremiah pushes his chair backwards so forcefully he rolls ten feet across the carpet of the OCC hexagon. 'Not a chance.'

I follow him halfway. 'Just hear me out.'

'It's stupid, there's no way in hell anyone in their right mind would sanction that.' He spins his chair deftly, and makes for his corner office. I follow him.

'Who needs to sanction it?'

'All sorts of people! The higher ups here, the higher ups in GMP. You can't just swan off and do something like that. God, you're pushing it. I mean, being in the field in any capacity was pushing it, but what you're suggesting here...'

He enters his office and swings the door shut, but I catch it. I hold my hands up and follow him in. 'I'm ex-military. You know they might go for that. You know it might get me in the door. Not just with them, but with the Dog of the Moors too – if it's him.'

What I've suggested, somewhat cheekily it appears, is to try to infiltrate the Mancunian networks of the extreme right, more-or-less in an undercover sense. I try to drive the point home that I'm the best man for the job. 'I'm not a copper. They don't know me. What they can find out about me, should they chose to, is that I was dishonourably discharged for murdering a fellow soldier in a mercy killing. I know a lot of soldiers who'd support that, and be angered by the brass' decision to scrub me out. Stick it to the man, and all that. They seem to be actively recruiting disillusioned soldiers – *hello*, isn't that my calling card?'

'I'm not sending someone who is tantamount to a civilian, *untrained*, into an undercover situation. Not on my watch. No way.' Now behind his desk, he pulls his glasses down from where I'd missed them in his nest of hair, and places them on his nose.

'You used to go for this sort of thing before,' I remind him.

'And look where it got me. Look where it got *you*.' He's referring to the unofficial missions he's sent me on, and how the last one ended badly for us all at a turkey farm in Cambridgeshire, filled to the brim with walking Christmas dinners and a cavalcade of stars from the global criminal underworld.

'I understand, but mate, we got *results*.'

'Results that we're still cleaning up now.'

I move around the front of his desk and face him head on, pleading my case. 'It's building, Jeremiah. You can see it, and I can see it. It's all over the internet. The far right and their drugs are a growing presence in Manchester and now you've got the murder of an undercover officer and warnings across the city. This is heading one way, somewhere bad. *Our White Christmas*. This is escalating to something.'

'You're guessing at best.'

'If we had the chance to stop something terrible happening we have to do what we can.'

He shakes his head, but the conviction is less pronounced. 'We keep combing the intel, build a bigger picture, wait for something concrete. People are never going to stop blabbing on Facebook, it's the nation's favourite pastime.'

'I'm not going to sit on Facebook when I could be finding out the plan directly from the horse's mouth.'

'No. The answer is no.'

I'm not angry with him, but I'm bloody frustrated. 'What's my role here?'

'Admin assistant and special advisor to the OCC.'

'Really?'

'I had to come up with something on the spot, but yes that title would cover it.'

'And who knows about me.'

'A couple of the real top dogs and the people in this department.'

'And they all think I'm Tom West.'

'Not the top dogs. They know just who you are. Which is why I can't go to them to sanction any undercover op, especially when undercovers are murder targets at present. They'd never let you loose.'

'Then don't. Tell them I'm having a few days leave. It's just before Christmas, it'll be fine. Everyone has time off around Christmas don't they.'

He doesn't answer, and that makes me think I'm getting somewhere.

'Give me a couple of days off. Hell, I just became a dad, anyone would allow that! And I'll check in with you from time to time. Unofficially. And I'll have a word with Okpara out of courtesy.'

Jeremiah thinks on this. I've put him in some awkward situations before, so me waiting for an answer from him is hardly anything new.

'You really think they're planning something?'

'I'm convinced. It's building to a point. And I've got a really good idea of how to get inside them.'

He sighs, and as the sigh finishes, he's already talking. 'I literally don't want to know… Today is Wednesday. Friday is Christmas Eve. 9.00am Christmas Eve you report back here ready to get back on your desk. 9.00pm tonight and tomorrow, you call me on my personal mobile. I'll debrief you, and you fill me in.'

'Thank you, boss.'

'Don't you dare let me down here, Ben. Grosvenor really swung for the fences when he convinced me to take you on here. I wouldn't want to let him down either.'

'Got it. I won't. I've learned from my mistakes.'

'Off you go then. Go and join the extreme right.' He sighs so fiercely it whistles at the end.

Chapter Eighteen

I decide to keep it simple as possible. Just me, the streets and a couple of things I put in my pocket before I left home this morning, just in case Jeremiah let me loose. I grab the 8.10 train from Birchwood station, and watch my fellow commuters head into Manchester, their nearest urban employment hotbed. Businessmen in suits, school kids in uniforms, holidaymakers with huge square suitcases on wheels on their way to the airport. Mums and babies going for a day out. Cyclists guarding their bikes with apologetic scrupulousness. Men and women freshly scrubbed going to find work. Everyone's there, life going on. The train clacks through stations, funneling in more humanity as it goes.

I'm tuned into people usually, but since the investigation has taken a political slant, I now find myself more and more alert to unrest, and reflective. The political leanings of the everyman have been pulled to further reaches thanks to a number of influences, including the rhetoric of certain parties and their respective online propaganda machines, and with this divergence has come a true separation of political ideologies. The centre appears ever less a safe zone upon which you can take a side with little at stake - now, that same centre is a knife edge. You pick a side and you're straight down it, plummeting helplessly to its farthest point.

But it's not just that. The results of the EU referendum were so close at 52% leave and 48% remain. It illustrates that the natural state of this country at the moment is to be split almost in two. And as I look across the people on the train, it's visible. People keeping themselves to themselves. This is now a nation where showing your political colours isn't a point of pride or active enthusiasm, it's like sticking up the Vs. Same with the national flag. A visible St George is now tantamount to a racial statement, a holler for nationalistic supremacy.

How did this happen? Just how much has the government failed us, in allowing the nation to split so drastically on their watch? While they sit at cushty Westminster, eating complimentary steak dinners, bickering over the mundanities of cabinet life and who can wangle what expenses claims to their own benefits, their nation is being torn in two. While certain politicians lobby, lie and finagle for power, the true purpose of their democratic appointment has been lost - the protection, governance and well-being of the people. The electorate - who has been consequently given the cold shoulder - maligned and discarded by the very people who they voted for. As a soldier, in my job, like so many others, if things went to shit on my watch, it was on me. We are held accountable for our failures - we all are - but they are not.

The country is ideologically shredded - and it's in broad daylight. It's not something I ever thought I'd see in my lifetime, but a couple of careless years by those in power, and you've got a nation in a state of fracture.

The train bends towards the city, passing through fields of wavering green and over the Manchester Ship Canal, which itself ambles along under dark iron bridges, but soon I can't see out. The windows of the carriage have filled with condensation thanks to cramped exhalations. I can just make out Irlam Station on my left, its refurb job completed it seems, an old Victorian station house resurrected to former glories. It seems they've even added a traditional signal house, which is a lovely hat-tip to nostalgia. I'd hop off for a full English, if it weren't for the tick of the forty-eight hour clock in my head.

Before long, we've swept through quieter industrial zones, and are approaching Piccadilly station, yet again. It's the end of the line, and I'm part of this giant organism that pours itself from train to platform out up to the main concourse. I know where I'm headed today. It's a sadness, but it's an obvious start.

Once out of the station, I head down the exit ramp into the hard, grey light of a frosty city morning, white chunks of brushed slush texturing the concrete at my feet. The high rises take a step back to allow Piccadilly Gardens to breathe, but there's scant tree life there - what there is, however, is a high number of homeless.

Manchester's homelessness problem has been much-documented, but nothing has come close to slowing its boom. There are groups all around the concrete square, small congregations leaning on each other for warmth in what I can only imagine are the most trying of circumstances. Unless, of course, you're medicated. Which is at once the rhyme and reason for so many here. The legal high, spice, put two dirty, synthetic hands around the neck of the city's less fortunate, and forced them into a life of zombified, outdoors addiction. As I said, it's a sadness. These human husks wander the city like a slow-growth army of the walking dead, and nobody in authority can do anything to help them.

I walk straight through the middle of the gardens, to a commercial coffee shop on the cusp of the shopping epicentre right next to it. I take mental notes as I go. I'm looking for the right one.

By the time I'm in the coffee shop, I've picked my target and order two coffees and something called a breakfast pasty, which looks like something you could fix a dented car bumper with. With the foods in hand, I'm back in the gardens. Far side, there's a group who all lie on the ground in mismatched bundles of sheets, duvets and sleeping bags. Just to their right, as if part of the group but not quite, sits a man with glassy eyes that don't speak so much of substance abuse, but of weariness and real cold.

'Hi mate,' I say to him. 'Mind if I take a seat?' He looks at me like he can't quite understand that I haven't stared straight through him, and after a second, nods to the floor next to him. He's maybe forty, but looks sixty, with greasy blond locks fleeing from under a snow cap. A jagged blond moustache sits on his top lip, given added weight and prominence by the hollowed nature of the cheeks that rest either side of his haggard face. His eyes are open, both figuratively and literally, and he has only one leg. On the lapel of a rumpled peacoat, he wears a battered poppy.

'Welsh Guards. Iraq and Afghani,' I say.

'12th Regiment, Royal Artillery. Iraq,' replies the man.

'Ben,' I say, and extend a hand. Our lives have gone different directions, but at heart we are the same. Ex-warriors who don't fit in anymore. We shake, and I hand him my spare coffee.

'Henry,' he says, taking the coffee. He doesn't say thank you, and I don't begrudge him that. He's probably waiting for the moment I reveal my hidden camera and tell him if he wants to keep the coffee he's got to drink his own piss or something.

'No catch mate, just a chat. All these guys ex-forces out here?'

Henry has simply put his mouth to the opening of the coffee lid, and is breathing in the warm air from within. When he speaks, his breath floats up and over our heads. 'Yeah, some are. Some just go to the army surplus store on Division Street, get some clobber there, thinking they'll get more charity if people think they used to be a soldier. They soon realise that nobody gives a shit about that anymore.'

I look at the people in the group next to us, and survey them. One man is being sick into a takeout carton. This is a chronic fall from grace.

'What's the ailment here?'

'Spice, mostly. Still legal, ain't it. But they're making it harder and harder to get your hands on.'

'What do they go to instead? If they can't get spice?'

'I don't know. I've got enough problems of my own.'

'Have you noticed any change out here? Any new faces? Any change of mood?'

'I dunno, but I know it's easier to get hold of.'

'What is?'

'Anything you want. Especially heroin. Lots of foreigners seems to be on that.'

'New pushers?'

'New pushers.'

'Any here?'

Henry thinks carefully, and closes his mouth while he does so. A small dog pops out of the sleeping bag wrapped round his feet - it's a destitute little thing, a white matted coat with mucky splodges that could be fur, could be old crap. Its gaze is forlorn, and if I was a soft-sort, I'd be setting up a direct debit. The best I can do, is pull out the breakfast pasty, split it in two, and give half to Henry and half to the dog. Henry looks at it like it's a foreign object, food of the most bizarre composition, which I suppose it could well be, while the dog has already inhaled it by the time I take a second look.

104

'There's a few here who sell and use,' Henry says. 'You could have a chat to the bloke on the edge of the circle, far side.'

'The one that was sick into a takeaway carton?'

'That's the one.'

'It had to be, didn't it...'

Looking at the guy closer, if I thought he was in a poor way, I was obviously underselling it. He looks dead, somehow animated and kept alive by the purge that he's still enacting. I thank Henry, and go back to the coffee shop. Another coffee, and another breakfast pasty, for as long as I think it'll stay in that guy's stomach. I approach him with both outstretched.

'Look like you could do with a bit of a settler, mate.'

He looks at me as if I just spoke Greek, but within seconds, his hands have flown up and grabbed the offerings. 'Cheers mate, you're a diamond.'

'Rough night?'

'Like every night, innit.'

'I'm after a bit, if you get my meaning.'

He starts chewing with a near wild gusto. Retching his stomach in half has clearly done no harm to his appetite. 'I dunno what you mean?'

'I'm after some smack. You got any?'

'Are you fuckin' stupid?'

'Assume I am.'

'I wouldn't have any on me now.'

'So where can I get some from?'

'Me. But not now.'

'Then you're no help to me.'

'Hang on, hang on.' His eyes are flying all over the place with the embers of last night's bender burning bright. Now he's not emptying himself, I see that he's about my age, probably younger. Pipe-cleaners for arms and legs, he looks like a kid's drawing of a garbage wizard come to life in a way they never imagined.

'Look I need it, I'll pay good for it, you've just got to tell me *yes* or *no*.'

He turns to the people around him, all prostrate and frozen in place. 'Here y'are, just keep an eye on me stuff for a minute, alright?'

Nobody answers or murmurs, but he seems to take that as a *yes*.

'Let's go for a walk.' He gets up, coffee in one hand and half consumed pasty in the other, and strides lankily out of the gardens. I nod to Henry as I go, as he watches, chewing slowly. I say nothing more, just walk - but I do keep an eye on whoever might be watching as we go. I don't pick anything up.

At the edge of the gardens, we cross the tram tracks, and head into the Northern Quarter. I keep a couple of steps behind him, in case he breaks into an escape, even though I don't know why he would. The frost has thickened here, only a couple of hundred yards away from where I met this Garbage Wizard, and chunks of white slush congregate in the gutters and on grids.

'Not far, not far,' he says, as we round Vinyl Exchange - where I used to go for cheap second hand CDs back in my student days. A nostalgic smile threatens, but this is all business. Another quick right down a shallow, narrow alleyway sees us faced with a row of overflowing industrial bins and a door recessed in bare brick.

There's a buzzer, which he thumbs. A scratchy dial tone rings out, followed by a 'hello?' in a voice that carries the reluctant croak of the freshly woken.

'It's Kezzer, can you buzz us in?' says Garbage Wizard, as I guess what Kezzer could be short for.

'You what?' says the voice.

'Come on, it's business, let us in?' Kezzer pleads, and it works. The door clunks, and Kezzer pushes through without pause. I stay close behind, as the stench of piss hits me like an uppercut. We're at the bottom of a narrow stairway that's damp and stinking. Takeout menus are strewn all over the floor, but they're soaked into a slush of urine-fermented promo-print. There are needles about. Old ones, rust tipped. Bad spot, this.

The stairs are wooden, the bottom two steps covered in the detritus that covers the floor as if it has evolved sentience and has decided to start a slow climb out of its own filth. Kezzer walks through it, but I hop straight up to step three, and make a mental note to wash my trainers regardless. We pass up one flight that's entrenched by bare brick on either side, and come out on a landing that, while filled with less rubbish, still carries that smell. Junkyard tat lines the wall - a few old golf clubs, some cardboard boxes, and, somewhat frighteningly, a filthy kiddies' highchair. There's only one stairway it seems, and this is the one and only floor. It's a weird establishment, with a filthy white door at the end of the landing which has no handle, just a plate for a Yale lock that looks far newer than anything else here.

As we walk, the door opens, and a bloke comes out - and to my horror, I hear a baby cry from within the rooms behind him. I shudder, and think of my own little one, safe at home. Surrounded by love. Surrounded by cleanliness. This child might have the first part sorted, but I can't picture the latter.

'What?' asks the man, by way of greeting. It's clear he knows Kezzer. He's another ratty human specimen, shorn of healthy weight, exhibiting the now customary sunken cheeks and cheekbones you could cut a steak with, wearing a black baseball cap that reads OBEY in big white letters, blue jeans that have frayed boot-cut bottoms, and a Manchester City shirt that has faded to an off blue-brown under the arms. Oddly, a perfectly manicured goatee graces his face.

'It's business. Don't forget my finder's fee,' says Kezzer. He hangs back from the man, and allows me to approach.

'I'm after some smack,' I say, cutting to the chase. The man looks at me, head to toe with a cocked head, weighing me up.

'You don't look like you need smack.' True, but I've got a story cooked up ready.

'Not for me. It's like Kezzer says, it's business, I've got some regular users that need a regular supply. This isn't a one-time thing.'

'Mention my finder's fee,' Kezzer whispers with scant subtlety. I glare at him to shut it. His eyes are electrified with the prospect of cash in hand.

'I don't know you,' says the man.

'I do,' says Kezzer, revealing the extent of his desperation.

'I'm good for it,' I assure. 'If it works out, it would be regular.'

We stand there, and I have to start breathing through my mouth because of that smell. It feels like a gas attack, growing ever closer, and just at the point I begin to taste it, I turn around and start walking down the stairs. 'Look, the money we're talking about is obviously too big to trust with a couple of wasters in a piss-filled shoebox. Offer's off the table.'

I walk all the way down the stairs, and out onto the street, where the frost-bitten air hits my throat with the bite of tequila. I take a second, waiting for the thump of shoes on the stairs behind me - *got 'em* - and then start walking.

I head back the way we came, and have made it only to the end of the alley when Kezzer catches up with me. 'Easy, easy. Give me your phone.'

I stop and look at him in such a way that accuses him of questioning my sanity.

'So I can type something in it, dickhead,' he says. I hand it over, and he types with familiarity. 'Right, you go there, tell them Kezzer and Desmond sent you. Des is making the calls now. Whatever you discuss, you owe twenty percent to Des, and ten percent to me. I'll be in the gardens, find me there.'

'Alright,' I say. 'Last question.'

'Get on with it, I'll be lucky if my stuff's still there.' He stamps his feet impatiently as he talks.

'Why was that guy killed the other night?'

Kezzer stiffens. 'Just do the right thing, OK. By me, by Des. Don't do something to get us in trouble.'

'But why was he killed?'

'It's a message innit?'

'Who to?'

'What difference does it make? Everybody. The man, the government, the pigs, the politicians.'

He mentioned political elements twice there. 'What's political about it?'

'We all need to look after ourselves, don't we. They want to take our livelihoods away, don't they. Always want to fuck the little fella.'

'D'you know who did it?'

'Don't be asking any of this shit when you go *there*. I've got my eye on a finder's fee, not helping stick another dead body on the street, least of all my own.'

'*They* did it? Who I'm going to see?'

'Just go now.'

I look at the address on the phone, and swallow my surprise when I see I know where it is immediately.

Chapter Nineteen

It's another brisk shot across town, and I'd ordinarily be happy to walk it - but I'm buoyed by the progress I've already made in such a short time this morning, so I grab an Uber. It has me down the other end of Deansgate in a flash, aided by most people having made it into work by now, and drops me off in the courtyard outside Beatham Tower, the giant structure and tallest skyscraper in Manchester, under which the city centre cowers hoping to keep in its good graces.

In the lobby, suddenly hit by a gust of hot air as I cross the threshold, I'm hit with an echoing chamber, a Christmas tree so vast a family of owls could still be in it unaware they've been moved, twinkly piano, and the soft notes of the freshest linen. Aside from the tree, it's just as I remember last time I visited, when I chucked a fellow out of one of the top floor windows. Don't worry about him, he was definitely fit for it with what he'd been up to, but it was one of the things that really started me off on the damn spiral I found myself on.

Security here has always been tight. Best way round security? Act like you own the place, and do it with a smile. To that effect, when the concierge and lift security look at me, I jangle my keys at them and flash them a sweet one. They're the house keys to Carolyn's house, but there are some stellar apartments up there over the hotel that occupies most of the tower - I could just be another resident.

It works and I'm in the lift, selecting the 18th floor as per Kezzer's instructions. With the tower having forty-five floors, this is less than half of the way up. It'll still be in the hotel section, if memory serves.

The lift scoots heavenwards, and in a flash I'm on the right floor. 1834 is the room. Best foot forward. Let's get a look at the next rung on this ladder. Everything smells fresh over a base note of expensive cleaning products - not the kind that makes you lunge for an inhaler, but the kind you could scrub a newborn in. Only the best.

Following the signs, I arrive at room 1834. Nobody outside. The whole area is quiet, save for a handful of doors open further down the corridor letting the buzz of hoovers ring out from within the rooms themselves, with cleaning carts loitering outside.

I don't know what I'm walking into, but I have a plan. I'm unarmed, but I don't think I'll need it - although I wouldn't mind Okpara's cheeky telescopic difference-maker. With a knuckle, I knock on the hard, wooden door.

Seconds advance. Ten seconds. Fifteen.

I bring my hand up to rap again, but pause as I hear footsteps on the other side, and the door opens with that soft hiss of fire-protective strips on the edges of the frame. It reveals a man who appears unassuming - medium-heavy build, fat-necked and silent. He stares at me with eyes soft as chocolate buttons.

'Kezzer and Desmond sent me,' I say. The man nods, his hair in gelled spikes that don't waver at all. He leaves the door open and starts walking back into the flat. So far, so good.

I'm expecting hostilities any moment, so I keep sharp. The plan is to charade them into giving me the once over. If they're finding high-level combat operatives useful, I want to put myself in the frame.

The hallway opens out into a large bedroom, with an expansive view over the city. It's frankly marvelous, with the cranes overlooking a glassy cityscape that looks on the up, literally. I can even see the giant, rotund inflatable Santa Claus that sits over the Christmas markets in Victoria Square, rendered as small as a kid's bath toy by the height of my vantage point. What's frankly less marvelous, but not surprising at all, is the handful of renta-goons stood admiring that same view, who all turn to meet me.

The room is small, and I take it in for things I can use in case things go pear-shaped at a rate of knots - however, it's a pretty basic layout. Corridor with wardrobes leading into a double bedroom, bathroom behind the wardrobes with a door by the bed, a small seating area by those floor-to-ceiling picture windows. I wonder what the story is here, and why these guys are in it.

'He's here,' announces the chocolate button-eyed goonie who let me in, and the congregation turn. They're a mixed bag, but there's something unmistakable about them. Upright, coiled, mobile. In decent nick. They're all cut from the same cloth as me.

This is going to work.

The three men approach, hard gazes with the safety off. Jeans, workbooks and bomber jackets. I'm already wondering if any of them are the rooftop-pissing MOD spook, Brett Scarborough. The middle man is a crew-cut blond with an unseasonably deep tan, but his eyes reduce the temperature considerably.

'You needed something?' he asks, in a reedy voice like a needle scratch.

Keep solid. 'Smack. Those two fellas said someone here could help me with that.'

The room stills.

'Who told you that?' It's the tanned guy again, but the men on either side of him ask the same question with their body language.

'Kezzer.'

'You know him, do you?'

'Yeah, I know him. Well, as well as you can know a transient spice zombie.'

That gets a chuckle out of the man on the right. Similar crew cut, with patches all over his bomber jacket. Nasty sneer, but its mean spirit isn't directed at me on this occasion. 'He is a fuckin' melt isn't he?'

'You're not lying,' I reply.

'How much you after?'

'I'm needing half a key.' Half a kilogram on a first meeting should show I'm interested and serious. Not too big and not too small. I knew a few of the boys back in Afghanistan used to barter everything from chicken nuggets to ammunition for raw opium direct from the poppy fields. Once I was driving a truck after a patrol and they were smoking it in the back. I only realised when the fumes had my driving erratic. I know what it feels like to smoke, and I've got to say, I could see the appeal. If you had nothing else to do or live for, that is.

'You think we've got half a key to give to someone we've never met before?'

Time to play smart, as horrible as it will be. If the data is right (God, I'm loving this data stuff, all of a sudden) these guys like a certain kind of rhetoric. 'I'm good for it, and I'm on the level. I've got a house full of dirty foreign smackrats that need looking after.'

I feel bile rising in my own throat. I've never spoken like that before. In any other company I keep, this comment will have been greeted by outraged silence before someone called me out. But here, a ripple of cackles let me know I've played the role spot on and scored a positive hit. 'Where's this house then?'

I think of all the stone cottages out near Bartoni's ice cream shop. 'It's out near Rossendale. Our old supplier went away, and this lot will be crawling the walls, halfway to eating each other, if I don't get it sorted soon.'

Blondie's interested. 'How many have you got in there?'

'It's always around about fifteen.'

'A half key won't scratch fifteen itches for long.'

'I really need five keys, but I wasn't gonna be the dickhead who wandered into a new supplier's and asked for that. Not my first rodeo, hoss. And I've got a couple of other houses in the offing too. I'm looking for a business relationship, not a one-time thing.'

The street value of five kilograms of genuine heroine, not the diluted black tar, is anywhere between twenty-five to thirty grand. At the prospect of serious money being made, there's an unmistakable buzz between them.

'I'm thinking bacon here boys.' It's the man who hasn't spoken before. Pale as a milk tooth, he's lithe with lizard's eyes, slow blink and all. Clearly the oldest of the group, but he's got the tautest energy of the lot. His face has the shape of a trowel, tapering to a strong pointed chin, with a blond buzzcut over a high wrinkled hairline.

'Hey, hey, what do you think you're playing at?' I ask, insinuating outrage.

'I'm thinking golden tickets don't just drop out of the sky and when they do, it's because they're too good to be true.' He steps closer, tension in his walk, and starts pawing at me. The other men do too, and this would be bad if it weren't for the fact I hoped they'd do this.

'There's something here,' one of them says, pulling out what was in my inside jacket pocket. You have a good look at that gents. Their voices suddenly scrap over each other's.

'Shit, he's a soldier,' says Patches.

'I knew it,' says the Tan-Man.

'No, you fucking didn't.'

'What's the story, pal?'

Patches holds up the only army keepsakes I have. The two things that made me proud, that still do to this day. I brought them with me today for that very reason - soldiers, especially infantry, love the bones of each other. My records were wiped, all achievements taken back - but the army couldn't take back my memories, or reclaim a couple of the things I said I'd lost. Therefore, Patches, rather aptly, is holding up the patch of the regiment I served in, the Welsh Guards, which is a small rectangle of navy fabric slashed across the centre by a red band, over which sits centrally a golden leek. And in his other hand dangles a trinket.

'It's a fucking CGC,' says Lizard Eyes. 'Shit, you cheeky bugger.'

I was awarded the Conspicuous Gallantry Cross for stuff that would never ever make the papers - like so much that actually went down in the dust and heat. Those fields, especially south in Helmand Province, were lawless at the best of times. Anything went. And the fighting got dirty. On one occasion, I just fought the dirtiest and saved some of our guys, and they gave me this. I was supposed to have given it back, but, well, y'know, the horrors of that night must have been so ingrained that I'd just *forgot* where I'd put it.

The men pass the silver cross around like a piece of circumspect treasure - might be worth something, might not - but it's confused them enough for me to tell them some truths I think will help them take to me.

'Welsh Guards, Iraq then Afghani. Captain. I was dishonourably discharged, but managed to keep the medal. Told them I'd lost it.' I don't tell them about the Iraq Cross, The Distinguished Service Order, the Military Cross and the George Medal, all of which I was awarded but none of which I was able to keep. But the business that led to the CGC... I felt I had to hold on to *that* one.

'How does a captain in the Welsh fuckin' Guards end up running a house full of smackheads?' Lizard Eyes has a good look at me, and it's very clear now that he's the leader of this posse.

'They kicked me out, left me with nothing. I've given everything for this country' - I glance at that silver medal to really drive the point home - 'and when I come back, I didn't even recognise any of it anymore. None of it. It wasn't even ours no more.'

Again, I hate saying these things. But I've got to keep burrowing into their good graces.

This was how I felt, minus all the racism. I didn't recognize the country, but it was nothing to do with the ethnic composition of its people. Conversely, I'm a man with a keen eye on the history of our country, knowing that multiculturalism is a pillar of what makes Great Britain great, so the diversity on our shores is one that I've always celebrated. No, the disillusion I felt was directed more at government, and my superiors. Those that sent a man into the spit of gunfire, the spray of blood, for reasons no more coherent than power and a demonstration of it. I came back to find the political elite of the country at total disconnect of the people it governed, a split that clawed ever wider as they squabbled for seats and political territory, forgetting the very people that put them there.

'Couldn't agree more,' says Lizard Eyes, taking the cross for himself. 'I never got one of these.' He eyes it appreciably, turning it over in his hand.

'You lads served too?' I ask.

The answers flood in.

Patches: 'Iraq and Afghan.'

Tan-Man: 'Afghani.'

Chocolate Buttons: 'Afghan.'

'Iraq twice and Afghan.' That last one was Lizard Eyes.

'We on the level then lads? Can we talk proper business?' I ask.

'Aye, we can talk proper business. You have cash?'

'I was looking for eighteen hundred quid for the half key.'

'I'd be after two and a half grand - normally. But because of that CGC we can call it two K.'

'I'd appreciate that.' I offer my hand, which he shakes firmly. 'Tom,' I say.

'Nicolas Raine,' says Lizard Eyes, before introducing the others. Patches is Kev, Chocolate Buttons is Mac, and the tanned guy is Winks, giving them the impression of a shite version of The A-Team. I shake with them all.

'What's the story with you boys then? Disillusionment, rejection, combat stress, the usual story?'

'You could say that,' replies Winks, going back to the window and thumbing out a cigarette. Pretty sure it's no smoking in the building, but that ain't stopping this bronzed badass.

'You have the cash here?' asks Nicolas. If he's the man behind the undercover's murder, I need to tread very carefully indeed.

'No, but it's nearby,' I say.

'Same with the H. Meet later to exchange? In fact, we could drive it out your way - I wouldn't mind taking a look at the zoo you've got together over there. Good for the soul, that shit.'

Think. 'I wouldn't be bothering mate - a long way to go just to see some spear-chuckers pulling faces on a dirty mattress.' I feel physically sick, while these guys laugh.

'Alright, how long do you need for the cash?'

'Give me a couple of hours?'

'Yeah. We've got a bit of work to do ourselves.'

I don't like the way he said *work*, and I can't help sticking my nose in. 'Busy day planned?'

'Oh aye. There's a march later, and we're working security.'

'Well, unofficially,' remarks Mac, while he plays on his phone.

'March?' I say.

'Yeah, St George's Patriots,' says Nicolas. 'You a follower?'

Play dumb. 'I don't spend much time online these days, what's it all about?'

'Taking the country back. Our country. Britain for Brits, not the worthless, godless rats who sneak about killing kids with rucksacks full of bombs. Policies to help *us*, not the benefit scroungers who come over here looking for handouts then kill us for it.'

I have to suppress a sigh. This is one of the most tired old arguments of the modern political landscape - and one that is on notoriously shaky ground. 'Sounds good. I can agree with that - I didn't watch my mates got shot up so that foreigners could come over here and take our tax money.'

'See, that's it. That's the problem.'

'D'you want to come along?' It's Mac again. 'With that CGC there, you've got as much reason as any to take it back.'

'Is it that woman Helen… ummm…?'

'Broadshott, yeah,' fills in Mac. 'She's gonna make the SGP a serious option again. A lot of people in this country feel the same. We're going to take back the country by force, and she's gonna help us do it.'

This is scaring the crap out of me. I can't believe that a lot of people in the country feel the same, despite Mac's assertions. There's the usual spread of the political ideology that has characterised the UK of the last hundred years, then there's this all new sense of injustice and militance that is downright frightening. I glance around the men, and I can see they're committed, but not just that - Nicolas is smiling with something akin to wishful romance in his eyes.

'I hadn't heard of any demos on the streets today?' I ask.

'Then you haven't been paying any attention.'

Winks butts in now. 'Man like you should come down. In fact, a man like you should be part of it. The cause needs you. Medals and all that show we're not just cranks.'

I wouldn't be caught dead at one of those things. However, the slogan *Our White Christmas 2019* looms into view. The best way to get a look at this entity and see what it's capable of is to get up close for a look-see. 'Can I come with?'

'Yeah, that's a good idea,' says Nicolas. 'We're marching through the Christmas Markets, underneath the big Santa, down there.' He points out the window at the cheery ball of red and white on the street below. 'March starts at one. We'll handle business afterwards.'

And as easy as that, I'm in the club.

Chapter Twenty

When I checked my watch, and saw I had time, I immediately hopped on the tram, placed a quick call, and headed straight to Bury. From there, it was straight up the M66 in a taxi until it petered out in textile country once again. Now, as I pass Bartoni's Gelateria (now closed), the cab driver's little Seat hatchback bounces around like it's never seen roads like it and can't get over how fun they are.

I get to the top of the road, which became a muddy track a couple of hundred yards before it reached the end, and it finishes in a frost encrusted turning circle with a rusty gate and a cattle grid. To the right of the gate, stands a metal turnstile in a steel cylinder, big enough for one at a time. There are a couple of cars here, both dog-walkers' specials in old Land Rovers, so I give the driver a twenty pound note with the plea for him to wait for me, and take the stile. Once through, I'm out onto the moors itself, and the wind chill hits.

It's freezing out here, but it doesn't quite reach the marrow thanks to the sunshine. The ground at my feet is long silver grass that crunches with every step and, as I look up and across the roll of the hills, seems to go on forever - interrupted only by the grey geometry of dry stone walls and the hardier plants that carry my namesake. I take a one o'clock bearing, and walk. That's where he said he'd be.

The hike is invigorating, the air even colder and cleaner up here, which is like a much-needed bleach scourer on my lungs. It's beautiful, peaceful and I love it. There's an eeriness to it too, and that could be down to one of a couple of things. Either it's my sudden change within half an hour from the mad city bustle to this bare earthen solitude, or it's the fact that I know this is where a twisted serial killer disposed of his bodies. I feel it may be the latter, as I see Bartoni himself on the crest of a rise, silhouetted by the bright blue backdrop of the clear heavens. He nods as I get nearer, his form clad in a green wax jacket that's had its money's worth, his grey shoulder length hair fluttering in the wind. On his feet are some hybrid of walking shoes and wellies, like a rubberised hiking boot, which is a much better choice than my trainers, already on the cusp of sodden.

I thought he was looking at me, but when I reach him, he's still gazing back from whence I came. I turn to see for myself, and the sight is breathtaking. An all-encompassing panorama of Manchester and its surroundings, for miles in all directions. The city lies central with the hills of Snake Pass and the trails towards Sheffield and Yorkshire behind. I feel a pang in my torso somewhere. My home was that way, and I'm looking at the route I used to take home from university on weekends. I say *was* because there's nothing there now. My home is empty, and I've no idea where my parents are.

It hits me for the first time since we found out Carolyn was pregnant. *My parents now have a grandchild.* What would they make of that?

'Food for thought, eh?' says Bartoni, catching the vibe.

'Easy to see the big picture when you can see the... well, y'know, the *big picture*. What do you prefer I call you?'

He nods to the city, then left and right to its environs. 'Back when that was my parish, I was Richard Barton. Round here, they know me as Ricardo Bartoni. Since you're blurring all sorts of lines, just call me Dick.'

'Thanks for meeting me then, Dick.'

'I haven't been able to think of anything else since you three came by the other day.' His eyes still haven't met mine, but, instead of being preoccupied with what's in front of him, they've glazed over to another time entirely. 'I thought he was gone. A fart in a stiff breeze - caused a bloody ruckus then off he went.'

'I assume, with you bringing me out here, that this is where they were found?'

'You're standing where the fourth was dug up.'

I look down as if I'll see something, as if there'll be blood pooling at my feet, sponging out of the grass, but there's nothing. 'I'm sorry,' I say, and move a stride to my right.

'Now you're on the second.' Catching my panic, he continues with a wry smile. 'I wouldn't stress it. Nothing there now. It's all up here.' He juts his nose upwards in a short stab.

'I might have met him. Or at least, this guy's our best candidate given the evidence.'

'Tell me what you've got.'

'DNA at the scene.'

'Blood? Sweat? Semen?'

'Urine.'

'He pissed at the scene?' He frowns.

'The urine doesn't fit?'

'If it's him, that would be a first.'

'It was at an observation point of the scene.'

'Would make more sense. We never checked the peripheries of the crime scenes specifically for urine stains. Would certainly fit with his more animalistic tendencies to mark territory. Go on, give me the profile, bit by bit.'

'Ex-military.'

'Could work, definitely. Time frame?'

'Iraq, Afghanistan. Now retired.'

'Could be OK.'

'Current age late-forties.'

'That's definitely right. The profile I came up with at the time would have him that age now.'

'You keep saying *he* - male would fit then?'

'Yes, every statistic in serial killer history would suggest that the perpetrator of these crimes was a bloke.'

So far so good. 'Six two,' I say. 'Physically capable.'

'Yes.'

'Blonde.'

'Yes.'

'Hair colour matters?'

'A 1997 study from Princeton's Behaviourial Science Department suggested that across serial killers in the age bracket determined here, twenty-five to thirty-five years old at the time of the offence, 78% were blonde.'

If I didn't get it before, I now realise it fully: Bartoni lives and breathes this case. He catches my pause and looks over at me, running a hand through his short beard. 'Keep going,' he says.

'A taste for the theatrical?'

'We both know that's right.'

I'm pulling Nicolas from the hotel room earlier up in my mind, looking at all his characteristics in fishbowl, the way he carries himself, the way he speaks, the way he moves.

'Confident.'

'I'd imagine to a fault.'

'Precise.'

'To a point.'

It's my turn to say, 'That fits.'

Bartoni unzips his jacket and takes out a hip flask. The clink of the cap sounds tinny and foreign up here, and he takes a slug, before tossing it to me. 'Warm yourself up.' I do as he says. It feels like it gives my epiglottis a hot shave, and, my God, does it hit the spot.

'Political,' I say.

'Yes.'

'Really?'

'Do you want me to quote another study?'

'Humour me.'

'DeMontford University, 2016. Serial killers often show a distinct proclivity towards political activism. Fits their sense of causal proactivity.'

'You've been working on this profile since retirement?'

'We're talking at the gravesite of his finest work - what do you think?'

I offer no counter. 'Did the study say which side of the political fence they'd fall in?'

'Pretty equal findings. The only thing to note is that they would be pushed to the furthest point of their chosen ideology.'

That fits right. 'Racism?'

'Oh yes. An innate hatred towards particular types of people is a common feature - regardless of their chosen victimology.'

'All this applies to our man.'

'And you just met him?'

'Yeah.'

'Did he feel right to you?' Barton's gaze is pressing now, the wistful faraway look cast aside.

I take a moment, because I interpret Barton's gaze as hope. For him, the Dog of the Moors has never left him, having cast a shadow over his career. It'll always be the one that got away, but as I look at him now, it's not his professional pride that's at stake - it's the people that this monster hurt. It's the chance to bury the past properly, and give closure to so many people that need it. Not least Barton himself.

'I have to be careful what I say here,' I say, 'because I'm truthfully not sure. But if he's been able to commit these crimes and hide in plain sight for decades, he's definitely able to fool a layman like me.'

Barton moves closer. 'But you're not a layman though are you, *Tom West*? I spent my life looking into what people are really like, the person that's actually there when they think no-one else is looking. I know you're no NCA dogsbody, and no beat-cop advisor. You're a military man too, I know that, but you've seen what life is like on the hardest side of the tracks, and yet you still throw yourself into it to fight it some more. You've seen what darkness is, what killers are like. Did you see that in this man?'

His incision is deft, precise and eye-opening.

'I'm no expert, and certainly no profiler. But I know a bad-egg when I see one – like the boys that thought camo gave them a blank cheque. This man definitely fits the bill, but biting chunks out of his victims is simply not something I can pass a comment on.'

'I'd like to meet him.'

'I don't know how to arrange that - but I'm working to get close to him. I'll be keeping an eye on him.'

Barton drops his head, then turns in the direction of his ice cream shop. He suddenly stops, and speaks.

'What's your real name?'

'Ben.' I realise I haven't hesitated. 'But keep that to yourself.'

'Call me anytime, Ben. I'll do anything I can to catch the bastard.

Because heaven knows that one day, I'd like to move on from haunting the moors myself.'

He kisses his fingertips, then waves them at the ground around us in a fond gesture of short-term goodbye, then leaves.

I'm left there, in the quiet cradle of a serial killer's canvas, left to think of the importance of Nicolas, and the true crime story of the Dog of the Moors - not just in terms of this case, but in the wider scope of our northern culture and of societal safety. Amongst the true physical facts to hand here, one is very obvious and glaring: there is still, after all this time, a depraved mind loose amongst the innocent.

What really happened here? Why? Was it the work of Nicolas the SGP security man?

'Grab yourself a coffee on me as you go past,' shouts Bartoni, his voice on the breeze, having morphed back into the kindly ice cream seller on leaving the scene. 'And you can have some beer if you want it.'

I get up with a slight smile, intent on taking him up on the former, and relieved that I've got a bit of a walk to come up with an excuse as to why I can't accept the latter.

Chapter Twenty-One

I spend lunchtime having a sandwich in Mulligan's (that pub certainly got under my skin), and read up on articles on my phone's web browser, trying to amass a better picture of the extreme right corner of the country, and more on Helen Broadshott. By twelve thirty, I'm borderline terrified and depressed, and no amount of salt and vinegar crisps will be able to fix it.

Broadshott had used crimes perpetrated by ethnic minorities as a key component of her xenophobic rhetoric, all the while, ignoring similar crimes committed by white Brits. She's also fully embraced Facebook for its ability to spread unchecked and unverified propaganda. I read an article which took a whole raft of her online examples of *immigrants doing bad things to British people* and managed to disprove every one, illustrating concisely that there were in large part photos misrepresented and taken out of context, overlain with inflammatory sayings and snazzy graphics. What she was doing was tantamount to brainwashing, and precisely equal in nature to what extremist groups the world over do to gain support. Tell lies and use fear.

This ailment wasn't just a symptom of the extreme right however. The far left was just the same, and the more I dug, the more I saw the same tactics in use by the supposed super-liberal left – something I didn't know existed until I looked into it just now. It leaves the conclusion that social media is a lawless breeding ground of unchecked political extremism, thanks to the delivery of an online soapbox to all and sundry.

I ring Jeremiah and filled him in on everything. He listens to me for a full five minutes before making a statement of his own, 'Handle it with care, OK.'

'Will do, boss.'

'And try to establish what the connection between drugs and this extrem-eright group are. I can't work out the link, other than it being these boys' little side hobby.'

'But then again, the data shows there's just too many of these right-wing loonies who are also pushers - that can't be coincidence either.'

'You and bloody data - an all-new love-affair for the ages.' He sighs, before conceding, 'You're absolutely right of course.'

I check the time. 'Gotta go boss. It'll take me twenty minutes to get to the markets, especially at a brisk goose step.'

I hang up, pay and get going.

I can hear the boos from Deansgate, and they only get louder the closer I get to Albert Square, the centre point of Manchester's yearly Christmas markets showpiece and venue for today's vent from the extreme right. The Christmas markets are one of Manchester's premier seasonal attractions, with a visit to them a staple for many locals and further travelers too. I've never quite seen the appeal - something about spending hours queuing in the freezing drizzle only to be served an overpriced mug of lukewarm mulled wine never truly captured my imagination - but from what I could tell, they were always jammed. And today, two days from Christmas, is no exception.

I walk into the square, emerging from the side street thoroughfares I'm much more used to, into a fractious, politicised Winter Wonderland, with rows of small log cabins complete with fake frost on their gables, masses of people in wooly hats, Christmas songs and steam billowing though the chilly air, against a backdrop of placards and signs proclaiming messages that are far from any kind of holiday spirit I've ever heard of - as the town hall itself and that gigantic glowing Santa look on from the back.

Go home.
Britain for Britains.
St George's Patriots.
Proud to be British.
British is BEST.

All interspersed with the red and white of the St George's flag.

I take a second to lean against the streetlight on the other side of the square, saddened.

How have we, as a nation, allowed this sentiment to flourish? Eighty years ago, we led the fight against a potent brand of fascism that was masked as patriotism, and helped beat it back with our allies so that future generations wouldn't suffer the same fears we had. How have we forgotten?

And after looking at the flavour of the Facebook sentiment, a lot of my ex-colleagues, men I've fought with on the broad team that is the army, feel that this is what they fought for. The right to reclaim the country for some spectral notion of a pure Britain. Worse still, they believe that our forefathers, those mighty generations that beat the Nazis, fought those fights for the same cause they argue now. So that Britain can be ours. My grasp of history is fair - and this is not my understanding of my military forebears at all. *This* is not what Britain fought world wars for.

I know now that there's growth of the extreme left too, who believe they've got a moral highground - an easier postition to adopt. For every extreme right gob there's an equally extreme and unreasonable left-leaning opposite. But in this country, after the horrors and circumstances which led to the world wars less than a hundred years ago, how can there be justification or reason for *any* kind of extreme viewpoint?

Back to business.

The main square is pedestrianised, up tight to the steps of the town hall, in front of which stands the platform for the massive Santa - which, on closer inspection, isn't inflatable. It's a solid model, constructed with bright red and white lights on a metal frame, all of which must weigh a ton. In front and to the side of the platform stand rows of SGP protestors, facing the customers in the square, as if condemning their enjoyment. I've only been here a few moments, and the crowd is swelling. In response, a gathering is forming on the edge of the markets, as the more combative of the revelers respond to the affront.

None of this looks good.

Suddenly, a loud speaker beeps an obnoxious attention tone, and a woman's voice blares over the scene. 'Happy, are we?' The tones are jovial and encouraging. 'Enjoying our mulled wine? The pretzels? The hot dogs? Having a nice time?'

Heads across the markets turn to look for the source of the voice, which seems to be coming from near the town hall itself. It seems as if it's the Santa itself bellowing at us, a sensation which only serves to add more surrealism to the occasion. I feel like I'm in an alternate reality.

Someone appears next to the Santa, up on the platform with it. The figure clambers across one of its splayed legs to stand between them, and proudly comes to the front of the platform like a rock star in a cream trouser suit and long blonde hair. I need no guesswork to conclude that this is not just the owner of the voice - this is Helen Broadshott. Spokesperson for the St George Patriots. Mouth of the extreme right. And in my book, stirrer of a lot of unwanted shit.

'Merry Christmas!' she shouts. Many voices return the gesture, in both ever-growing groups. I could laugh at the almost helpless insistence on such festive civility, despite the divisiveness of the occasion. 'Enjoy it. Drink in every drop of this festive season. Lord knows that, with the way things are going, it won't be like this for much longer.'

A first couple of *boos* ring out from under the cabin roofs. Police have arrived on the edge of the square, yellow jackets pouring from unit vans. This could get ugly. For everyone's sake, I hope the revelers have had enough mulled wine to soften their outrage.

Broadshott turns to the huge Santa, and surveys it up and down. 'Despite all the history and traditions that should stand to protect it, Christmas is on the endangered species list. It soon will be no more. You can wave goodbye to all of this.' She casts her left hand out across the square, a gesture to encompass all. 'Instead, you can look forward to Eid markets. Hannukah markets. Diwahli markets. And Christmas markets will be banned. Too offensive. Too *in your face* for our immigrant brothers and sisters. And the funny thing is, it'll be the snowflakes that bring down Christmas. What an irony that is!'

You could hear a pin drop, for all sorts of reasons. She's speaking horrors here, but she is a fantastic, mesmerising orator. Composed, dramatic, imbued with a Freddie Mercury swagger and posture, she's electrifying. I look at the faces on her side of the divide gazing up at her, their eyes wide, lips parted in half-smile hypnosis. It's love, that is.

'You were promised things, weren't you? Not just my friends here, but my new friends in front of me, enjoying one of the last pure Christmases on these shores.' More heads are looking now. She's engaging them. And at the edges of the square I can see more listeners of all kinds emerging. This is becoming a cauldron. 'You were promised freedom of choice. You were promised democracy. You were promised fairness and equality.'

Any hoots of derision have stopped.

'But all we've been given is a forced compromise. And we've been expected to choke it down like the humble pie David Cameron had to shovel when the EU referendum didn't go the way he expected.' That brings cheers from her supporters below her. 'No, no - he didn't think the country actually wanted that, did he!'

The police are now funneling along the divide, keeping the two sides apart, forming a human barricade between the markets on the square and the SGP facing it - some of whom snarl in reply.

'Don't antagonise our public protectors, please,' Broadshott appeals, directing her words squarely at her followers. 'These are the men and women who have had compromise forced on them the most, and have to choke it down more than anyone. You see, regardless of their beliefs - regardless of what *they* hold dear - they are here to keep us all safe. Some of them will no doubt have a lot to say about the key issues here - particularly in light of the way their brothers and sisters have had their uniforms unfairly tarnished in recent years by the very PC compromises that are eroding our national culture.'

My God, she's having a go at getting the police on her side now. She's like the wizard from Fantasia, conducting both a spell and concerto at the same time. I catch myself, and realise that I too have moved forward. Tension and fracas - I'm unwittingly drawn to both. My natural role and place is to be sorting trouble out, and my subconscious has moved me closer to where it might kick off - for better or worse.

'The very badges I see in front of me, as I meet our brave police officers around the country, are forever under siege. To tone down the cross and crown. To make it acceptable for all. I ask you, when we visit other countries, do we demand change to ensure our comfort? Do we make them alter their cultures just to satisfy our selfish needs? The answer is *no*.'

It's disturbing. As my eyes glance along the row of officers in front of me, I see that a great number are of Asian heritage. What must they be thinking, as these words, delivered with however much understanding, can only drift between them causing seeds of distrust and antagonism between themselves and their colleagues? But she's talking bollocks anyway, no matter how compelling. We, as a nation, from what I've seen, are a nightmare when we go abroad. The supporters of our national football team inhabit whatever capital city we happen to be playing in like a virus, soiling its streets with loutish behaviour and violence - and that's just one example. I spent some time tracking criminal ex-pats on the Costa Del Sol. Everywhere I followed them, the locals were expected to make compromises to please us. I spent the whole time embarrassed.

But like everything, the minority spoils it for the majority. I have got to believe we are not all like this, despite the extent of my disillusion. I must believe as a country we are better than that, but when I'm faced with this kind of scene, on the cusp of Christmas no less, where an extreme right spokesperson has a captive audience in a major city centre while parading in front of a giant Santa, my faith has a huge crack in it.

'We are all brothers and sisters in the same fight. A fight for sovereignty. A fight for our own country's sense of identity. The fat cats in Westminster will exchange all that sovereignty for their own portions of power, carving up our national identity until they're rich and there's nothing left for us to be proud of. They're all doing it. Every last one. Not one of them will speak the truth, but I assure you I always will.'

That brings a cheer from her supporters, and a lot of gruff masculine grunts of praise. Suddenly there are *boos* from behind us. Another party has entered the scene. Pushing through the crowd in the markets, is a wild diverse crowd with their own flags and banners. Banners with the European flag, and a couple of homemade signs that read 'BroadSHITT'. Their faces are contorted with rage, spitting froth and ire as potently as those they've come to quell. Now, the SGP supporters are stepping forward, teeth bared in challenge, with a row of police in front of them.

I didn't even know we had this here, but here it is - an extreme left, borne it seems to combat the sudden growth in the extreme right. And looking down on them, I can see Broadshott is smiling.

'I can see we've been joined by our friends who think we are here to cause harm. But note this, everyone who has been here since I started speaking knows that this has been an occasion of peace and understanding, right up until now. The civility of this moment is being set upon by this militant snowflake left.'

There is genuine rage at this comment, and the new crowd jostles tight to the police, who are at risk of being overwhelmed here. I've got to do something.

'And remember this. What sets this great nation apart, what always has, right through history, is our capacity for civility. The Saudis still behead people in the streets, right across Africa there are bent elections decided well away from the phoney polls, and you don't even want me to go near Myanmar. We are the elite of civility. Or at least we were until these violent leftists showed up. So, despite what your sanitised social media and your snowflake press outlets will have you believe, who are the real villains here? Us, who'd keep the UK in a state of civil sovereignty? Or this shower, who'd sell off every last acre of England's green and pleasant land for an avocado and hemp sandwich?'

That does it. There's an eruption and the yellow line between the two sides dissolves. The noise clicks up a handful of notches in an instant, windbreakers rustle angrily as limbs flick out, and some scamp somewhere starts playing Jingle Bells through a PA system. Fists start to fly, Broadshott bellows 'Merry Christmas!' as she disappears behind Santa, and the clatter of horses' hooves bullet the air, as a mounted police unit arrives.

It's a mess. I don't know what to do, whose side to join. Both sides are wrong. The extreme point of any political standpoint is wrong. It offers no compromise, no room to negotiate, scant chance for middle ground to be reached - and again, all I can think about, is those supposed leaders down in Westminster who let the country split on their watch. Who allowed this kind of scene on British streets. They're the real cause of this, not the misguided reactionaries in front of me.

Before I really know what I'm doing, I'm pulling a policeman out of the melee by his arm and shoulders, who was being crushed by four inflamed people and lots of swinging fists and feet. One of the SGP try to grab my lapel, assuming I'm part of this extreme left gang, so I twist back and out, pulling him forward a touch. The loss of balance lets me cream cracker him with a right hand. There's a sudden surge behind me, as if seeing the strike gave more life to the crowd at my back, only to be met by a push from the front. I'm caught, punches are raining this way and that, someone's thrown a banner over our heads, while horses start pushing a way through us, and it feels like the closest I'll ever get to a modern day reenactment of the Peterloo Massacre.

In the empty wake left by one of the mounted officers, in the split second before the crowd fills the vacuum, I catch sight of Broadshott. She's being led away from the bottom of Santa's platform, two bouncers in front and two behind. To my surprise, I see that the four are none other than the men I came here to meet. Nicolas, Winks, Mac and Kev. They look like her personal security detail. I try to follow them, as they duck the crowd. Broadshott is easy to keep a fix on thanks to her bobbing blonde hair, and as I get to within five yards of her, leaving the maelstrom churning behind us, a figure in jeans and a green parka steps from the crowd, arm cocked facing her. I don't know what it is, but my moral compass won't let anyone get hurt, and in an instant, instinct has me pouncing at the man, grabbing his arm mid hurl, and twisting him back into a heap on the floor with his arm up his back. As I drop him, a strawberry milkshake pops from his grasp, glooping all over him.

I remember this started happening back in the summer, this *milkshaking* of right-leaning figures. Like it was an acceptable thing to do. It's still assault at the end of the day, and if one side is using any kind of violence to intimidate or quell the other, no matter how silly and harmless a splash of milkshake is, then you've run out of arguments. A failure of words is a failure of reason - and I can't see a reason it should be done. And a milkshake is one thing. Tomorrow it could be a brick or stone, just like I thought it was today. I know Broadshott inflamed the situation, and you could easily argue would get her just desserts (quite literally) but it still is not something that will promote peace.

'You *fucker*,' the man seethes at my feet, but I know there's no fight in him. He was after a headline, this guy. Wanted to go viral. Speaking of social media, there are camera phones everywhere, so I duck back again - but it's too late.

'You fuckin' *legend*!' The shout comes from the group I was tailing, who've stopped to watch - Winks is pointing with glee. The men are smiling, and Broadshott herself is looking at me with appraisal. They start hustling forward again, and Mac turns and gestures a *come on* with a paw. I follow them as they round the corner of the square, into a side street, batting away anyone who dares come close.

I cover my head, shield myself from the camera phones, and follow.

As soon as we are round the corner, a white van guns forward, headlights flashing. It's been parked there, suddenly called into duty, and the door slides open as it reaches us. Inside is plush dark leather in two rows, one facing each other. All of them pile in, and they turn for me to hop in too.

Hoping my conscience won't keep me awake forever on it, I jump in. The door shuts, and we're away before I've registered the clunk.

Chapter Twenty-Two

We are travelling at speed through the back streets of Manchester city centre, the mood in the van jubilant. I sit on one side, facing backwards, alongside Winks and Mac. Opposite sits Broadshott, flanked by Nicolas and Kev. Not one of us wears a seatbelt, and more than half are laughing. Broadshott and I are in the minority, and she looks at me carefully.

'Well that could scarcely have gone any better,' she says, without breaking eye contact. Up close, you can see why she's got so many middle-aged men's knickers in a knot. She says what they want to hear and packages it as well-to-do *totty*. She's fantasy material for the down-trodden, average man, and not just that, she champions them. 'This outfit's a new one, and I think it hit all the right triggers. And I'm glad I don't have to throw it.' She's still looking at me. Mid-thirties, dirty blonde hair with a carefully unkempt flow. Thick crimson lipstick, but that's the extent of the glamour. She's naturally beautiful with an extra-large side of *cut-your-balls-off*, bedecked in a trouser suit so tight you can see she's got a giant smartphone in her pants pocket.

'You've got Tom here to thank for that.' Nicolas extends a hand to gesture in my direction. Sirens flock in the other direction, spitting blue shards into the van, a handful of which hits his face like the touch of a higher force.

'I don't like people taking the piss,' is all I can say. It's the truth, but I don't know what I mean by it. Broadshott still hasn't broken eye contact, and it feels like I'm being stared down by an elite predator.

'And I like people to take the initiative,' she says. I look away. I can feel heat up my neck.

'We met Tom earlier, invited him down. Been doing a bit of business. Didn't know he'd be so useful!'

I don't know what the phrase *business* means between these people, but the casualness of the way it's been used here makes me think all present are aware of its true meaning. 'Some good things afoot?' Broadshott asks, while pulling out her phone. She has to wiggle her pelvis up out of her seat to get at it - a movement that is not lost on Winks and Mac, who follow her every squirm. She doesn't mind at all, as if every movement is currency to keep her supporters sweet, but it's the fact her eyes are still on me which keeps me unnerved. I feel challenge in it, and I try to hold her gaze, but while she thrusts her groin out at me across the gap between the seats, it feels too sexually provocative and I have to look away again, conscious of any inappropriateness.

'You'd love them. Right up your street,' says Nicolas.

A couple of seconds later, I check back. She's still looking, but there's a slight knowing smile. She's got her phone now, thank God, and sits down. Thumbing the screen expertly, she finally breaks eye contact, and I thank God again.

'These numbers are outstanding,' she says, her eyes glinting with glee. 'Hashtag Broadshott is already trending in Manchester. Hashtag Our White Christmas, too. They'll be national within fifteen minutes, looking at this. The live stream of the speech has had forty thousand views already. Facebook will be electric too, going off of that. As for Instagram…' She jabs her thumb again. 'That's excellent. Fifty thousand views, top trend in the north west. Merry fucking Christmas.'

I know now that her every movement is calculated for maximum impact and control.

'That first pic we put up has had over two thousand shares already. The one of you straddling Santa's leg before you started speaking.' It's Mac talking, looking at his own phone, his lips smearing in a smile to reveal cracked teeth.

'Estimated impressions on that?' asks Broadshott.

'It'll be about 1.2 million within a few hours.'

'Outstanding.'

These guys are way more clued in than I pictured. There's no leaving it to chance here and hoping something sticks. This is a concerted, composed effort to make waves, and harness the powers of social media to force a message home. And with numbers like that (*1.2 million views by the end of today!*) they're achieving it with aplomb. This is modern politics, away from the archaism in that old building under the big clock down South. This is digital propaganda fed directly into the pockets and cerebellums of potential voters and young minds. The fat cats in Westminster won't have the cream for much longer. This is changing the face of politics in this country - and every day that ticks by, the old generations and ways of doing things are fading away, and when they've gone, who'll be there?

By the looks of it, the St George Patriots and the extreme right.

'You have the agreed amount?' Nicolas asks, his head cocked back, chin forth like he's got an eye on the end of it that could do with a gander at me. Time to play ball.

'I do.' I'd run to the local branch of Natwest in the Spinningfields commercial district, and withdrawn two grand I'd saved from my rather basic NCA salary. But, because the house Carolyn lives in came from a fund attached to the Protected Persons Scheme, there's no mortgage to pay, just utilities, and I'd managed to put together the makings of a little nest egg which I hope I'll get back when all is said and done.

'Good, good,' Nicolas replies, and he leaves it there. I keep quiet, but the first buzz of urgency rings out. I need to start picking into these guys - I've only got another day, and those hours will suddenly run out.

'Have you got anything else planned before Christmas?' I ask. 'Any other events you're going to make an appearance at?' I smile lightly, as if I can't wait for their next political jape.

There's no immediate answer. The silence is kind of stoney. Broadshott is looking at me again.

'We're nearly there now,' says Winks, looking out the window as streaks of drizzle race along the tinted glass of the window.

'We'll have a good chat inside,' says Nicolas, and with that, I'm sure of two things. One, I'm about to be very alone with these very dangerous ex-military madmen and their supposed Queen. And two?

They've definitely got something in the offing before Christmas.

And from the way my jokey question was received? It's *big*.

Chapter Twenty-Three

The van sweeps off the street and passes beneath a rising metal barrier, into the hungry dark of an underground parking facility. I curse myself that I hadn't paid much attention to where we were going, and now I have no clue as to where we are. We are still, surely, within the confines of the city. The car sweeps a couple of left turns as we head deeper underground, around pillars and past other parked cars. I feel us slow, and turn to look through the windshield, over the driver's shoulder, to see another barrier rising, lifting a sign reading *residents only* as it goes.

Broadshott must have noticed my interest. 'Home,' she says. So, she lives here. Interesting. A couple more turns, and we pull in to a quiet corner of the car park that features two wide spaces up tight to a cage whirring with steel industrial machinery. It could be the air-conditioning unit.

The van doors slide open immediately on stopping, triggered automatically, and out everyone piles. I merely follow, as they head straight to a wooden door opened by a key fob panel, which Broadshott activates with a keyring from a clutch purse the exact same shade as her suit. It must have been in the van while she was whipping up that riot. Suddenly we're in a reception area for a couple of lifts, and one is en route.

It's a squeeze to get us all in the lift, so the men line the sides while the much slender Broadshott stands in the middle looking up with a confident smile. 'Give a girl some room,' she says with a cheeky grin, illustrating she clearly has no problem at all with such proximity to these men who worship her.

After a few moments of acute awkwardness, the lift door opens out directly into a reception area - and it's bloody gorgeous. A huge Christmas tree beckons us inside, swathed in silver and metallic blue tinsel and ornaments, with warmly glowing fairy lights. The entrance area is completed by a chaise longue upholstered in cream leather and dark wood lines the walls. All I can smell is pine, and that invokes the nostalgic prod of the Christmasses of my youth on the rare occasion we were allowed a real one.

We turn from the left, and there's a whole flat here, and it's only at this moment that I realise the lift opened right out into this - *her*? - apartment. The central living space we enter is very large for an inner city flat, and everything is in that same upmarket dark wood. A long kitchen island stands with a pale marble top, right in front of a matching set of appliances and cupboards. In the middle are two deep cream sofas facing each other, with a low coffee table in between, on which sits nothing but an Alexa virtual assistant speaker. To the left of them, on the wall hangs a gigantic flatscreen TV that must be at least sixty inches - which Broadshott approaches with a remote. In the far corner stands another Christmas tree, this one as big as it is wide, next to a set of huge patio doors which reveal a terrace outside, and the taller buildings of Manchester beyond. We haven't gone that high up, because almost everything around us is taller, but it's still a very impressive sight.

'Help yourself boys,' she says. 'And open me a Prosecco while you're at it.' The men make themselves at home, clearly having been here before.

As the TV turns on, I watch her walk behind the furthest sofa, and climb onto something. As I move towards the kitchen, I see it's an exercise bike. She starts pedaling while she watches the news, still in her suit. She raises her arms when she sees that she is the main story on BBC News 24.

'Fucking jackpot,' she says, and her legs pump quicker. I'm bemused, and actually relieved when the familiar tinny cold press of a beer can is pressed into my hand. It's Mac, and I nod to him, before popping the tab.

'Tom,' says Nicolas. He's by the breakfast bar, cracking open his own can, beckoning me over with a flick of the head. As I approach, he turns to a door off the kitchen area, and pushes it open. He holds a hand out for me to stop, says 'Just hang here for a sec,' and I wait obediently by the door.

'Half a kilogram, wasn't it?' comes the muffled voice. I hear a *thunk* and a hissing slide, as if something smooth was just dragged across the floor. I'm desperate to look inside, but don't want to look overeager. Within thirty seconds, he's back out with a small brick no bigger than an Amazon Kindle.

'We have them prepackaged, varying weights, ready to go. If you want to weigh it, be my guest, I'll bring some scales out.'

I hold it up to feel the weight, let it bounce in the air. In 2013, the Royal Army stopped issuing the Browning 9mm as its standard sidearm, something it had been doing since World War Two. Its replacement was the Belgian Glock 17, a handgun I became just as familiar with. It was quite a bit lighter than the Browning, by over a pound - and clocked in at approximately six hundred grams when unloaded. I can still feel that weight in my right hand as I think. This block of smack feels slightly lighter, and therefore good enough for me to believe the weight is as promised.

'That feels about right,' I say. I reach into my jacket pocket, and take out the white envelope of cash I was given in the bank. Two grand, when delivered in fifties, doesn't look or feel like a lot, but the dent it left in my account certainly did. I hand it over, having a firm silent word with myself to get that back.

'A pleasure,' he says. 'See how your livestock feel about that, then come let me know if you need anymore.'

'I will. Thanks for sorting it out. Kezzer wasn't wrong. He was at me for a finder's fee, but I suppose I leave that to you?'

'Kezzer will be lucky not to get a kick up the arse for his trouble. He's a junkie, and it's a right shame. He was one of us. A good old serviceman. But once you've gone down the opiate route, you're no better than all the rest. Kezzer's a mark, plain and simple.'

'And Desmond?'

'Funny bugger, that lad. Hear he's got a young one living over there in that shit-tip with him. Can't believe the authority's let him, or if they even know. He's mixed blood though, and so's that baby. Even more I think with a darkie mam, so I've been told. Can't help them now.'

I force myself to smirk, if only to stop myself from throttling the guy. I'm going to have to use this as fuel to take them down, and add each callous, racist remark as a log to my fire.

'Thanks for this,' I say. 'Should keep them happy for a while.'

'You mentioned you'd need more?'

'I will do. Will that be a possibility?'

Nicolas smiles. 'There's enough in there to go around, don't you worry about that.'

I force a smile back. 'Alright. I'll see how they take to it, and I'll be back. Can I get a number or something?'

He winks. 'Did you like what you saw today?'

I don't know whether he's talking about the bizarre mahogany drug caché or the demonstration earlier, so I go with the latter. 'Yeah,' I say, turning to face Broadshott, who's still pedaling at pace now with her hands stretched over her head. 'She's the first person in the public eye in ages who I've heard talk about the country I want to live in. The country I killed for.'

Nicolas puts a hand on my shoulder. I want to twitch away but I don't. 'Then you know how we all feel, and why we're here.'

I smile and nod. We clink beers and I drain mine. In a daft knee-jerk response of machismo, he does the same. I take the can from him, and head to the cupboards and root out the bin.

'Listen. Come back tonight. Take care of your business, then make yourself available tonight. We've got some things going on and an extra pair of highly trained hands could be very useful.'

Bingo.

'Cool, OK.'

'Phone,' he says, and types just like Kezzer did only hours before, and when he gives it back I head for the door.

'Tom's just got to go and feed his pets, but he'll be back later,' Nicolas shouts to the others, who holler various goodbyes. Broadshott waves, smiling with that same knowing arrogance.

I take my brick of smack, and head for a breather, bursting to clear my head and make sense of all I've just seen.

138

Chapter Twenty-Four

I walk back into the NCA headquarters, straight up to the OCC regional office headquarters, and drop that half kilo of heroin square onto Jeremiah Salix's desk with a clunk. 'This is what's funding Broadshott's political livelihood,' I say, pointing at it with disgust.

Jeremiah looks up at me, then back down to the dark parcel. 'You're kidding me?'

'No.'

'You brought a block of Class A *here*?'

'I'm hardly taking that thing home.'

'Jesus Christ,' he says. I reach for it, but he bats my hand away. 'Don't touch it! For Christ's sake... We need to establish a chain of evidence.'

'To who? I'm not an undercover, remember? I'm an idiot having a few days off.'

He considers this. 'What you do in your spare time is up to you. Just get it off my desk, will you?'

I pocket it.

'Heroin?' he asks.

I nod. 'And it's none of that shit diluted or cut up with anything lesser. This is the good stuff.'

'Sit down. Tell me everything.'

'Is Blake about? I think she should be in on it.'

Within a few moments, Blake and Catterall have joined us in Jeremiah's office, which has become more of a squeeze. I stand by the desk, and let the team leaders take the chairs.

'I've spent the day getting to the bottom of this new heroin network here in Manchester. It's Helen Broadshott, the extremist group called the St George Patriots and a handful of ex-military boys who have pretty much fallen in love with her.'

'You're serious?' Blake says. She's staring goggle-eyed, swapping between me, Jeremiah and Catterall - who's just ruined his perfect hair by throwing his hand properly through it. I go on to tell them about Kezzer, Desmond, and just how easy it was to burrow into the drug network if you show enough need and have enough cash.

'They hooked me up with contacts at the Hilton Hotel, who were able to help me out with a proper weight. When I got there, it was a team of four ex-military guys who gave me a price. They heard about my own military career, and asked me to join them at a demo in Albert Square because they thought I might like what went on.'

'Shit, the riot at the Christmas Markets?' Catterall says.

'You got it in one. Before long, it was extreme right versus extreme left, but make no mistake, I saw Broadshott's supporters in person. They're in love with her. They'll do anything for her. Without really meaning to, I stopped her from getting milkshaked. Turns out the four boys I met at the Hilton are her personal private security team, who funnel heroin as a sideline. They took me to her flat, at least, she behaved like it was her flat - a swish place in a building called The Quad just off Oxford Road - where they gave me the heroine. Suggestion was clear that they had a lot there. Kilos and kilos of the stuff was the implication. For me, it was clear that the heroine trade is funding her political aspirations.'

Everyone is silent for a moment, but I have one more thing to add. I pull out Nicolas' beer can from my pocket, which I'd pretended to bin.

'The dregs at the bottom of this. See if it matches the black ops ghost man who's piss we got a DNA match from. If it does, I've got him.'

'I… don't know what to say at this point, but we've got to try, haven't we?' says Jeremiah. He looks exasperated yet blown away, in a bizarre combo of tired excitement and adds almost under his breath, 'How do you do it?'

'He seems to be the leader for me.'

'And you think he could be the Dog of the Moors?' asks Blake.

Truthfully, I'm not sure. Maybe it's because I still hold a shred of bias that no military man could do such a thing as murder a bunch of people then nibble on them up a remote hillside, but having said that, none of their behaviour is anything to write home about. 'I don't know yet. He introduced himself as *Nicolas Raine*. See if that flags anything up.'

I take a moment, while compiling my thoughts. There are a few things that aren't clear in my head, and it's like having a bunch of different threads that have all split, and now are jumbled. 'Broadshott has engaged the extreme right fully to her cause, with a vested interest in the underground narcotics industry. She openly taunted anything and anyone leaning left, and this promoted a violent response. But, what's her motive? Is she seriously trying to get into parliament?'

'I don't follow,' says Blake.

'Does she genuinely have political aspirations?'

'She doesn't have a party, so she can't be that fussed,' says Catterall.

Jeremiah thinks out loud. 'No. You're right. She's got a militant gang of thugs pushing hard drugs on the streets.'

'Yes. So why is she doing this? Why politics? You're serious about getting onto the ballot sheet, you join a party and get campaigning, start pressing the flesh, put yourself about that way.'

'He's right,' Blake says.

'We need a full background profile for Broadshott,' says Catterall. 'We need everything we can get on her from the day dot.'

Jeremiah is thinking, and the three of us find ourselves stilling before he eventually speaks. 'We do have a file in here. It will need to be expanded but for now, what we know in broad strokes is as follows. She's privately educated, parents deceased, the last of her inheritance got her through boarding school but couldn't stretch to university. That much knowledge is clear in the public eye. She's not being funded by mummy or daddy's money anymore, because there is none. The situation with her funding has always been a grey area, but I think we can put that to bed now, right?' He looks at me.

'Right,' I say. 'She's got piles of heroin in her flat.'

'OK. So, she's self-sufficient. How does a private school girl here in the UK suddenly become a narcotics baroness?'

None of us can answer, so Jeremiah answers his own rhetorical question. 'We need to go digging. Catterall, you're on it. Uncover every last thing you can find about Helen Broadshott. If she's got dirty magazines under her bed, I want them pulling out for us to nosy through.'

'Got it, boss,' Catterall replies.

'Blake, get those social media profiles out, see if West here can identify any of this security team. If he can't, get full descriptions from him and get finding them.'

'Sir.'

'And West?'

'Yes sir?' I reply.

'Don't buy any more class A drugs on the job, will you?'

'I'm not on the job, sir.'

Jeremiah sighs. 'Of course, you're not.'

Chapter Twenty-Five

I feel like it might be a late one, and I've got no idea when Nicolas would like me to be available from, so I check in at home while I'm on this side of the city. Works out well, as I get back just before five in the afternoon. This will give me the chance to let the traffic go before I head out again.

I open the door, expecting to be hit immediately by the energised voices of the young ones, burning off their post-school excitements, but it's quiet, save for a plinky-plonky xylophone sound from the far end of the corridor, where the kitchen is. I follow the sound and hear the sing song voices of the kids tv presenters, which are abruptly shouted over by Carolyn, 'Is that you, daddy?'

Daddy. I've not even heard my own kid say that yet, but the very idea of me being a daddy is still one that thrills me. A long time ago, an old girlfriend told me she'd been pregnant but had got rid of it, and I didn't even get a say in it. It was her choice, of course, her body, and quite understandably we weren't in the greatest position to have children. But it tore a hole in me, and that's when I knew how much fatherhood truly meant to me. 'Daddy's back,' I say, with a smile. In the kitchen, Carolyn is at the sink up to her elbows in foam, while Jam is swaddled in a blanket, fast asleep in a rocker on the small dining table. On the draining board, sit four small baby bottles, two of which are washed while the other two are caked in a creamy foam. I sneak up behind her, wrapping my arms around her and into the foam. I nuzzle into her neck, right through her hair, and get a whiff of that coconut that still electrifies me since the first time I got close to her. She's not changed it since I told her of that memory.

'Let me do it,' I say.

'If you're going to be this close to me, let's both do it,' she says, and leans into me. I can feel myself melting.

'Nobody in? It's very quiet.'

'They're at school, remember? The nativity dress rehearsal?'

Damn this slippery grip on domesticity. 'Of course.'

'Busy day?'

I infiltrated the extreme right and bought a half kilo of heroin. 'Yeah, pretty active.' I left the parcel in a locked drawer at work. Didn't know what else to do with it. 'And I'm afraid this is just a fleeting visit.'

I feel her tense slightly. I wish I didn't have to be out so much so soon after Jam's birth. I did all the reading before he got here, I've got an idea of how much support she needs at a time like this - and I'm desperate to provide it. But there's the bigger picture than the five of us in this house.

Hell, that's been my problem from the beginning. There's always a bigger picture with me.

And duty. There's always that too. I thought family would shift my priorities, but surely, by being out there and playing an active part in making the country safer, surely the safety of my own family, who walk these same streets, has been equally prioritised?

'They're not back for half an hour,' says Carolyn into my ear.

Now it's me that tenses.

Chapter Twenty-Six

As I'm hopping into the car with decidedly more spring in my step than there was before I got home, my phone pings and I'm wondering what Jeremiah's got for me now - but it's a number I don't recognise. The soft blue glow from the phone screen washes my face and douses the car interior as I read.

WE'VE GOT A SURVEILLANCE JOB. MEET IN 20.

Then there's a postcode, followed by the sign off.

N.

Nicolas. It can only be Nicolas.

I put the postcode straight into Google Maps, and the red line that forms across the simplified topography looks too small. Horribly too short. He's sending me nearby.

My synapses buzz. Half-expecting a loop of piano wire to pass over my head, I jump out of the car.

It's quiet. It could either be that pregnant silence before imminent violence, or the perfect stillness you could encase yourself safely in. I've learned never to trust either.

After a moment, watching the houses and the street, orange cones falling from streetlamps into small front gardens, I check the map.

Two miles, that's it. Next village along, a little hamlet called Moorehill. There's a central street with a bunch of cutoffs, down which the postcode leads. I know just where it is, and no longer need Google's guidance, so I hop back in the car, and make tracks.

Within five minutes, I'm there, but I stop two streets along and leave my car. My old habits and the effects of my surveillance training are leaking back into the present. Don't arrive at the location and announce your presence with a car engine - especially one as throaty as the crapwagon I drive, which I picked up for under a grand to get me the ten minutes to work every morning.

I get out of the car and weigh up the surveillance conditions, and it's only now I realise how cold it is. It's arctic out here. Surveillance ordinarily involves a lot of sitting about with your eyes peeled, and warmth is always a priority. I have a little look in the back of the car, to see if there's anything that I could use and luckily, there's a picnic blanket folded up back there, which will work great in a pinch. I tuck it under my arm, lock the car and get walking.

As soon as I enter out onto the main road, I see the dark shape of a man underneath a streetlamp a hundred yards away. The figure waves to me, before dipping back out of the downwardly fanning amber. It can only be Nicolas, and he clearly knows what he's doing too.

It is leafy and rural here, lined by hedgerows and quaint cottage homes. This central street has a couple of pubs on it and a community park. I can just about make out rusted swings and a frozen hard football pitch in the murk of the expanse.

As I get closer to the streetlamp, the figure in the shadows hisses 'this way,' and starts walking. He's wearing a beanie hat pulled low over his eyebrows and a bomber jacket zipped a little too snuggly. We pass a pub called The Horseshoe, its beer garden sheltered by tall ice-tipped conifers, then a small village gallery. It's still open despite the hour, the lady behind the counter, beyond the glass in the brightly lit shop, is the first sign of life I've seen since I got here – aside from the man I'm following. We walk another fifty yards, before Nicolas stops, and points over the road at a large house skulking behind iron gates. It's the biggest home on the road by some margin.

'That's it,' he says. The building is two stories tall, red brick, with a pitched slate roof right along the top. Two bay windows adorn the front, either side of a grand wooden door stained by dark wood. A brace of cars sit in the driveway, both smart, clean and relatively new, but there is surprisingly space for much more considering how close the property is to the road. A fir tree stands on a small lawn wrapped by fat, multi-coloured fairy lights, and white twinkles line the eves. 'This is the home of Michael Bennett, MP for West Lancashire, Labour Party.'

He hands me a small cutout from a bigger glossy photograph. I can barely see it, so I look for a little light from one of the streetlights, angle the snap at it and can just about make out a middle-aged white man with close cropped grey hair, twinkling blue eyes, and boyish features edged by the odd wrinkle. He wears a suit, tie and broad grin. 'So, who's he?'

'Ready for anything?' he asks. It's a weird question, and one that I can only answer positively if I'm to make any progress.

'Ready for anything,' I reply firmly.

'He's a piece of shit, for a start. You might recognise him from Prime Minister's Question Time, or maybe the front pages of whichever dirty red top you happened to glance at on the petrol station forecourt. Once squeaky clean and extremely influential, now scandal-tarnished but still carries real heft. It seems having skeletons in the closet only enhances your political impact.'

I'm lost. I've no idea where he's going here. 'OK…'

The breeze hisses softly, snaking cold fingers up my legs, as he goes into all the details. 'I'm afraid it's nothing more exciting than your bog-standard affair with the nanny. His wife, Henrietta, is a career-orientated gal, a bigwig at Liverpool legal firm Walker Fish LLP, on track to make partner within the next two to three years. She's clearly been putting the hours in, and the nanny essentially brings up the kids, of which there are two. Well, daddy was a bit naughty and arranged for the nanny, a tasty-looking Czech lady called Natalya, to move into the family home on a permanent basis, and he has a nasty habit of sleepwalking, let's say. Caught in the act more than once, not by his wife, but by somebody with fairly bog bollocks, and more than a little financial backing.'

I look to him with my eyebrows raised, and he offers a slight bow, before continuing.

'We used infra-red to track his movements from one end of the house to the other, and prove that the heat was increasing on arrival in the nanny's room. We were about to blackmail him, but it all counted for nothing when the red tops managed to out him in any case, when he got extremely careless on a business trip to the south coast. Yes, even though the family had separate rooms from the nanny on the visit, he still couldn't keep his parliamentary dick in his pants. A member of the public caught him in the act, and made a beeline for the local paper. All that effort for nowt.'

'What were you going to blackmail him for?'

'He's spearheading a shadow cabinet initiative, meant to come in if Labour were to get in office at the next elections. It started off a stupid shot in the dark until suddenly it got everyone starry-eyed. Either way, he commissioned a report which got him a load of stats and evidence, and it's proven so popular in the polls that it looks set to be considered by all parties. It seems that whatever happens, unless he admits it was all falsified or he fucked it up somehow, this policy could become law with or without him. We can't let it happen.'

'What's the policy?'

'Legalisation of all currently prohibited narcotics.'

I take a second. 'Everything?'

'Class As downwards. He wants everything legal and regulated. Not a good combination for those of us with pets to feed.'

'Why's it so popular?'

'This study of his argues that full decriminalisation would result in a lot of societal positives. Mass long-term reduction in diseases usually communicable via needle share, thanks to clean needle facilities. Registering users offers more pathways to help, means less addicts. Eventually, the suggestion is that legalisation now would reduce drug use across the board within twenty years, to the point of it being irrelevant. He says it would solve the UK's drug issue. Factor in to this that it would free up police force resources so other crime would fall. Murders, thefts, assaults, organised crime, all reduced in one big go.'

All those sound great to me. 'Is he sure? Is the study watertight?'

'Who knows… It's a big gamble. But, it's proven so uniquely popular that it's collected a definite cachet.'

'So where does the SGP come in?'

Nicolas turns to look at me and all I can see is the black of his pupils. I feel the temperature dip, but it's gone nowhere.

'You're on the level aren't you? You're genuine, aren't you, Captain?' Statements, not questions.

'I am.'

'You've seen how quickly cash changes hands here haven't you? Like this afternoon?'

'Yeah. A quick two grand to the SGP.'

'That's right. You legalise drugs, then our revenue stream dries up. He gets in, or that policy becomes real life, and our market goes with it. Why get your stuff illegally when you don't need to anymore? They can go to a clinic, get their gear without all the shame and stigma, and shoot up safely. Then they can get the help they need to kick it. We're shit out of luck, and shit out of money.'

'You need the policy gone big time then.'

'Yes. Now usually, you could just remove the problem. Pop Mr Bennett out on an unmarked moor and bury him…' I can't help but notice the pointedness of his comment as he continues. 'But his idea has so much traction, it would only pick up steam. Then he's a martyr, and his cause is so much more potent. No, he needs to stand up and say he was wrong. Say he got it so wrong, and it would be suicide for the country, and everything goes back to normal.'

'That's what you were hoping he'd do with the blackmail attempt?'

'Yes. The moral compass of the country depends on this. We can use narcotics to control the weak, thin the herd and remove the undesirable element. This is for England.'

This is all kinds of fucked up.

'So what now?' I ask.

'We keep an eye on him, because we need him to be here tomorrow night. We need him here, in this vicinity, twenty-four hours from now.'

'Why?'

'If you come through on this one for us, I'll tell you in the morning. The payday for all of us will be worth it.'

'How so?'

'Helen needs this. She needs the cash to keep coming in. If we pull off this thing tomorrow night, and she keeps her revenue stream, we're all in line for a Christmas bonus.'

'Why me?'

'We're cut from the same cloth, you and me - and the others too. But you were doing this on your own before you came to our attention.'

'Remind me what that was exactly?'

'Taking England back. Using whatever you needed to keep the vermin under your boot. This is our country - a white country - and you know it too. You were taking it back one filthy brown addict at a time, and you were turning a profit while you were doing it. Not fucking bad.'

I want to be sick. I want to drag him behind this privet hedge and choke his racist neck until his eyes haemorrhage and burst from their sockets.

But... tomorrow night. I only find out what they're planning if they get to tomorrow night. I swallow acid and force a grin.

'You got it,' I say. 'Let's take this country back.'

Chapter Twenty-Seven

Nicolas takes me deep behind the hedge opposite the politician's house, where the lights are on dimly inside. Interestingly, the land opposite is a bare field with very little cover, an undulating sparse meadow left on the fallow cycle of the arable rotation. In daytime, from Bennet's bathroom, I guess this would be a good view.

We walk two hundred silent yards into the field, and just as our feet begin to crunch into fresh frost, cracking it as quickly as it forms, I see a black shape on the ground before the crest of a shallow rise.

Being marched into a field with the only suspect we have for the Dog of the Moors, this villain who could be capable of so much, is unnerving in the extreme. He can't be fixing to off me here, surely? On the edge of a village? It's hardly the Dog of the Moors' usual way of things.

The bag takes shape, and it's boxy at one end tapering as it gets to the other. Nicolas unzips it, and pulls out a tripod with what would look to the casual eye like an professional SLR camera.

'Batteries are in there,' he says softly, pointing at the bag, as he walks to the top of the rise with the whole lot. 'I assume you're familiar with this?' he says as he goes.

'I am,' I reply in equally hushed tones.

'Good. It's a good one this. Would cost over thirty grand new, but I nicked it off a surveillance job I did in the private sector when I came home. Said it fell in a river. It fell in my bag, more like.'

He sets out the tripod legs, which are no more than eighteen inches apart, and the unit sits about two feet from the ground. This must be the unit he used on that roof-top in Manchester. He points the lens back to where we just came from, at Bennett's house - which looks doubly warm and inviting from this distance.

'You keep an eye on what goes on through the night. Take the photos of anything you think could be useful, and by that, I mean anything that he might not want going public. Anything at all. The nanny's gone now, so I'm not expecting 'owt. But we need to know what he's up to, and we've got to keep him here until tomorrow night. There's nothing scheduled in Westminster that should see him needed in the capital, and his personal diary is clear.'

'How've you got his personal diary?'

'Never you mind.' I can hear the smirk in his voice. 'Intel is intel. Just make sure he's not going anywhere. Mac will be here at five to take over. Leave the unit with him, get some shuteye, then, all being well, it'll be showtime.'

'OK, got it.'

'Contact me on the mobile in case of anything, but failing that I want hourly check ins.'

'OK.'

'This is for our country. And taking our country back. Don't forget it.'

'Aye, aye,' I say, and as he walks away, I place my eye behind the view-finder. I worked with thermal imaging units in the past, on excursions and exercises in Afghanistan. The terrain is different, the shapes not the same, but the colours make me right at home.

I pan up from the retreating shape of Nicolas, whose breath clouds around his head in a spectral blue haze which billows and dissolves with each step. Behind him, the house comes into view and the auto focus locks in on the building. It looks like a kid's crayon drawing on a blue piece of art paper, in lines that are clean yet colourful and fuzzy round the edges.

My training has me looking for power centres. When I was doing this in Helmand Province, you'd look for those first because that's your primary route to take out the power of the target location. The buildings I'd be looking at in those settings didn't usually have as much power as this - this guy's house is lit up almost absurdly, and the glare from the Christmas tree outside and the fairy lights along the guttering isn't making the image easier to process. For me, that is, as my eyes struggle to get used to which lines matter and which don't. The equipment is military grade, and handles the task with ease.

The walls are a blue green at one end, and more of a yellow at the other. It seems like in a lot of larger homes, the family inside seem to congregate at one end. Nicolas said there'd be two kids in there, and with it being almost eight o'clock now, they're probably winding down for bed.

I'm glad I bought the picnic blanket. It's a big piece of luck, because, since it's huge, I'll be able to wrap myself in it. I spread it, wrap it around my shoulders like a cape, and sit down again.

What on God's green demented earth am I doing here?

I quickly check the tripod and unit for anything amiss. I do the same for the bag and its contents. It's listening devices I'm looking for, and there aren't any.

I pull out my phone. Battery on fifty two percent. Not ideal for a full night. I reduce the brightness of the screen to its lowest capacity, and switch off location services, bluetooth, and close down background apps - anything that could contribute to a quiet loss of battery. Then, I call Jeremiah, who picks up almost immediately.

'Can you talk?' he asks by way of hello.

'Yes, can you?' I keep one eye through the viewfinder.

'Yes.' One last check through the scope but Nicolas is gone. 'I need intel and fast. It's situation relevant.'

'OK, just let me scoot to my terminal.' In this most silent night, I hear the whir of his wheels through the static. A door clunks, then, 'OK, what do you need?'

'I'm currently in a field a couple of hundred yards opposite MP Michael Bennett's house. I'm on surveillance it seems until oh five hundred, when I'll be relieved by Mac, the SGP security guard I briefed you on earlier. I'm monitoring the property via FLIR.'

'Let's keep the military speak down to laymen's terms, OK - what's FLIR?' Jeremiah asks.

'Forward looking infrared,' I reply. 'I'm quite used to it. Vantage point with these things is key. The one they've set me up with is perfect.'

'Did they tell you why they've got you there?'

'They need me to monitor all comings and goings, and alert them if he's going anywhere. They need him here tomorrow night. Something is scheduled to happen, somewhere, nearby it seems. I think this is Our White Christmas. They've not told me what it is, but apparently I'm on board if I do this for them tonight. And whatever it is, this guy's crucial to it.'

'Why Michael Bennett?'

I tell him about the new policies, and how it will wipe out the SGP's income stream – as well as their own secret desires to control those elements in the population they don't approve of. 'There's already been an attempted blackmail plot to silence him. Is that something the ranch would know anything about?'

'I've not come across anything off the top of my head, but I can certainly feed it into the data networks, see what comes up.'

'Can you do that, then call me back? Nicolas said they've got access to Bennett's personal diary - we need to know what's on there, and what is so significant about tomorrow night. That means we need to know the SGP's diary as well, including Helen Broadshott.'

'OK. Hang tight, I'll be back asap.'

'Ok. Jeremiah?'

'Yeah?'

'There are kids in this house. I don't like where this is going.'

'Can't say I do either. Over and out.' He hangs up, and I watch, as the lightest snow begins to tumble, and it's so quiet I can hear every flake land.

Chapter Twenty-Eight

An hour has dwindled by with very little external movement or sound, save for the occasional car dopplering by on the village main road, and the distant cooing of an owl in a copse a quarter mile to my west. The house is cooling, the stronger colours on the walls slipping to a quieter blue, and the children have started the bed time routine. Through the windows, I catch bright glimpses of the kids as they pass through downstairs to head up to their rooms. No adults accompany them, and it's apparent as they pass between a couple of rooms upstairs before stopping in two separate ones at the end of the house, that they are obedient buggers putting themselves to bed without fuss.

There is zero movement from any adults for another half an hour, until a smallish one goes to the bottom of the stairs and pauses for a couple of moments. I suppose this is Henrietta, checking that the kids are quiet and in bed as they're told. A little later, I catch my first glimpse of the bigger adult - the target surely, Michael Bennett. He passes the large bay windows to another room, before returning. He stops to look out through the window, and for a moment I worry he's seen me, however improbable that may be. I soon realise I'm OK, as he tilts his head up to look at the soft snowfall, and I clock that in his hand is a dark blue object. It's a squat cylinder, whose colour denotes is ice cold. I realise it's a beer can just before he pops the tab. I smile. For some reason, that seems absurdly normal for an MP.

An everyman with a solid plan to change the country. Who'd have thought it. He might even have my vote.

Both he and Henrietta head back into what I guess is the living room, and things go still once more. Until about an hour later, the colour of the walls around that living room get slightly lighter. It's almost imperceptible, but it gets more obvious by the minute. Maybe they've started a fire, but, as I look up to the roof, I see no smoke, let alone a chimney stack. As I consider them having played with the thermostat, Henrietta passes the bay windows again. She is a much hotter than she was before, and she's pulling a t-shirt on - *ah*.

My phone buzzes in my pocket, and I grab it. Jeremiah.

'Aloha,' I say.

'It ain't that warm,' he says. 'I had to get a few clearances, but I've got something for you. Have they been up too much?'

'They've been just fine.'

'Good. I've had to play it carefully because what we're dealing with here straddles a number of departments, particularly Extortion Command, and because our work here at the OCC often dips into blackmail, I need to keep that relationship sweet.' Jeremiah, as head of the North West's Organised Crime Command, always has to juggle plates like these. 'I've said we'll keep them in the loop with developments, as it helps with their inquiries.' He's always been good at it too. 'My counterpart over there is a geezer called Donnelly, who seemed to play it straight with me. I obviously had to fudge where our intel came from, as everything you're doing is so unofficial I have to pretty much pretend it's not happening.'

'Understood.'

'Donnelly confirms there was a blackmail attempt on Bennett, but it never took hold. They said he was having naughty liaisons with the family nanny, and the blackmailers had evidence by way of infrared images of the house. They caught him in the act. I have the pictures here, I'm going to send them through to you now, alongside the reports.'

'I think him and his wife have made up, by the way.'

'How nice. Either way, the fact that the original blackmailers used this FLIR stuff, and you're sat there also using FLIR stuff under the supposed blackmailers' instruction, confirms for both myself and Donnelly that the blackmailers in question are one and the same. Donnelly is delighted, as their inquiries were stalling, and this blows it wide open for them.'

'Glad we could help.'

'Always a team player, aren't you Ben.' He hasn't used my real name in a while, and it catches me cold. He must be enjoying himself, caught up in the matter at hand, defaulting back to how we used to operate in the old days. 'Donnelly's team have had the Bennetts on their radar ever since the blackmail attempt, so they were interested to hear you have word of a mole on the inside of the MP's circle, feeding information to the SGP.'

'They had a name?'

'They're looking at everyone, employees past and present. One name stands out, but there's another that's also of interest. Check your phone as we go, so you can look at the pictures while we talk.'

I do just that, opening the email that duly arrived as Jeremiah prompted, and open the PDF. 'You got it?' he says.

'Yes.' I don't even need to put the phone on speaker, it's that quiet. I just hold it close and look at the screen. 'I'll go straight to the images.'

'OK, see the guy that looks like a security guard?'

It doesn't take me long to find it, after I sweep past a few infra-red shots I'll go back to later. I stop on an image of Michael Bennett getting out of a car at what appears to be a party convention, red placards waving in the background. The man holding the door open for him is a tall, well-built man in a suit. He looks every inch the private security career professional, particularly in the way he scans the crowd. 'Got it.'

'Darren Gallacher. Dazzer to his friends and colleagues. He's been with Bennett as part of his security detail for five straight years.'

'Where is he tonight?'

'Security's only called upon for public engagements.'

'How do they know he's the gob inside?'

'Without causing offence, he's got a military background the same time frame as yours, and we only have to look at what you did today to know how easy it is to form quick bonds in this corner of society, especially with those credentials. Donnelly tells me his voting history also suggests a more right-of-centre leaning, despite his line of employment. It's always the little things. Also, move on to the next picture I sent you.'

I obey. 'OK, who's that?' The woman in the picture is the very definition of homely. Early forties, frumpy, cardigan-packaged, unkept hair in a birds-nest tangle. The bags under her eyes alone suggest that she has raised four-plus kids, and her hips look stout enough to have fired them out like a cannon. In the picture, she stands by a gate, leaning over to look across a sun-blazed field.

'Phyllis Longmuir. Domestic goddess. One-time cleaner for the Bennett family, now deposed, the reasons for which we've managed to get a bit of traction with. She had very light fingers, and some of Mrs Bennett's jewellery went missing, and by *missing* I mean it ended up in dear Phyllis' handbag. She was sacked soon after discovery, and that is why she is on the shortlist. She has definite motive for wanting to get back at Bennett.'

I scrunch my nose, speculating the connection.

Jeremiah answers my silence. 'She's Darren Gallacher's mother. Remarried.'

Ah.

Jeremiah continues. 'She'd been the cleaner for a while, got her son the job in security in the beginning, no blips in her employment record, one day had a proper brain fart, pocketed some jewellery and got sacked, most would say rightly so. But she protested her innocence. Her lad bit his tongue, but for me, that gives him motive to let a few details slip.'

'For me too.'

'And Donnelly.'

'Can we bring him in? The son?'

'EC are trying to get a fix on him. This close to Christmas, organising anything's a bugger.'

'Do EC have any idea what to expect tomorrow night?'

'Zero intel.'

'So we're on our own?'

As soon as the words leave my lips, I realise that *I'm* not. My eyes had been casting about at what I thought was random, but I now realise it wasn't random at all. I was regularly checking the target house through the viewfinder, between glances at the field's perimeter - and the soft glint I caught, which was a millisecond of reflected moonlight, deep in the field almost four hundred yards to my four o'clock, was unmistakable.

Another lens.

Trained on me.

This watcher is being watched.

And they'll have seen me using my phone.

Shit.

'Gotta go,' I say, before hanging up. I'm conscious to make my actions as unhurried as possible, as I navigate through the phone file manager to delete everything Jeremiah just sent me. If I get caught with the dossier, I'm as good as dead.

I wipe everything, including Jeremiah's contact details just in case and try not to look behind me.

It's got to be the SGP, keeping an eye on their new asset. Seems I'm not quite in the inner circle just yet.

Chapter Twenty-Nine

Aware of the eyes on my back, I play it straight for the rest of my stint. I phone once an hour to check in, and do very little else. My targets went to bed soon after I realised I was being watched, and the middle of the night passed without incident.

Things went very quiet at eleven, and I heard a couple of distant doors open and close, with a couple of yelps in between. Dogs being let out for a final whizz in the bushes before curling up for the night. Cats at the back door waiting for their human servants to let them in to do the same, albeit much more sinisterly. From there, that owl keeps me company, and from midnight, a car doesn't even pass through the village. It's still.

At one in the morning, the clouds moved on with the slow drift of an unmanned oil tanker, taking the snowfall with it. The night it left behind was crisp, bright with moonshine and redolent with the kind of beauty you'd only ever get from Britain in wintertime. I sit hunched in it, go through my heat conservation routine of wiggling my fingers, stretching my legs, and monitoring my breathing. For a while, I start enjoying myself.

Because of the crystalline texture to the air, I can hear everything, and my watcher occasionally betrays his presence thanks to the brittle snap of dead twigs in the copse. Turns out, while it might be good for staying out of sight, his hiding place is not so grand for keeping quiet. I never once let on I've heard anything, but on the inside I'm tuned into his frequency.

At five to five, whoever it is moves through the copse. He's quieter, because he's concentrating, but there must be so much frozen debris, like twigs and leaves, all over the floor beneath the spindly treetops, that I hear it all. It goes quiet, and two minutes later, he emerges at the opening to the field that I used with Nicolas hours earlier. It's no coincidence, and I recognise the burliness of the man's shape immediately. It's Mac with the confectionary eyes, and he's come to take over - having spent the night watching me.

He's not walking with any urgency, and I keep it cool. I'm going to let him think he had the drop on me all night, and use it to my advantage. As he gets closer, I see he has heavy footfalls, making it clear why I heard him in the copse, and he's dressed as he was yesterday. It all adds up to make me think he's not really a field man. He crests the rise, and stands over me.

'Anything?' he asks, turning to the Bennett property.

I remember to adopt my role just before speaking. 'Nah, they went to bed, and it's all been quiet. Nowt happening, sleepy night in by the looks of it. You volunteered for the early shift?'

'Yeah, I like an early wriggle. Not much of a sleeper.'

Not much for keeping still either. 'Cool. Well, batteries down there in the bag. Nicolas told me to go and get some shuteye before catching up with you gents later.'

'You check in with Nicolas?' I can tell he's trying to make it sound as unloaded as possible, and I'm suddenly grateful again I wiped it.

'Yep, as I was told.'

'And you didn't tell anybody else did you?' Now, if I didn't know that he'd watched me use the phone, I'd lie and say of course not - but that would ruin my progress within the group. 'Nah, I just checked in at home. We had a baby a couple of weeks ago, and there's night feeds and all that going on. Had to tell the wife I wasn't going to be back tonight for arse-wiping duty.'

'I didn't peg you for a family man.'

I look up at him to see his face is flat with suspicion, and he's still trying hopelessly to convey polite disinterest - when we both know he's digging. He can't have been a covert operative in Afghani - he shows none of the traits or skills. I think he volunteered for this assignment, which hints he too may have his own point to prove. 'Neither did I. She sent me a few pictures and whatever, I think it made her feel better. I'm not that sentimental I'm afraid.'

161

'It's nice making them, but that's about it,' he says, as he drops to his knees.

'You're not wrong there.'

'This fellow is no stranger to that either, is he?' He nods to the house, the ground crackling under his weight. 'Smashes the babysitter, and in no time at all he's back giving the wife a good seeing-to.'

'I noticed.'

'Some men have it all.'

Fairly grimmed out, I creep up onto my knees, my legs creaking and muscles straining with the cold. 'Catch you later?'

He looks at me with an amused expression. I can't tell if it's threatening, or just the usual jostling that testosterone-fueled men give each other when their territory welcomes another. 'As you say, Captain.'

Deciding to play it safe, I give a mock salute with a smile, and walk off. I feel his eyes as I go, and my animosity towards this group - this band I might have fought alongside, and God knows, without checking it might emerge that I actually did - grows to the point where I know, just as I know myself, that I'll have to see this through.

Chapter Thirty

As soon as I'm back to the car and heading away from the scene, I've got the phone out again. After a lifetime of being given coordinates, times, weights, speeds and distances, numbers get stuck in my head pretty well, as if on entry they're granted a special level of importance. Ask me what we watched on TV two nights ago, and I'll go blank. Ask me what my best mate's phone number was in primary school, and I'll spit it out before I've even remembered his surname. Jeremiah's number is easy to recall and type back in, and as it rings, I recall there's only one time I noted a number down, worried that it was too important to rely on even my good memory for these things. As sure as the Manc rain, it was Carolyn's.

'Hello?' Jeremiah answers. His voice is a choked croak.

'Catching forty?'

'No, no, I was… Yes. What have you got?'

It's such a short distance that I'm almost home. 'Not much extra happening. The house went quiet at eleven and was still dead when I was relieved just now.'

'OK. Probably didn't need to wake me for that.'

'You told me to check in.'

'I… did, yeah.'

'There is one bit of news however. They monitored me all night. Had a man behind my position. He wasn't very good at it, but he was there.'

'Seems they don't quite trust you yet.'

'With good reason, you could say.'

'Absolutely. Well nothing's happened here either, so you best get a couple of hours rest then get in here for eight. I want you, Blake and Catterall in my office with a plan.'

'Got it.'

I hang up as I park outside Carolyn's house. *Our* house, but I'm still not sure I've earned it.

It's still as dark as any night that's preceded it, as I get out of the car and head down the drive, the only difference to last night being its loss of colour, now that all the fairy lights up and down the street are off. Makes the day feel more serious. Portentous. It makes me pause.

I shouldn't really go in, and take any time off here. Something is going down in a matter of hours, and I've got the chance to stop it - but I can't stop anything if I'm staring at the back of my eyelids. However…

The value of sleep was always something that was laid bare to me, as it is to all soldiers. You take it when and where you can get it. If you're told to sleep, you damn well do so. Jeremiah's words were to get some, so that's what I'll do.

I key the door as quietly as I can, and the still-warmth of the house greets me once more. I slip off my shoes, and shrug off my coat, before creeping up the stairs. What I've learned in this fledgling family setup, is that if you're noisy any time past five in the morning, the kids will wake and think it's time to be up and at 'em.

I sneak into Carolyn's bedroom, and see immediately that Jam is in there with her, asleep. A chubby little fist pokes from the sleeve of a babygro, resting on Carolyn's shoulder. I can't help but smile. Little man has been holding the fort while I've been out. He's a good one already. I slip in next to him, careful not to squash any of his starfished limbs, and feel that security that only being with your family can provide. It's such an overwhelming feeling to me, so fresh in its newness, that as soon as I close my eyes, I'm gone.

It feels like only seconds later, when I hear whispering by the bed that is so loud it comes off as slapstick. My senses have me up before either my son or Carolyn.

'Do you think we can get mummy up yet?' says one.

'Yeah, it's Christmas!' comes the reply.

'But it's not Christmas day.'

'It's Christmas Eve, who cares!? Nobody sleeps on Christmas Eve.'

'We do!' I whisper, only just a little less theatrically. The two children by the bed burst into giggles. '*Shh*, shh, your mum and little brother need their sleep!' I roll off the bed onto the floor at their feet, my arms and limbs tangled, and sit in front of them.

'You made us jump,' says Jacob, his hair as mussed and crumpled as his Avengers pyjamas, as he falls onto me. This is a first. I've caught him before, in playtime. But he's never dropped into my arms before without gravity ensuring it. And after a second, Grace does the same, and I've got one on either knee. I'm overcome by a warmth and pride that's set fast in my chest. We sit in it, for just a second, the three of us.

'You guys ready for Christmas?' I say, normalising the moment.

'Too excited,' replies Grace. I jiggle her shoulder. *Keep that excitement alive, kiddo*. Once you lose it, it doesn't grow back.

'He better have everything on my list. That stuff is non-negotiable,' says Jacob, and I can't help but smile at his boldness. I think of Carolyn, and our conversations a couple of months ago, such as how prepared she was. I know 'Santa' is ready.

'I'm sure he did,' I say.

'This will be your first proper Christmas with us, won't it?' the boy says. 'It will.'

'What did you do for your other Christmasses?" asks Grace. She'll go far this one. No stone unturned and all that.

'Whatever I used to do, it won't be near as good as this one.' I squeeze them, and Jacob's head falls to my collarbone.

'We used to see our Grandpa at Christamasses. And a few other uncles. They all went away though.'

'I heard.' I'm reminded immediately of how complicated this could get for these kids. They saw those people as family, yet it was me who killed them and took their place. How does someone possibly explain that to anybody, let alone a child? 'This will be a great Christmas though.'

'Yeah - are you coming to the nativity?' asks Jacob, his head suddenly snapping up.

Shit. 'When is it again?'

'Tonight,' answers Grace. 'Twenty-fourth of December, at 7.30 pm. Be there or be square. If Mr Clay stops interrupting on the speakers and lets us get on with it, that is. He's interrupted every rehearsal we've had.'

Shit. 'I've not had a chat with your mum yet, but of course I'd like to. Work has been very busy –'

'See, I told you he'd have work,' says Grace, looking at Jacob, as if they'd had a bet before they rustled me out of bed with the Laurel and Hardy schtick.

'Can you get out of work? Pull a sinky?' Jacob asked.

I smile. 'If you mean, pull a *sickie*, then no, I can't do that. But I can try to get out early.' I really don't want to let them down. It's such a big deal in our relationship, not just this moment, but them asking for me to be involved in something so family-orientated as watching their school play - something a *father* would do - is something I don't want to have to say 'no' to.

If we can find whatever it is the SGP are up to today and wrap it up, I can make it tonight. I don't want to let these beautiful kids down. Where they're concerned, I want to be the kind of guy that delivers. That's what Grace and Jacob deserve, especially after all the hurt and upheaval they've been through.

'I'll do my cast-iron, gold-plated, pinkie-promised best,' I say, squeezing them tight.

Chapter Thirty-One

'Well, looks like you're a hero,' says Jeremiah, chucking a copy of The Sun in front of me. I lower my eyes, struggling to even bring myself to look at it. Notoriety is so far from what I want, and I half expect to see my old mugshot as a front-page splash, staring back up at me. 'Dairy products are the new leftist weapon of choice, it seems, although the more centrally minded would rather it was still merely words used as artillery. By keeping the peace, you're a national darling.'

I open my eyes, and see the image. It takes up the whole front page, with a grand headline splash proclaiming 'A NATION DIVIDED', over a grainy, blurred image of Broadshott walking, the SGP minders either side of her, and a milkshake spilling near her feet, caused by a mysterious arm, and another arm blocking it.

'That is, until you jumped into the getaway vehicle,' says Catterall.

I look at him with an eye roll. 'You think that's how I wanted it to look?'

'What the hell did you expect?'

'Enough,' says Jeremiah.

We pause, and I don't know whether it's good or bad.

'Are there any pictures of me?' I say.

'Mercifully not. Just your back as you hop into the van.'

'Then we're good. It's a footnote. I need to get you up to speed on last night.'

Blake and Catterall sit opposite me in Jeremiah's office, while the man himself sits behind his desk, as I fill them in on all I know. I'm up by the wall, bouncing my shoulder blades against it, my body a coiled conductor of nervous energy. I couldn't sit if I tried.

When I'm done, a charged silence sits heavy in the room, almost daring one of us to speak. I fill it. 'Anyone got a concrete idea? The way I see it, we've got eight hours, at a push, to work out what their plan is, and we all need to be on it.'

'But, if what you're saying is correct,' says Catterall, 'you're part of the plan too. Give it a few hours, they'll fill you in, then we hit it. Go wherever you're sent and head them off at the pass?'

'We could do that, I suppose,' I say, 'but it feels too much like lying in wait.'

'I'm not sure they fully trust him yet either,' cuts in Blake. 'That's why they're waiting so late, keeping him on the edge of arrangements. He's part of it but not fully. It's like they recognise his usefulness, but he's not inner circle yet.'

'That's very true.' It's Jeremiah this time. 'And considering this is all supposed to be off the books, it's not like I can call in any favours and get an armed unit ready to go wherever we need them. He's not supposed to be in the field, but he has a way of getting what he wants.' He's nodding at me.

'Besides, they're all laying low,' I say, 'or at least that's what they told me. Said they're keeping their heads down to keep sharp for tonight.'

'Who else will know about it? Who can we lean on?' asks Caterall.

'I don't think anyone else knows about the core plan. Just the security team, one of whom looks like The Dog of the Moors.'

Blake suddenly leans forward. 'The security team… this is Helen Broadshott's security team. She must know.'

I catch her wavelength. 'Christmas Eve, will she be doing something that needs protection?'

Catterall starts to buzz in his seat too. 'Most politicians make a show of whatever it is they do around the festive season. Like to be seen to do the right thing. I could check her social media channels, see if she's mentioned anything, and check her entries and updates for this time last year to see if she has anything she habitually does around the holidays.'

'Good thinking,' says Jeremiah. 'And if they're not with her, we'll know she's alone.' He looks at me with a pointed focus, but there's mischief to it. More than a hint. It's a dirty smile. 'But you know where she lives.'

'You could go down there on some pretence?' says Blake. 'You could distract her while I take a look at the place.'

'What premise would possibly take me down there?'

'You're not married are you?' she says.

'No, but I'm with someone.'

'How long ago was it between this one and your last one?' I'm confused with this line of questioning, and Catterall looks completely lost.

'Ten years, why?'

'I knew it. You're a good-looking bloke, West, but you're clueless around women.'

'I won't deny that.'

'You said she was looking at you funny yesterday. How funny?'

'Intense funny?'

'West, you moron, she was *flirting* with you.'

'You're kidding me, aren't you?'

'Nope.'

'You weren't even there!'

'Women know women.'

Jeremiah can't help but get involved. 'You stopped her from getting a milkshake chucked all over her, then she looked at you *funny*. She wants you, West.' He's positively delighted, his eyes shining as I squirm.

'Fuck off,' I say.

'I think we have to play on it.'

'How clearer can I be? Fuck. *Off*.'

'If we can come up with a plan, a clear-cut way we could get the info we need, which may well prevent whatever it is they've got planned for this evening, then you've got to go for it.'

'No.'

'For Queen and country,' says Jeremiah.

'Don't you say that to me. I've given everything for this damn country and you know it.'

'And it needs you to give some more.'

'Two days ago you were moaning about me being in the field - now you're pushing me headlong into it!'

'If we can prevent harm from coming to a politician and his family, then it's our moral obligation to take it.'

I think of Carolyn. I don't like the feel of any of this, but I can't have anyone getting hurt. There's so much already on my conscience that I fight with myself daily. Any more when I could have prevented it is not going to help my head in the long run. I've just got to a point where I'm settling, and this feels like a spanner in all the works.

But…

Duty.

Here we go again.

I sigh. 'I'm listening.'

Chapter Thirty-Two

This is a terrible idea, and I can't wait for it to be over - and if it doesn't work? I'll be having serious question marks about what the hell it is I'm doing with the NCA.

I ring the bell at the front door, as snow starts to fall from the grey heavens, that sit ashen and obese over the entire city centre, and the air carries that white noise both visually and aurally. The intercom is answered, with a solitary buzz. I try the door and it opens.

How -

Before I even finish the thought, I see the camera embedded in the middle of the glass door, fashioned as a peephole. Whoever is up there has seen me.

God, I hope it's her, but at the same time, I hope it's not.

If Nicolas were to catch me here, what on earth would he do? What would I say?

I remember the route to the room easily, using the lift then the short corridor walk to the normal front door I exited from yesterday. Nobody is about. I remember when I lived in the city it flushed empty on the cusp of Christmas, as the inhabitants fled the hubbub to go back to their respective quieter family hubs in other areas of the country. With Manchester's returning role as a true northern powerhouse, population has soared, but that all had to come from somewhere - which is exactly where they end up going back to when work is out for the holidays.

I'm at the front door to the apartment, the dark wood of the door impressive in a subtle fashion, and I knock with false confidence. It swings open, I smell warm cinnamon and linen, and Broadshott stands there.

She's partially hidden by the door, although I can see her hair is held up by what looks like chopsticks (I've always wondered how that's done), and she appears to be wearing a dark towelin robe of some kind, which makes her blonde hair glow in the contrast. Her look is direct.

Blake might just be right.

'Yes?' she says.

'You remember me?'

'I do.'

'I wondered whether I could come in for a chat.' Her gaze is so forthright I have to look away.

'Come in.'

I cross the threshold, and start walking to the stairs which lead to the main body of the flat. As I pass her, I smell fresh citrus perfume that is so strong a nostril-full would probably get you halfway pissed, and must have been sprayed on liberally and recently.

Up the stairs, and my eyes are open for anybody else in. 'Are we alone?' I ask.

'We are,' she says, as she takes my arm and leads me into the main body of the flat. It looks just like it did yesterday, as we head towards the sofas. I don't like this. This feels like unfaithfulness, and in plain terms, it is. But there's a reason for this. It might save lives.

She directs me to the sofa and I drop onto the middle, the cushion so forgiving I sink a good foot. Broadshott sits next to me, her knees tucked beneath her, and her whole body angled towards me. Even I can read that body language. It's then I notice the bare legs, the painted red toenails, the bathrobe that could have been nicked from an upmarket spa save for the personalised stitching on the breast pocket, and her fingernails resting on her own neck.

I feel like gulping.

'What does T stand for?' I say, turning slightly to her, trying to act as confident as I can.

'What?' she says, momentarily thrown.

I nod at the letters on her chest. 'HTB?'

'Oh!' she says, and laughs so throatily it's a surprise. 'Teresa.'

'Like Mother Teresa?'

That causes her to burst into deep laughter again. Either she's laying it on thick, or she's a bit unhinged - and I think in this case it's a little bit of column A and a little bit of column B.

'That's just me, isn't it,' she says. 'I'm a real Mother Teresa.'

'The saviour of the people,' I say.

'Why are you here, Captain?'

'It wasn't like I could get to know you better yesterday, with that lot here.'

'You want to get to know me better?'

'I knocked on your door on Christmas Eve, didn't I?'

'Are you my present then?'

I smile, but I need to get her out of here. I need to get her into her bedroom. I think she likes directness so I say, 'Where do you sleep, Miss Broadshott?'

Her pupils fill her eyes with a sudden vacuumed rush, and I know I've got her. 'Down there,' she says, nodding to the stairs we just came up.

'I'd like to see that room.'

She stands, takes my hand and pulls me up. Her fingers interlock through mine, and I'm caught immediately by how rough they are. She's no stranger to work, but not just any work – proper hard labour. She takes two steps to the stairs but I pause. 'I'll follow you,' I say, as I let go of her and walk to huge patio windows, miming as if to check them over. 'Old army thing, I'm afraid. A soldier is taught to know all entrances are secure before he lets his guard down.'

She's quiet so I turn to her. She's looking at me with fascination, a hand on the polished banister. 'Whatever you need, Captain - because I do hope to help let your guard down.'

I smile, and turn back. Through the glass, on the vast patio, I can see Blake and Okpara hunkering down behind one of six patio sets. Just where they are supposed to be. Okpara nods at me, and I can see he's wearing his sandals in the snow again. I make no indication I've seen them, and try the key in the door. After making a show of unlocking it, locking it again, then turning back, I turn but, shielding the door behind me, I unlock it again one final time.

'Lead the way,' I say, and she extends her hand.

Here we go.

Chapter Thirty-Three

I blank out everything that's happening. It's too intimate already, and nothing has even happened yet. Broadshott pulls me into her bedroom and the door is thrown closed. She cocks her head to look at me while she turns the lock with deliberation.

'Better?' she says.

'Better.'

She pushes me back onto the bed, and I fall as the mattress hits the back of my knees, taking my balance. The bed offers as much firmness as the sofa - which would be none - and I tumble deeper into the folds of white quilting. The walls are all white too, and the finishings are all cream. Wardrobe, dressing table, occasional chair - all in heavy ivory.

Please, please can Okpara and Blake be in that room already.

Broadshott is looking at me, but her firm assertiveness has taken a softer sheen. She raises her chin slightly, a very small move that shows that she really is, despite the repugnance of her political beliefs, a beautiful woman. Some men would find this all somewhat arousing.

'You're nervous around women, aren't you?' she says.

I'd rather we stuck to talking, so I offer a slight nod.

'It's OK,' she says. 'I don't mind if you are.' There's a kindness to her gaze now. 'Were you away for a long time?'

'Yes.'

'No family?'

'Was never back here enough to start one.' A statement which is true - mostly.

'Women?'

'What about them?'

'Not many notches on the bed post?'

I shake my head slowly. 'Not many.'

'That's OK,' she says. 'I understand. I don't know what you've been through, but I can very much imagine it.'

'Best left in the past.'

She moves down to my shoes, and starts undoing my laces. One by one, my trainers are pulled off. It's weird. A sickly mixture of almost parental care and eroticism seems to guide her actions. I've got to slow this down. James Bond would be busy quipping her robe off, whereas I'm trying to get this godforsaken seduction to stop.

'You've been home a while?' she says, while peeling off my socks.

'Yes.'

'Settling in OK?'

'It's taken me a while to find some kind of balance, but I think I'm getting there now.' Oddly, I'm responding with what sounds like the truth.

'I'm glad to hear it.' She puts my socks neatly in my shoes, and places them on the floor by the bed. It's... atypical. 'Can I take your coat?'

'I think that would be helpful,' I say, and that's as close to a super-spy one-liner she's going to get. She helps me out of it, climbing onto the bed to help sit me up and pull my arms through the sleeves. I can smell myself. The nerves.

'You're tense,' she whispers. 'Do you ever switch off?'

'Not really, but I'm trying to work on it. You don't need to be on constant alert here at home like you had to out there.'

'I can't imagine how hard that must be. On your mind - and your body.' She puts her hands on my trapezoids, and starts to knead them like ropes of dough. 'Do you get enough sleep?'

'No. Never.' This has quickly become therapy, but with a strange psychosexual flavour. Her voice is little more than a low, understanding breath as she coos into my left ear.

'I think you should sleep here in this bed. You'll be safe here. You can let me look after you.'

I manage to croak, 'I'd like that.' She lies me down, then comes around to straddle me.

Carolyn. All I can think of is her, and how quickly this could tilt to betrayal if I let it - but now Broadshott is rubbing my chest, with a softness that once again can only be described as maternal, and I'm lying there looking up at her and questioning what in the Oedipal hell is going on in her head. It's like she wants to mother me then seduce the shit out of me, all in one go, like she gets off on the role as carer for a soldier returned. Maybe that's it. She's surrounded by soldiers after all. Maybe she likes playing mother-hen to all sorts of shell-shocked chickens.

Maybe I need to get the hell out of here.

I realise I don't know what to do with my hands, so I lay them at my side, either side of her knees. She's sat on me, but I'm not aroused or anything - just supremely uncomfortable.

'The tension is right the way through you,' she muses, almost to herself. 'Do you think you'll ever get over it?'

'One day at a time.'

Something that's making me even more uncomfortable is how easy I'm finding answering her questions, however opaquely. With Carolyn, she knows I have a serious past, and a catalogue of skeletons in a lot of different closets. But we leave it there. Maybe I actually *do* need to work through it at some point. It's nice for someone to ask if you're OK, because you spend your whole life trying to convince yourself that you *are* without ever asking the question of *yourself.*

She's looking into my eyes, and it feels genuine. It feels like she does care, like she wants to ice mental bruises. But then I remember what she stands for, and when I look in those eyes through that filter, all I feel is pity and injustice. This woman uses racism and political extremism as a lubricant to her own secret goals, which is the control of heroin into Manchester. And now she's leaning in to kiss me.

She's tentative, lowering herself to my face. I do nothing to lead her forward, nor do I lift my head to meet her. She senses my unease.

'God, you are broken, aren't you?' she whispers hot onto my cheek, where she plants a series of gentle kisses.

Despite the keenness of my moral compass, my body is awake to this kind of touch now, and I feel I couple of responses down below.

I can't.

I take her shoulders and lift her as I stand, gently moving her onto the bed. Sod this for a game of soldiers.

'Poor baby,' she hushes demurely from the bed. This woman is something else, none of which I can articulate. 'We'll get you there.'

'I…' I'm genuinely lost for words, because I'm scrambling for an excuse.

'It's been a long time, I understand.'

Go with that, Ben. 'Yes. I'm a bit out of practice.'

'Let's take it slowly then. We'll get you there.' She pats the bed, and I'm running out of things to say, and there are sticky situations I've been in in my life before but not one of them has prepared me for this.

And my phone rings.

Thank God. It's the signal. Okpara and Blake have been in and out again.

I fumble it out, and it's the first time Broadshott looks dented at what's happening.

'Oh shit,' I say, back into pulling off this deception. 'It's my wife.'

'You're married?' she says, betraying a slight puncture to her mystique.

'Yeah. I'm sorry, I'm confused.'

'You must be.'

'Yeah. I've got to go.'

'We can continue this another time if you like? Schedule something in so we can take a bit more time?'

No, thank you. Not on your life.

'Yes. I'm sorry,' I say, as I grab my shoes. 'Don't get up, I'm embarrassed enough as it is.'

She says nothing, but watches me with those beguiling eyes, that offer a mix of predation and understanding - as I back out of the door with my shoes, socks and dignity all just about intact.

Chapter Thirty-Four

My shoes are back on before I'm even at the lift, and I spend the ride down getting my heart rate down. I'm not cut out for *that* side of any undercover work, clearly. When I get to the front door, I taste the sweet tang of sanctuary immediately on sight of Okpara's white rhino idling on the street opposite - the man himself behind the wheel, Blake in the front passenger side. I run over and jump in the back, and as soon as I'm in, we're away.

Blake turns around immediately, her cheeks rouged by the chilled air up around the fire escape I know she just clambered down. They also dimple with glee. 'I was half expecting to see you come out of that door in a gimp suit with a ball gag in your mouth.'

'My brain definitely feels that way,' I reply, as Okpara deftly switches lanes on approach to the traffic lights, prompting me to fasten my seatbelt. 'She is one complicated woman.'

Unlike his driving, Okpara's voice is cool, calm and collected. 'It goes deeper, my friend. Much, much deeper.'

'You found something?' I ask.

'We found a lot in that room - a *lot*. Your intel was spot on - I think what they say round these parts, is that you smashed it.'

They spend the drive back to HQ filling me in on the contents of the office. They had divided the tasks, Okpara tossing the room while Blake photographed everything with her iPhone, which had already beamed the images to her iPad, which in turn had already sent them to the OCC intranet. Jeremiah was on them now. The documents that had been photographed were being converted to PDF by Catterall, and we were all headed back to pore over them, the OCC oiled and firing on all cylinders.

Okpara wants his Chief Superintendent to rain festive brimstone on Broadshott and her SGP security boys. They were building a case, rock solid in the eyes of anybody who cared to take more than a passing glance, but utterly inadmissible in any kind of court. It was a quandary for him, and for his relationship with the NCA and its Organised Crime Command. The urgency which prompted our inventive raid on Broadshott's home was prompted by Jeremiah, who saw the potential threat to life this evening as high enough to warrant a disregard of protocol, but on the stipulation that anything they turned up was to have come from a confidential informant.

That couldn't quite work for Okpara, who was called firstly as a courtesy action (Jeremiah keen never to stand on any GMP toes) and also because of his investment in the case - but now he'd seen what she had in there and looked upon the filth that was going to flood the streets of Manchester in the dual name of profit and racial cleansing. Something that, as a proud Maasai, he was damned was not going to happen on his watch. But he didn't have the luxury of throwing together raids at a moment's notice. He couldn't hijack the findings of informants registered to another organisation. But he was going to try. He was going to march into the superintendent's office this afternoon, bolstered with their findings and that brick of heroin I bought yesterday, to try to guilt her into action.

'What about any plans for tonight? Did you find anything?' I ask, beginning to get frustrated. 'That's what we really came for.'

Blake and Okpara glance at each other. 'Nothing sprang out at us. But we've photographed as much as we can. We'll have to go through it all. There'll be a lot to wade through. It was a bit of a treasure trove.'

'Every hour is going to count here,' Blake says, almost to herself.

My knee starts to bounce. Please say we got something. *Please*.

'We got a bit of extra news while we were waiting,' she says, and I catch her watching me in the wing mirror.

'And?' I say.

'Jeremiah called. DNA results in. It *is* Brett Scarborough you're dealing with. He and Nicolas Raine are one and the same. He's the one-time black ops man, and presumably the Dog of the Moors.' There's a pensiveness to her statement, as it seems her own fears of the man she once worked with have just come true.

I breathe out. *As if we don't have enough to deal with.*

Chapter Thirty-Five

Blake and I enter the hexagon, closely followed by Okpara, who says rather bluntly, 'I'm seeing this through. And if you try to stop me, I'll show you first-hand how that lion went down.'

The whole command is in, all members of both teams. Even some people I've not seen before, sat at the central conference table, facing the expansive information wall beyond them - where Catterall is active yet again, pinning up everything we have. Efficient bugger is really pulling his weight here. My respect for him creeps forward.

We are greeted with a pensive excitement, and I see Jeremiah move into view at the head of the table, having finished circling it. He's a ball of energy, constantly moving, the chair no constraint to his vibrancy, as he points at the three of us. 'Listen to these people. Look at this board. No such thing as a bad idea here. We need anything and everything.'

Heads turn to look our way, as Jeremiah motions us to join him at the front. Okpara pauses, knowing this isn't his wheelhouse, but Jeremiah gives him a *don't mess with me* look and he trots over.

'West, in your words, tell them everything about last night and yesterday with the SGP. I've filled them in once, but in case I've missed something, let's have it straight from the horse's mouth. If this threat is real, we're running out of time.'

I do as he asks, while Catterall continues to arrange the printouts for digestion behind us. When I get to the part about the trip to seduce Broadshott, I glance to Blake to bring her in. She steps forward and takes over.

'This is about following up the matter of our murdered undercover, and in our main suspect for that crime appears to be part of a group who have issued another threat of violence, scheduled to take place tonight. It is our intention to stop their plans and apprehend our suspect using the information at hand. The office at Broadshott's house has a concealed bookcase doorway to a small area that appears to have once been a panic room. Now, what we found in Broadshott's hidey-hole suggests all manner of different crimes, but the clearest was concrete evidence of narcotics. All that business will be part of a different investigation, and are to be viewed simply as supplemental info. DCI Okpara will be following this one up with GMP once the threat has passed. So as things stand, the information we found amounts to corroborative footnotes of bad news and nothing more.'

'Tell them what you found,' instructs Jeremiah, eager to press on. 'For the sake of completeness.'

'Around a hundred kilograms of heroin, appears to be of a high standard. Three hundred grand cash. Four firearms. A number of documents, which are being scanned and placed up behind us by Catterall. If there's anything in there that suggests what's going on tonight, we've got it here now. We were thorough.'

The room has that start line purr. All the components are locking into place and start to hum with cohesion.

'And you're sure this woman runs the SGP?' asks Fredericks, an officer with the thickest Irish brogue I've ever come across.

'She does. And a heroin empire operated by some extremely sympathetic ex-soldiers. She's our main villain here. We just have to find out what she's part of tonight. We unmask the plot, tie her to it, and bring her in – then raid her home, and we already know what's there.'

'Is anyone on Bennett and his family?' I ask.

'Yes, we've got eyes on him,' replies Jeremiah. 'It's only a couple of our lot, not official surveillance or anything, but when they move, we move. Have you heard anything from Nicolas Raine?'

'Not yet, I suppose they're all still laying low.'

'For everyone's information, Raine is our chief suspect as the murderer of Officer Kyle - and logically, we think he must be the Dog of the Moors.' That brings out a few murmurs. That legend obviously still has deep, stubborn roots. 'Anything jumping out?' Jeremiah spins to regard Catterall, who's now on a chair taping paper to the wall just below the ceiling.

'Not for me yet,' he says. 'Aside from that one over there.' He points to his right, but because of his precarious position, I go across to help point to the one he's after.

'This one?' I ask, pointing to what looks like a legal document, in terms of typeset. Except for an ornate calligraphy that's been used solely for the title.

'That's the one.'

Calligraphy is sometimes a bit too ornate for me to get my head around on first viewing, something I've never been sure of the reason for. Maybe my brain just appreciates things simpler.

'Yeah, that rang a bell too,' says Blake. I look to her, then Okpara - who nods with solemnity. 'It was a series of pages bound by a clip. By the looks of things, the following pages are the ones stuck up adjacent to it.'

It's then that I realise what one of the biggest words on the front page reads. *Manifesto*.

Jesus Christ. In this day and age, here in Britain, we've got an extremely popular neo-fascist politician who has been working on a manifesto - a manifesto she obviously has serious hope and application for. Any doubts that I had regarding her aspirations for actual office, that the heroin trade might be enough for her in terms of influence, have been put to bed and tucked in tight.

Broadshott could be going for a Fourth Reich here.

'Is the creation of a fascist manifesto enough grounds for arrest?' I ask.

'Not by itself - and again, you'd have to answer the question as to how we got it.' He turns to the team. 'Fredericks, Alberts - can you both focus on that document please? Please try to break it down as quickly as you can.' All the faces look to him for instruction. 'It's now two in the afternoon. Every minute is crucial. Work together, work alone, whatever, just find something that tells us where they are going and what they are going to do. Christmas is cancelled until we get a result.'

I check my phone, as the room springs into activity. Nothing.

Come on, Dog of the Moors. Get in touch.

Chapter Thirty-Six

Blake, Okpara and I gravitate around each other, a solar system of just three planets, while we bounce ideas. We seem comfortable in each other's company, in so far that a working relationship has clearly been born. However, nothing seems to be forthcoming. We trying things out, turn things over, every person in the office crowds in front of the display wall at one time or other, with Catterall playing the bizarre role of supposed secretary to the wall itself, fielding questions like *have you got any more of this*, or *any more of that*?

I sit, just looking, thinking, calm my ally. Staying cool when things go down has always been something I'm good at, and has helped me out so many more times than I can adequately describe. These are the best minds in the NCA, trained specifically to look for criminal traits, and we have centuries of collective experience between us. We'll find this.

But what are we missing?

It's then, at 6.00 pm, that my phone goes.

It's Raine.

A text, that reads: 6.30PM. JUNCTION 9 M62. BE READY. WEAR BLACK.

My mind goes blank, and I share my screen with Okpara and Blake.

'That's near here,' Blake says, her brow fused and wrought with concern.

'Very,' confirms Okpara. 'You think they're on to you?'

I mull it over for just a second. 'It's a possibility, but the same thing happened last night. I was leaving home, when he sent me instructions to meet him just five minutes away in the next village over. It all felt very convenient.'

184

'I don't think you can go. I think this is a set up,' Blake says. She's dead serious too.

'What choice do I have? We still have no idea what the plan is, and if I don't do it, then we won't find out until it's over. I have to go with them, and try to stop it. Whatever it is.'

We sit in silence a moment, but I break it with, 'what do you think, Ollie?' It's the first time I've ever used a personal term with him, and he takes it seriously, shifting in his seat, before his eyes rest on the floor.

'I'm a bit of both,' he says thoughtfully, with a reticent smile.

'Please elaborate,' says Blake.

'Time is short. Now shorter by the minute. We have to go with the best option, however dangerous. I recognize on one hand, it seems ridiculous to go with them. But on the other, it seems even more ridiculous not to.'

'So?' I ask.

'Given the choice, I'd go.' He nods at Blake. 'You'd go.' Then turns to me. 'You want to go.'

His logic is faultless, his assessment a direct hit.

'OK, it's done. You keep working on it, and let me know as soon as you have something.' I look at all the people around the conference area. 'Now, who's wearing anything black?'

After a quick whip-round, I've got a black peacoat, black jeans, a black jumper a couple of sizes too small, but my trainers are dark navy and because they're as comfortable as a bad habit they're going to have to stay. There's talk of wiring me up on the fly, but I don't want to risk it. Anything with these guys, especially whose ranks include a neck-severing psychopath serial-murderer, could lead to bad news and a swift, nasty ending. It's time to go, join up with these guys and hope I can get a call out to the good guys at some point.

Okpara rises to shake my hand, takes my wrist with his free hand and says solemnly, '*Tumunyana*, my friend. Good luck.' I nod my thanks, while Blake surprises me with an arm around my shoulder as we walk to the door.

'Don't break any laws, arms or noses,' she says. 'And whatever you do, don't try to seduce anybody, OK?'

'I'll do my best on all fronts.'

She smiles and as we reach the door, Jeremiah appears.

'As soon as you know where you're going, call it in to us,' he says. 'If you can give us details of the threat, do it. I can't believe I'm saying this to you again, but we're in your hands.'

'You're all talking like I'm about to walk the plank here, I - where has *that* come from?' My eyes have caught something on the display wall I'd completely missed.

'What?' asks Jeremiah, as his eyes attempt to follow mine. I march to the wall. *That* wasn't there before.

'When did that get put up?' I say.

Catterall comes over, breaking off from another conversation. 'I just put it up five minutes ago. Fredericks noticed that there was a legible imprint left on one of the documents - the one above it must have been written on with a biro or a marker or something similar. Like a trace. We don't have that document itself, but we do have what it says. I magnified it, brought up the contrast, and stuck it on the wall. Sadly, it doesn't like like much, more like a bunch of idle doodlings.'

I look at the image. To the layman, indeed these scratches do have the qualities of the random - as if someone was on the phone, listening to something important, and was just making shapes with their pen on the paper until the good stuff came up. It's two and a bit lines of shapes that look like geometrically aligned glyphs. The second line loses it halfway through, as the shapes captured from the top sheet fade to nothing. But I know what they are.

'They're not doodles, Catterall,' I say. 'It's a pigpen cipher.'

'A cipher?' Jeremiah says in surprise.

'A simple one, but yeah. In Afghanistan, ciphers like these were used to swap messages within the ranks for those people who were after something you shouldn't be trying to get hold of. Drugs mainly. You'd scratch these symbols onto the frame of your bunk, to send quick messages.'

'You're kidding?'

'They obviously found a use for it back home.'

'Would you need a key to break it down?'

'Not usually. It uses a standard key, but even if they've adapted it, a specialist shouldn't find it too hard. The Enigma Code, it ain't.'

Blake grabs my arm, and says with authority. 'You're going to be late if you don't get going.'

'I know a guy,' Jeremiah says. 'We'll decode it, and we'll text you what it says. Hope he's not signed off for Christmas yet.'

I check my watch - six fifteen. I've got to get going if I'm going to make this.

'Alright, let's go. But let me know as soon as you know anything.'

'Got it.'

Chapter Thirty-Seven

The only spare bit of land at junction 9 of the M62 is the parking lay-by for a vast landfill, which doesn't really settle my nerves about meeting these guys one bit. Would be very easy to pop one in my head, and drop me into all that rubbish, never to be seen again. My guard is up, and I button the collar of my new coat up to match it.

It's dark, the snow is still falling lightly, as it has all day, but never quite enough to stick properly. From my spot, I can see the cars on the motorway below, drifting slowly through the falling flakes, which are now lit up orange by the sodium flares of the street lamps. It's the first time I've felt quite festive and Christmassy.

Christmas.

Dammit, usually I couldn't give two shits about Christmas, but I'm a family man now. A baby that relies on me, and kids that are beginning to. And I forgot to let them know I've got to let them down on Christmas Eve.

I pull my phone out and hit a quick text to Carolyn. *Please tell the kids I'm so sorry, but I'm not going to make the nativity. Tell them I'm sure Santa will make it up to them. x*

I put the phone away, and feel like a poor excuse for a father.

I can't dwell on it because with a swish of tyres on melting snow, that familiar white van pulls up in front of me, and the door slides open before it's even stopped.

'Good evening chaps,' I say, as I hop in, and take the nearest available seat. I look around at them, as the door is slammed shut by Mac, I think. It's hard to tell as they are all dressed in bomber jackets and jeans, and beanies pulled down over their ears, every single one of which is black - even the driver, who I can barely make out but assume must be the same guy who drove yesterday at the demo.

'Evening, evening,' says Nicolas in a mock policeman's accent, which come off as sinfully creepy, especially coming from him. He regards me with focus. 'Ready for anything?'

What a question, given the circumstances. 'Ready for anything.' The car pulls off and I feel doomed to whatever fate I'm now hurtling towards.

'Good. Not long until we're there.'

The van falls silent again, and the atmosphere is subdued. It's a familiar one - all transports heading into a war zone are like this. It means I can't resist asking where we are heading any longer.

'So where are we going, gents?' I say, as if merely curious.

Kevin looks at Nicolas, who gives him a calm nod.

'It's time to intercept Bennett,' he says.

'OK, cool, where?'

'The only place he won't have any security with him.'

'And where's that?'

'You'll see.'

This is taking the piss now, even if I am double-crossing them. 'Come on lads, why the secrecy?'

'Good boys like us follow orders, don't we?' says Nicolas.

'Are you SGP or are you SGP?' says Mac.

'I want my country back,' I say definitively.

'Then you'll be right,' says Nicolas. 'All you need to do is stand where we tell you and look heavy going. Look like you can handle yourself.'

'Alright.'

Then the guns come out. A revolver each, except for me and Kev. I recognise them from the pictures taken in the office panic room at Broadshott's.

'None for me?' I ask.

'You won't need one,' says Mac.

If I didn't like how this was going, now I really don't. I frown slightly to show my displeasure, but let it go, and focus on the window instead. We are heading around the many round-abouts near Birchwood, and if we're not careful, we'll be stumbling on the NCA offices. That feeling of dread grows with every turn of the tyres.

'When we get there,' says Nicolas, 'your job is to deliver a message. Just a few words, to one person. Nobody will stop you, you just need to go up to him and say it. He'll follow you. You'll bring him to us.'

'This is Bennett we're talking about, isn't it?'

'The less you know at this stage, the better it is for you. It can never come back to haunt you.'

Christ, what are they making me do here?

'Nice way to spend Christmas Eve,' says Mac. I don't share the sentiment. My phone vibrates against my leg. I need to look at it.

Everyone has phones. Everybody. And each one of those people check it incessantly. When I got back from the Middle East, it caught me off guard at first. In the time I'd been away, everyone in the UK seemed to have grown a new electronic appendage that they couldn't go any serious period of time without consulting. Mac has checked his twice since I got in the car. Kev once.

Surely I can have a look. So, I do.

It's Jeremiah - and his words shake my very foundations.

CHRISTMAS EVE. 7PM. SCHOOL PLAY. MOOREHILL PRIMARY SCHOOL.

Holy-fuckin'-*shit*.

That's where Gracie and Jake go. The school play - they are in it tonight. Carolyn. And Jam. My son. *They're all there.*

Why Moorehill? That's round the corner from Bennett's house. His kids must go there too. Shit, he's popping out to watch his kids' play, but hasn't bothered with any security with it being a family thing at Christmas.

I look at the time in the corner of the screen, before putting it back in my pocket before anyone sees. 6.40 pm.

My family will be there. Ready.

'All alright at home? Baby OK?' Mac says, with a knowing smile that might carry a little extra bite.

'All fine,' is all I can manage, my mind clenching panic like a cinching zip-tie.

Looks like I'll be making the nativity after all.

Chapter Thirty-Eight

Twenty-five minutes later, the play is already underway, as I open the glass front door to the school. I breathe deeply, my mind a mess. As I enter, I catch the stillness one feels when there's a lot of life in one space, but it's all quiet. A lone voice is speaking. It's young, pre-pubescent. It's a child, loudly asking in stilted tones if there's any room at the inn.

Oh God. Literally, *God*.

Focus, Ben. At this stage, I feel like the only person in the area that can do anything about what's about to happen. But for now, I have to go along with it. If I don't, people are going to die.

Layout. Key it in.

The school is a low grey brick building, one story, all trimmed in blue. The assembly hall, where the play is taking place, is in the centre, with five offshoot corridors like spindles - one for the reception, staff room and entrance area (which I'm standing in right now), and one each for nursery/reception/year 1, years 2/3/4 and lastly years 5 and 6, casting clockwise around the centre in ascending age order.

I take the corridor, my trainers padding along the old green linoleum, to the double doors at the bottom. The walls are adorned with brightly coloured star charts, paintings and drawings, class photographs of smiling kids bright as polished buttons, collages made with dry leaves, a Christmas tree blinking softly with home-made decorations on every weighed-down bough. And right now, as I reach the door, I know a team of militant right-wing extremists has just entered this building - this place that is supposed to be a sanctuary for learning and development.

191

I look through the glass panel of the door, which is at the back of the hall, and I see the back of rows and rows of heads. The ambience is dimmed, the only illumination coming from the lights above the stage. Everyone in the room is facing it, upon which is a traditionally happy scene. Or so I've heard. I've never been to a nativity before, aside for being in the odd one I suppose when I was a kid - none of which I can remember. I'm saddened by the notion that the first Christmas play I've ever been to, as a spectator, is in circumstances like these, where focus and keeping my wits about me is going to keep everyone in this building alive.

I look at the faces in search of recognition. Everyone in the room is important, but there are a few that I simply have to keep safe. I can't see Carolyn - there are a few long-haired brunettes in the room, yet none of them seem to be her. Please let that be because she didn't come, and she's safely at home with our boy. I can't see the back quarter of the room, such is the angle of the door. She may still be in there.

I glance at the faces on the stage, trying to see actual features amongst the camel costumes, and multiple kids in keffiyehs as shepherds and other characters. But I can't quite make out the ones I'm looking for.

Focus, Ben. Truth is, I've never cared about anyone in this way before, and nobody who has ever come close has broken over into the combat world I inhabit. If I ever wondered about just how strong the bonds of family are, I fully get it now.

Follow instructions.

I slip through the door like a parent who's come late from a meeting that ran over, and loiter at the back looking for Bennett. They're up to the part where Mary's about to be visited by an angel. Bennett is about to be visited by a whole other force entirely.

I see him now. I knew he was tall, thinning brown hair with a grey sprinkle and a bald patch, so in the end he was quite easy to spot. I move position by a couple of feet, to catch his profile. Yes, got him. About the middle of the room. Of course, he had to be. A couple of heads have turned to me, catching movement in their peripheral vision, so I smile apologetically. I need to make a move. They'll be in position by now, and before I know it, the son of God will be here, the Frankincense and Myrrh

192

will have swapped hands, it'll be Merry Christmasses all round and my chance will be gone.

Mercifully, there's a central aisle which I'd missed, and I shuffle along the back row to take it - and as I walk down the middle of the crowd, I see that one of the angels is waving to me with a beaming smile. Gracie. She looks delighted but my heart plummets to a new place. I wave back with that same sheepish smile, and I see her day is made.

Please be safe. *Please.*

Bennett is ahead. Centre of the room, four seats over on the right. Next to him, his wife, whom I just about recognise despite this being the first time I've seen her without being etched in bold infrared hues. I keep low, get to the row, and motion that I need to get in. The old man on the end, who I suppose *was* enjoying a night out watching his grandkid's performance, looks at me like I haven't just lost my marbles, but I crushed every last one.

I need to get in, I mouth as politely as possible. A few seats over, Bennett has stiffened and taken notice. He's not one of those politicians who looks unwieldy and stupid when not in a suit. In this case, he's in a dark jumper and jeans, with a starched white collar poking above the neckline. I take the bull by the horns, and scoot to him in front of the three people next to him, who try not to make a sound of indignant protest. As I reach him, I see another sight over his shoulder I wish I hadn't.

Carolyn, near the back, holding the baby. She looks at me with a mix of pleasant surprise and confusion, a half smile playing across her face while her eyebrows bend a touch at the middle. Against everything my heart tells me, I ignore her and whisper in Bennett's ear.

'Mr Bennett. Right this second, there's a rifle trained on your youngest daughter's forehead. Follow me, look happy about it, and the trigger won't get pulled.'

Chapter Thirty-Nine

Michael Bennett, Labour MP for Warrington North, looks into my eyes to see if the awful words I uttered were true. My return gaze gives no compromise. He gets up, and follows me out of the row, just as, up on stage, Mary's about to wake up with a surprise.

First corridor offshoot on the left is where I'm headed, through the left-hand set of two double doors on the western hand wall of the assembly hall, to the left of the stage. The sign above the door, in a homely printed-out flow of A4 copier paper, reads *nursery, reception and year 1*. As we round the back of the crowd, I see a couple of people watch us go. I hope they're merely fantasising about the busy lives our politicians must lead, as opposed to anything approaching suspicion. Checking to see if Bennett's still there, I'm relieved to see he is, albeit white as a sheet.

As we get to the double doors, a woman with a name tag approaches us, wearing orthopaedic shoes and a tissue under her watch strap for any sudden snotty noses. 'Are you OK?' she asks.

'Yes,' I whisper back, before Bennett catches up. 'A bit of urgent government business this gentleman needs to attend to.' I flash her the most winning smile I can conjure.

She smiles back immediately. 'Oh, absolutely, of course.' Then she holds the door open for us.

Once through we walk along a row of coat pegs, all empty, the door to a dark computer room, then a small library, and the first classroom. I slow to allow Bennett to take the lead, and as he passes me, he looks back in the direction of the room we just left, and the stage on which his little girl stands for the last time if he doesn't do as he's told.

He then takes a good look at my face. A very good look. A very *I'm remembering every last fold of your skin so I can hunt you down later* kind of look.

One more classroom down, and we're there. Nursery. The classroom door is merely a wide opening, which suggests an open plan aspect to the learning offered here, and we enter to find the team in place.

A tripod sits in the middle of the room, light on. Behind, is a small kiddie chair in front of a clean whiteboard. Four figures stand around the centre, facing our entrance. Their beanies are now pulled down to reveal they were balaclavas all along, but I can see it's them, and from their shapes I can have a decent stab at who's who. Nicolas, Mac, Kev and Winks.

'Mr Bennett, a simple game,' says one of the masked men, although I recognise the voice immediately as Nicolas'. He gestures to the chair. 'Sit down, do what we tell you, and nothing happens. Your little girl's head stays in one piece, her brain stays where it is. All those memories, and things you've taught her - they'll all stay there. The things she could achieve, the life she might lead - they'll all still be on the table if you do as we say.'

'Anything,' he says, as he walks to the chair.

'Just so you know we aren't messing about, please observe, oh, I don't know… This pot of pens here.' Nicolas walks to the teacher's desk at the front, which is festooned with folders, pieces of paper, a computer monitor and a pot of brightly coloured pens. He turns to the far bank of windows, and points to the pot.

As we watch, the air is cut by a whizz, a crack, and a tinkle of glass, as the pot bursts in a rainbow fountain of ink, flicking a blotchy spectrum up the wall behind it. I look at the windows, and see one of them shaking to a standstill. It's an old school, with single-glazed windows, but the high-powered rifle that's evidently out there somewhere is being used by someone who knows damn well what they're doing. When the pane stills, I see a neat circle resting in its lower right hand corner.

The stakes leap forward again. Any notion that the sniper threat isn't real - and I've used that one before myself - has been dashed. And an all new, awful question forms in my mind - namely who the hell is that fifth member of the team?

'OK, OK, OK,' says Bennett, and confidence of negotiation shattered.

'Our man out there is now training his rifle back between your daughter's pigtails. So, you sit down and record the message as we instruct. If you don't bad things will start to happen.'

'OK, OK, anything.'

In the past, I may have been detached to this, in a professional sense. Not because I know this is wrong - because this *really* is - but because I didn't understand the bonds that are at stake for the subject of this negotiation. The *family* bond.

I'm now imagining being in his position while a professional trains a rifle on my baby boy's skull. I can't think about it. I physically shake my head to get the image out. This has to stop but *how*?

Nicolas is all business, while one of the others takes the tripod and points the camera at Bennett in the chair, the spotlight catching the sheen on his forehead. They've angled the camera so that the frame includes the edge of the Christmas Tree that stands in the corner, each bauble a different cartoonish farm animal. It looks like they're about to film an ugly hybrid of the Queen's Christmas message and an ISIS beheading video.

'I know you can improvise,' says Nicolas through the wool of the mask, 'so I know you can make this sound natural. All you politicians lie through your teeth every time you're in front of the camera, so I just need you to do that again today.'

'OK,' says Bennett, nodding, breathing out, drying his hands on his pants. *How do I intervene here?*

'What you're going to do, is passionately denounce your proposed policy of drug legalisation. Tell the world you got it wrong, that your research has shown faults, and that it is no longer a viable or recommended policy.'

I should have known something like this was coming, but I just couldn't, for the life of me, put my finger on it. And hearing it like this - *a fucking policy!* - makes what's happening here all the more unbelievable.

But that's just it, isn't it? This is Broadshott's income stream they're protecting here. And in turn, it's their wages, and their way of controlling the very people they seek to dehumanise. I've got to stop this... but Bennett hasn't answered.

He looks at the men around the room, the tear of the decision so richly composed on every one of his features. But there's something else there. It's defiance.

'Why?' he says. And there's real question there. I can tell right then and there, that he believes in that policy. 'The findings are accurate.'

'I don't give two fucks if they're accurate or not. Their accuracy is not in question. What is in question is the structural integrity of your daughter's head.'

'Just listen to me,' Bennett says, and he shifts in his seat, leaning forward. 'Just listen. This will save lives. This will change people's lives. Not just in the drug enforcement sector, not just for drug users, but for sufferers of crime everywhere. Legalise drugs, take away the demand, the mystique and the overwhelming pressure, and, with time, it all goes away. Society will benefit. Everyone benefits.'

He enunciated every word. This guy clichéd his wife with the nanny, might well be a weaseling career politician, but I *believe* him. His policy, the policy they're all talking about, right across the political gamut, might change this society for the better and for the *good*.

'I don't care,' says Nicolas. 'I really don't care who benefits, or who might get better, or if grannies don't get robbed in their homes anymore by smack heads who need to steal heirlooms for a fix. This policy ends tonight, and you tell everyone all about it. *Now*.'

'Let's negotiate about something else, please. This is an actual policy - none of this bullshit you'll read on buses, or you get promised and it never happens. This is a genuine motion that if elected I will enact which will save hundreds of thousands of lives.'

'Last chance.'

'God forgive me, no.'

And then things take a very dark turn in the nursery classroom of Moorehill Primary School.

Chapter Forty

It starts with a hand signal from Nicolas Raine - a sweep of forearm in Bennett's direction, ending with a whole open fist pointed at him. It seems primitive and over the top, but it elicits an immediate response. One of the masked men steps forward, and takes Bennett by the jaw. I step forward, but I'm stopped in my tracks by a blade appearing. The man who's holding Bennett has pulled something like a two-foot knitting needle out of his pocket, and is angling it at Bennett's neck.

I can't move. I don't know what I'm looking at. The surgical, precise element to the movement has me stuck in place, intrigue and confusion cloying like glue in my head.

Bennett is the same and rabbit freezes. Then the man in the mask looks twice, moves his thumb, then drives the blade straight through the middle of his neck, so far that it comes straight through the other side without argument or resistance.

Dumbfounded, I look to the masked man I know to be Nicolas Raine - who is turning away, and as he turns away, so does my thought process where he is concerned - because I now know he is *not* the Dog of the Moors. That title belongs to whoever that is holding a blade through the politician's neck, the man I thought was Winks thanks to their similar builds.

Bennett's eyes almost pop out of their sockets, casting to the ceiling and back down again, but when he realises he isn't dead or bleeding out, he calms a fraction.

The man with the blade speaks, low, even and easy.

'Don't move. It'll be bad for you when you move.' I don't recognise the voice. This is not one of the security team.

I've never seen anything like this. Bennett is breathing fine, no rasping, and this is exactly what happened to DC Kyle - a knife through the neck, avoiding both the windpipe and the oesophagus. With a couple of looks and a measurement with a digit, it's clear that his assailant has got this practice down to a fine art. And I was there at Kyle's post-mortem - I know precisely how delicate and precarious Bennett's position is. Any sudden move will be fatal - and at any moment, the Dog could whip that blade out through the front, and this room will get painted a lot more grimly than the exploding pens managed.

'Are you prepared to risk your life for this policy?' asks Nicolas. Bennett tries to speak, but it's obviously quite difficult with a sword through your throat - and I can't help but recall the nicks on the back of Kyle's oesophagus.

'Yes,' he whispers in a voice so scratched you can almost hear it bounce off the steel.

'That's a shame,' says Nicolas, as there's a moment of impasse. I don't think they were quite expecting him to be so resolute and committed, and he looks happier that it's his life at stake and not his child's (something I can suddenly empathise with). Who'd have thought it? A politician who actually *believes* in his promises and policies - and one who's willing to die for them at that.

Nicolas takes out his phone. 'Then we are going to have to start killing people until you do, starting with your kids. You've got two, haven't you?'

'Wait!' says Bennett as he tries to rise, but he screams in immediate agony.

Fearing I won't get another go - and fearing that it'll be my family they start to spray bullets at - I go for it.

I'm gambling.

Gambling on all sorts of things.

Gambling that they need Bennett alive for any of this to succeed its objective.

Gambling that the need to keep the knife still will keep the Dog in place.

Gambling that the confusion of my sudden movement will take Mac and Kev by surprise.

I start with Mac. He's bent forward, looking into the LCD screen on the back of the camera like the on-set cinematographer checking his framing is right - but because he's doing that and bending at the waist, stretching forward, pulling up the wool hem of the balaclava, revealing his neck. It's completely exposed right along the left-hand side.

Within that exposed piece of flesh, is the Vagus nerve direct to the brain, which is the nerve that measures the blood pressure in your arteries. Hit that nerve, and you don't even have to hit it that hard, just with precision, and you send a false signal to the brain that you've got an extremely sudden bout of high blood pressure. The brain reacts in an instant to drastically lower said pressure, but because there was no problem in the first place, it causes a massive drop in blood pressure throughout the body, and subsequent shutdown of the central nervous system.

Layman's terms? An immediate knockout.

I move at speed and strike hard and fast with the outside edge of my hand, and Mac drops, short-circuited into a crumpled heap. I don't hear him land, because I'm already onto Kev.

Since he's got his back to the partially shattered window, I gamble again - this time, that the outdoor shooter still has a bead on us, and that he's seen me move and is going to take me out. So, I push Kev by the shoulders to the window, using him as a shield. I hear the shots pummel his body before the window even shatters, chunks of glass tumbling into the window frame and to the concrete outside. The cold floods the room, as Kev becomes a dead weight in my hands, and I go down with him, rolling as I go under the edge of the bare window frame.

Two down. Result.

By the time I'm tucked against the wall, out of sight, and I turn to see what is happening in the room behind me in the aftermath of the gunfire, Nicolas Raine and the Dog are gone. Only Bennett sits there, terrified, unable to bring himself to move even a fraction, with a two-foot sword still impaled through his neck. As the falling glass rings its last, he tried to turn to look at me, but it's clearly agony for him.

I half expect his head to explode now thanks to a bullet of his own, but nothing happens. I imagine the shooter, the only one left who I suppose must be Winks, has likened executing Bennett to shooting fish in a barrel, when the fish themselves have already been speared. Like any half-decent nut job, he's going to leave him to suffer a bit longer.

'Where?' I say. His eyes go to the door.

Then the night outside is christened by gunfire so crisp you can hear the cold air split. I hear screaming from the assembly hall, now that the true gravity of the occasion has finally been realised.

Carolyn. The love of my life.

Jam Jr. My son. The chance I thought I'd missed.

Gracie and Jake. The kids who I know in this very moment I love as my own.

I need to go to them, but my duty - this stupid sense of fucking duty that has got me in so much trouble right through my life - won't let me leave Bennett. I cannot leave a wounded man. Me and the moral problem of wounded men have a troubled history.

I just have to pray that the kids and Carolyn are inside. All that gunfire was outside, and until just now, they were in the school hall. This is madness, like an awful cranked up twist on a school shooting.

Gambling again, I go to Bennett, prayers ringing again that Winks is preoccupied elsewhere, as the gunfire suggests. As I reach Bennett's side, it's so far so good.

'We need to get that out,' I say.

'Don't touch it!' he rasps. His eyes bug like a junky's at sheer euphoric peak.

'Michael, I can't leave you like this, and you can't leave it in there.'

'Don't go near it.'

'It'll be like pulling off a plaster.'

'Don't go near it,' he whispers now, on the cusp of passing out with fear, panic, pain - all of the above.

Gunfire again.

Closer. Frighteningly close.

Winks is coming to the school, clearing his path as he goes.

I stiffen. He stiffens. His eyes leave mine.

I pull it out as quickly and as straight as I can.

I stand there over him, holding the blade, as he realises what has happened. He doesn't blink, eyes wide, before they move around in their sockets with expectation.

We've got the same fear - that when I pulled it out, I hit something, ripped something, sliced something.

We stare at each other, until it's clear he's not bleeding. His throat is in one piece. He got halfway beheaded and lived to tell the tale.

'Like pulling off a plaster, right?' I say.

'I don't know who you are, but you're a maniac,' he says.

Then we're both up and running.

Chapter Forty-One

Bennett and I sprint back down the corridor to the main hall, and, through the glass fireproof panels on the door, it's obvious that everyone inside is panicking. My urge to get to my partner and my son is overwhelming - and Bennett clearly feels the same way. In this moment, across the diametrically opposed manners in which we came to this point, we're just a couple of dads in the middle of a crisis which affects our families in the most urgent and threatening of ways.

'In case you hadn't worked it out, I'm not one of them,' I say, as we peer through the glass at the ensuing mayhem. 'And what I had to say to you before will haunt me for the rest of my life.'

Inside the hall, everyone is on their feet, and chaos has taken firm hold. Some parents are pushing to the stage to grab their children, others are looking the other way to the front of the building.

'So, what are you then?' asks Bennett, while his head bobs up and down like a chicken as he frantically tries to spot his own loved ones. As his neck cranes, a thin stream of blood oozes from the visible wound in his neck.

'I'm with the National Crime Agency. Sort of.'

'Where the hell are they?'

Conceding the point, I pull out my phone. Four messages.

Blake: *Tactical Aid Unit en route.*

Okpara: *Hang in there, my brother.*

Blake: *10 minutes.*

Blake: *2 minutes. Hold on.*

I check the time on the last message. Two minutes ago. I'd imagine that a couple of vans of armed officers might accelerate the SGP's priorities, and they're probably what Winks was shooting at outside.

'They're here,' I say.

And no sooner have the words left my lips that more bullets start to fly, but this time, they're from the hall we are looking in to.

Winks has emerged from the entrance corridor at the back, and is pumping rounds into the ceiling. I still can only assume it's Winks because his balaclava is tight down over his face. He's shouting, but in the commotion I can't make out the words. The gun he carries gives all the message I need however. It's a decent looking rifle with a scope, no good for close quarters but could still put a bullet into you at 500 feet a second - bullets which are now peppering the cheap ceiling panels, raining chips and chunks of polystyrene down on the people below.

We've gone from secret intimidation to full on Nakatomi Plaza.

And now Nicolas is taking the stage. I definitely know it is Raine, because he's pealing off his balaclava. He looks ruddy and hot, but somehow puffed up like a turkey, buoyant with importance. Like this is his moment. The one he's waited for since his tour stopped and the war, for him, finished - only we know now in his mind it never did.

'Quiet! Quiet!' he bellows. 'It's Christmas, I know! I mean this is the last thing you need, isn't it?'

The crowd begins to quiet so they can hear him and face their circumstances. Stuck in a pincer movement, rock and a hard place, both with guns. You could make a break for an exit, but you'd get shot in the back.

'We don't want to hurt anybody, let me make that abundantly clear. But if we have to, my friend and I have hurt more people than I can count and we both still manage to sleep rather well at night. It isn't going to affect us that much, so don't force us into a decision *you'll* regret much more than us.'

The room is quiet, save for the harrowing percussion of sobbing children.

'In your midst, there is the spawn of a traitor. Where are the children of MP Michael Bennett?'

Bennett himself, next to me, reaches for the door handle, but I grab his arm to stop him. He looks at me with panic, but I hold fast, shaking my head. On stage, Raine has turned to the children still on either end of the raised platform, who are huddled in groups, not yet able to get to their parents.

'Which one of you lot is Michael Bennett's little girl? Is his young lad here?'

He stalks the group waiting for one to bleat and give the game away, but so far fear keeps them immobile and mute. Nicolas takes out his own pistol, and starts sticking it into crying kids' faces. 'Is it you? Maybe you?' In one callous wander through the children, rolling out threats, he's single-handedly dishing out years of psychological issues and nightmares.

'Where are your kids?' I ask Bennett.

'I don't know,' he replies breathlessly.

A crunch of glass behind us, and I grab Bennett to pull him under the tables in the computer room to our left.

'Shhh,' I hush him. 'Stay still.'

Footsteps down the corridor, and in the dim IT suite I catch a glimpse of Mac, striding past the door, his balaclava now pulled up, rubbing his neck. It was never going to take him out for good, the nerve strike, but now I wish I'd somehow done something to make the shutdown of his central nervous system more permanent.

I do a quick count of our adversaries.

Winks is in the hall.

Nicolas is in the hall.

Mac on his way to join them.

Kev is toast.

And the Dog is on the loose. In a primary school. Sweet *Jesus*.

Then Mac walks into the IT suite, carefully, each step deliberate. He must have got to the hall and realised, if we're not there, there'd be nowhere else to go.

He's cautious. Through the gaps between the chair legs, I can see him looking across the room, scrutinising every small bunch of tables. He reaches for the light, before lowering his fingers, thinking better of it. Old army rule. If you can see them, they can see you.

A howl of rage erupts next to me, and before I know what's happening, Bennett is up and screaming, charging at Mac.

'You *bastards*!' he howls. Any qualms I have about this particular politician having no backbone are fully erased, however stupid his move is. Mac knows he needs Bennett in one piece to fulfil his objective, so he lowers his gun to Bennett's moving thigh, and lets loose one round which, in the small suite filled with half size table and chairs, sounds louder than I've ever heard a pistol report.

Bennett goes down with a howl, clutching the flesh just above his knee.

'Scream all you like,' says Mac. 'You just get ready to say what we need. Now, where is the soldier?'

Bennett gasps through gritted teeth. 'Get fucked.'

Mac backhands the MP, and, using the distraction, I vault over the small table directly at the big veteran.

But Mac is wise to it, and sees me coming. He turns and fires where he senses my movement, and for a second, I don't know if he hit me or not. In confusion, I keep lunging at him, and it's only when I lift my hands up to grab his lapels do I realise I can't lift my left arm without blinding pain. It's excruciating, and as I struggle to do anything with any impact, he backhands me with the gun, right across the face. My nose has been broken many times, so I know the feeling all too well. I don't think this is a bad break, but it ain't going to look any straighter when I eventually look in the mirror again.

I stagger back, only for a second, and come forward again immediately. He's got the gun between my eyes, sticking the barrel into my forehead. It's still hot from when it was fired just seconds ago, which is just another source of pain on my body.

'I knew giving him a whack would bring you out,' says Mac. 'I thought there was something funny about you, but I couldn't place it. But it's weakness, I can see it now. You did your time, came home, and felt you hadn't finished. You're a bloody goody-two-shoes who doesn't know when it's over - who doesn't know it was all a lie. The only truth left is that you'll end up dying for that cause you can't seem to let go of, because the big difference here is that we need *him*, and we don't need *you*.'

He says it so matter-of-factly that I know my fate is sealed. He's been indoctrinated by his own new cause, radicalised by the influences around him. He's made his mind up. I'm having a bullet through the brain, no arguments. Other times in my life, I've been ready for this. Ready for this precise moment.

But not now. I've got too much to live for. I've got too much I need to see and teach.

I'm a parent now.

'Sweet dreams,' says Mac, as the gunshot rips the room.

Chapter Forty-Two

It takes me a confused moment to realise the gunfire didn't come from Mac's gun, and I'm doubly surprised to see him slump to the ground, not me. As he hits the deck, I see another gun behind him, raised in my direction, but it's in the hands of a man whose timing could never have been better if he tried (although my nose would probably appreciate it if it came a touch earlier) - it's Okpara, in a ballistic vest, holding a Heckler & Koch MP5.

'Thank you, my brother,' I say to him.

'You're both hit,' he says, lowering his weapon.

I point at Bennett, and the Maasai goes to lift him. 'I'm alright, the bullet passed through,' I say, finding an exit wound high on my left shoulder blade with my right fingers. It's been a lucky one, but will require some attention eventually. Straight through, but there's an underlying horrible dull sickliness to the sensation that convinces me that bone has been hit somewhere. 'What's the score outside?'

'Tactical aid units are here, with NCA and GMP. Any civilians that were in the entrance way when we arrived got out, but there wasn't many of them. It looks like the start of a standoff.'

'It's him they want.' I gesture to Bennett. 'You have to get him out of here.'

'I climbed in a broken window in a classroom back there. We can go out that way.'

'Good.'

'I'm not leaving my family,' says Bennett.

'Their plan is going to shit, Bennett,' I say. 'By getting you out of here,

208

we'll make sure it stays that way. If you're not here, they're more likely to try to call it quits.'

'I'm not leaving my kids.' It doesn't escape me that he doesn't mentioned his wife.

'I'll bring them to you.'

'You're staying?' Okpara asks.

'I'll be your man on the inside. All phones on.'

Okpara looks less than happy, but eventually accepts with a nod.

'If the situation looks good, and by that I mean they've decided not to start offing people, then come back with the big guns through that same window back there.'

'Got it. What's your plan?'

'I'm going to sort these bastards and put a dog on a leash.'

Okpara freezes. 'He's here?'

'In a school, yeah.'

'My God.'

'Time to move. You too Bennett, or I'll give you one of those smacks to the neck and you'll be carried out of here.'

He acquiesces, but demands, 'Bring me my children.'

'I'll do my best. What are their names?'

'Sam and Gwen.'

'Sam and Gwen, Sam and Gwen, got it. Now get gone.'

Okpara hoists Bennett up, which draws a gasp from the politician, and they start hobbling back down the corridor.

I test and stretch my shoulder. I won't be doing lat pulldowns for a while, but I'll be alright for whatever this night brings. Or at least I tell myself that.

I leave the computer room, and head back to the hall doors.

Everyone inside has been made to lie on the floor, foreheads on the lino. As I look around, I can see children and the elderly haven't been excluded from the instructions, and Nicolas and Winks are walking alongside the people on the floor, checking their faces. They're looking for people of value, namely members of the Bennett family.

So far, it seems they've been frustrated. As I think of the new geography of their predicament, I try to predict their new plan. They've suddenly got a room full of hostages, but the sure way to get Bennett back is to find his kids and trade them for him. Or, even better, threaten them until Bennett agrees to denounce legalisation.

As I look across, my stomach tightens as I spot Carolyn. Jam is lying on the floor next to her, swaddled tight in a cream fleece blanket. He doesn't appear to be upset, but my body feels the natural urge to reach to him. Winks is heading along the same row. Oh God, please.

No.

No.

His gaze pauses on Carolyn and my baby son, and he shouts for Nicolas to come over.

They must have followed me yesterday. I've gone soft, and in going soft, I've put them in mortal danger.

Nicolas tells her to stand up, or at least he must have because, although I can't hear the precise words, she gets to her feet and picks up Jam.

And on seeing her mum get picked from the crowd, Gracie, still in costume on the stage, gets up too.

No. *No.*

Nicolas Raine bellows at her, and she runs to her mum. I can't see Jake. Please be safe, Jake, *please*.

Chapter Forty-Three

I need to think of something, and that supposed genius moment of euphoric epiphany better come fast. My family have just been pulled from the crowd, and marched into the far corridor, into, if memory serves, the corridor that holds the years five and six classrooms. As they cross the threshold, and the door begins to close, I see Nicolas place a hand on Carolyn's arm and my son lets out one long plaintiff cry - which is suddenly cut off by the door swinging shut.

It's a sound that pulls a sickle across the front of my brain.

My shoulder wound is long forgotten, my shattered nose an afterthought.

Winks is stalking the middle of the room, shooting into the ceiling intermittently, keeping the threat level high - but he pauses for a moment, and pulls out a small St George's flag. It has been modified however, with a black cross over the red, diagonally from corner to corner in wobbly, smudged spray paint. He lifts the lower half of his balaclava, and wraps it around his chin like a bandana mask.

It looks like end-game behaviour. He's ready to die in that thing, and I think this lot will try to take as many people with them as they can. This is escalation.

I phone Blake. She picks up immediately.

'You're still inside,' she says, a statement not a question. Okpara and Bennett must have got back to the perimeter.

'I am.'

'I won't ask why you.'

I ignore her. 'Situation update. Three active enemies in the building.

One centrally, in the assembly hall, controlling the main bulk of the civilian hostages. I assume that's what they are now.'

'You'd be right.'

'One is in the south-east corridor - years five and six, with three members of my family. A woman, an eight year old girl and a baby.'

'Jesus.'

'The third is unaccounted for - but it's the Dog. Nicolas Raine is not the Dog of the Moors.'

'*Jesus.*'

'I'm in the south-west corridor at the entrance to the hall.'

'OK. Eyes?'

'On the hall.'

'OK, give me a sec to relay this to operational command.'

The line is quiet for a moment. Every last bit of me wants to back out of the building, go around the side, sneak in and take Nicolas Raine's head off for even dreaming of touching the woman I love.

But I've been on too many operations, in too many situations where the odds are so precarious that even the smallest thing might tip them, to know that my position - and my skillset - might save multiple lives by taking instruction and staying cool. I breathe, wait, and hope he hasn't touched them.

If he has…

Blake comes back on the line almost as an act of mercy, breaking the thought that was about to form.

'We're trying to get a line into the building, but they're not talking yet. If they had demands, usually they'd be getting ready to give them to us by now, but so far nothing.'

'I'm not sure the Dog is that bothered by the cause or whether he just sees it as a way to legitimise mayhem. If it's the former, then we need eyes and ears on the rear of the school, particularly the fields. When we were on our way over, that was our designated exit after the operation, with transport waiting for us across the first field where a road intersects the farmland. This might be the closest we've ever got to actually catching the Dog, so we have to do everything we can to bring him in.'

'Agreed, but the priority is the hostages.'

'Right. Can you cause a diversion? There's not that many of them, and I think I can get a few out in dribs and drabs through the window Okpara got out of.'

'I'll see what I can do. Where's clear?'

'North west corridor. Nobody there to my knowledge.'

'Hold on.' I listen, while Blake turns from the phone and speaks to somebody, I'm assuming in a command capacity, then she comes back on the line. 'OK, get ready.'

'Now?!'

'You weren't hoping to wait for a break in the calendar were you?'

I hold fast, before a small explosion crunches on the other side in the north west hallway. In the assembly hall, Winks' head cocks up. He appears to debate with himself, what the right thing to do is, but he can't persuade himself not to check it out.

While casting the rifle barrel across the prostrate bodies on the floor, he walks backwards to the corridor.

'Tear gas,' says Blake.

'One's on his way,' I reply.

'We'll have bodies at the window ready for them.'

I watch and listen, and as soon as I hear the door to the gassed corridor thump shut, I crack open the hall door and whisper to the nearest people. 'Keep low - come on!'

A mad scramble erupts around the doorway, never more than two feet off the ground, reminiscent of an urgent game of Twister. 'One at a time,' I hiss. 'Stay calm, classroom at the end of the corridor, out the window.'

I count as best I can, and it's at about thirty people when a volley of bullets takes out the glass of the door, scratching shards across my face. It hurts like hell, but I just add that to my injury tab, which I'll cover later.

'Get back in here now!' screams Nicolas from across the hall. My family isn't with him, which devastates me. The people halfway through the door push through, glass ringing out everywhere, and make the sprint down the corridor.

'I said *stop*!' he screams. I'm dragging a man in his fifties through the

213

door by his lapels, when Nicolas fires again. The bullet goes through the back of his neck, and hurtles out of his jaw, splitting it vertically as it went. The man slumps dead as blood drenches the front and back of his once-dapper pale blue festive jumper, and the situation ramps up a series of notches with its first fatality.

First fatality I know about - but I can't think like that.

I pull the man through, as a gross maroon smear follows him in. He's dead before I even stop dragging.

Real, grief-stricken screaming kicks off in the hall, and I'm looking at the man knowing that, by opening the door to let him in, I consigned him to this violent early death. It's another layer of guilt that I'll have to somehow learn to live with.

In the hall there's the sound of arguing voices, but again it's hard to pick the words out over the screaming - and I know that once they've worked out what's happened, they'll come down this corridor, looking for me. I head back into the IT suite and hunker down in the darkness again - and that's when I notice a real stroke of luck. Mac's gun, in the moonlight, is lying on the keyboard between one of the screens. He must have flung it there while taking a bullet from Okpara. It's a Glock 19 with only a few shots gone from the magazine, and it looks in decent order. It's a model I'm familiar with, and its weight feels perfectly natural in my hand. *Bingo*.

I could make a stand with Mac's gun, but that would only result in a firefight with hostages in between us. The smart move would be to back out, and reconvene with Blake and Okpara. Me being in here has already got one person killed.

But giving up this position means giving up the pressure - and I can't do that. I breathe out, trying to come up with something, and try to put the innocent man's death out of my mind. Glancing to the heavens for some kind of guidance, against all odds, I'm granted some immediately.

A skylight.

Chapter Forty-Four

I'm on the roof creeping between skylights which rest in wide rows, casting glances down at the scenes beneath them, and I've built a picture that I relay to Blake outside via the phone. I'm careful because of the light snowfall - falling off a roof now would be one of the more useless and embarrassing ways to go - and I canvas the whole floorplan in no time. I can't see my family, however. Nor the Dog.

Winks and Nicolas are still in the main hall, pacing the lines of hostages, now threatening them with more force than before. The escalation is alarming, but I'm trying to be smart and calm, and stop more people from getting killed.

From the front of the roof, I can see that the tactical aid units have established a proximity that is bordered handily by the blue-painted iron school gates and fencing, beyond which the scene is managed by what looks like uniformed members of Cheshire police. Blake and Okpara are in a huddle with a woman in tactical wear, and a plainclothes officer in a high visibility jacket, the four of which I'm assuming comprise the command unit. Beyond that, cars line the road in all directions, and a crowd has formed where two roadblocks set up at either end of the 'school warning' road-markings. Two helicopters buzz high overhead, only one of which look to be police. While I can't see the vans themselves, further down the road I can see the roof-mounted satellite dishes of news trucks.

This has quickly become a national incident.

Blake and I have been keeping the line open, while I report info to her on the fly. She comes back on.

'We've got Nicolas Raine on the line, can you see him?'

I shift back to a spot over the hall, and peer through the skylight. I spot him. 'Yeah, I've got him. He's on the phone. What's he after?'

'He seems to have dropped all pretense of the original plan. Not even asking for Bennett.'

That's good. It means that getting him out worked. 'So how does he want this to end?'

'He wants full extradition out of the country with five million pounds, and he's given us a list of soldiers he assures us were tried and imprisoned unlawfully.'

'And what if he doesn't get that?'

'Everyone in the building dies.'

'Oh, lovely.'

As I watch him, I see that he's been clutching, in his non-phone hand, a white rag, which he opens like a handkerchief. It's another modified St George Cross.

'He's going on about the country. About how we've let it become a genetic cesspool, and how we've allowed the good white Brits to be pushed down the chain of importance by lesser species. Those are his words, not mine, I hasten to add.'

'What are you thinking?'

'I'm thinking he's prepared to die for his ideologies.'

'Me too. We've got to do something.'

The fact I can't see my family is driving me insane, and keeps catching up with me.

'Can you do me a favour?' I ask.

'Speak.'

'Can someone go and check the north-east corridor, see if you can see my family?'

Muffled speaking.

'Okpara's on his way.'

'Thank you. I'll keep myself useful.'

'OK.'

I see Okpara, ballistic vest and automatic rifle over his shoulder, hop the fence and hurdle through the trees off the school path, heading through the school grounds to the corridor in question. 'If they move towards his position,' I say. 'I'll shout.'

I swap skylights for one a few over, so I can get a better angle on the doors of the hallway I want them nowhere near - but as I get closer, I notice a red light has started flickering through one of the skylights behind me. One I'd already looked down, and determined I was looking into the pitch-black void of an unused store room.

'Tell him to hold on for a minute,' I say into the phone, as I walk towards it. 'I've seen something.'

The phone drifts down to my side, as confusion takes hold. It looks like a disco light. I can now see some red and greens kaleidoscoping along the frame of the glass. *What in the hell?*

I peek my head over the edge and look down.

Oh my *God*.

The Dog is still here. And the situation is infinitely more dire than I thought.

Chapter Forty-Five

The room below is not big, but I can now see it quite clearly, thanks to the wall-mounted disco light that flashes rainbow strobes around the small place. The floor is padded, with mats lining the entirety of the enclosed space, and there's a tower of soft play blocks stacked by the wall, as well as a basket of teddies. I know what this is, because I've seen it in hospitals where some of the boys were struggling with PTSD. It's a sensory room, designed as a soothing safe space for children with behavioural or learning difficulties.

On one side, kneels the Dog, like a sensei in a dojo. He's removed his mask now, and I can see the top of his head, not the face. Light hair, short and spiked, but that's all I can see.

And on the other, kneel three quivering, blindfolded school boys, their arms tied behind their backs.

I'm appalled, sickened and bile rises in horror.

He's talking to them calmly. I've no idea what the Dog is saying, but he looks almost calm and understanding. The look of the scene below me is all wrong.

He's gesticulating with his hands to the boys, with wide, expansive, expressive gestures. One of the boys is shaking, and I can see clearly and to my complete horror that it is Jake. Carolyn's Jake. And from now on, *my* Jake.

No wonder I couldn't see him before. He had been hijacked by the Dog of the Moors.

It makes my decision all the clearer, in that there suddenly isn't one to make. I shut the phone off, jump in the air directly over the skylight, and stamp down onto the glass as fiercely as a can.

With a thud and no shortage of surprise, it holds fast. I jump immediately again, and this time, it goes, and I rain into the sensory room in a hail of glass and gentle snow. I land with awkwardness on straight limbs, but the padded floor stops me from breaking my legs or ankles. I'm getting my bearings, as the boys shout in terror. They can't see me, bless them, and I have to get them out of this room.

'Stay where you are!' I shout with as much authority as I can, but the Dog is bolting for the door. I grab his ankle as he pulls the handle, and light from the entrance corridor hits his face.

No *shit*.

I've got a positive ID on the Dog of the Moors, maybe the first person ever to do so.

And it's someone I've met before.

It's Helen Broadshott's driver. The very man that dropped us off tonight. The man who helped us escape yesterday. The man with the van is Ricardo Bartoni's all-time object of obsession.

As my mind springs recognition, he introduces a boot sole to my already pancaked nose. I have no choice but to reel back, but my hands have a hold. And I won't let go.

The slippery psychopath, this blight of humanity has revealed himself, betrayed himself. He couldn't bare being around the vulnerable without at least trying to have a little fun.

I'll show him some fun.

Try blindfolding me, you sick sack of shit.

I feel myself roaring without really knowing I'm doing it. The strike to the face only serves to embolden me and make me infinitely stronger, like when a boxer tastes his own blood. This fucker's coming in, and he's coming in with me - and I'm going up to Dick Barton's ice cream shop tomorrow morning to offer him this freak's balls as a trophy.

I yank him closer via his outstretched leg, and he has no choice but to hop towards me with splayed legs.

I'm not a Queensbury rules man. I've been in enough scenarios where you can't play fair just for the sake of form - and this guy has never played fair in his entire miserable existence.

So I punch him in the balls as hard as I possibly can.

He makes a sound like a hamster being stepped on, and I follow it with a forearm strike across his own nose. Under my speeding elbow, I feel it crunch and move, and once it's past his face, I see his conk is pointing in a direction so adventurous it would require a compass and set square to establish its angle.

Usually, that kind of strike makes a person fall into themselves so severely that whimpering is the strongest thing they can do.

But that does not apply to the Dog of the Moors.

This person is more supernatural animal than human.

He replies with a rageful cry of his own, this one more imbued with outrage and contempt than mine. He believes his own superiority. He created it, he lives in it, he believes in it.

He uses it to swipe across me face at a speed and ferocity I was not anywhere near ready for, and with it I feel a series of red flashes across my face, and the heat of blood oozing down my cheeks from multiple wounds. I didn't even see what he was holding, but it did the job.

Blood floods my eyes. I can't see anything, not really, and I feel the claret flow freely. I respond with punches, but I don't know where to direct them. I can hear the boys behind me whimpering, I can feel their fear.

I can't fail them.

The Dog wins it by slipping something into my stomach. It's not a long blade, but it goes in without argument. I gasp because the feeling is categorically unpleasant. I don't know the extent of my injury, but like any warrior who doesn't know he's dead, I keep throwing. I hit him hard in the jaw, which spins his head. He shakes, ragged, but holds consciousness. For a second, I admire his granite chin - and whatever it is he pushed into me falls out.

'You crafty bastard,' he says, with a genuine, honest-to-god *smile*. Then he pushes me back, and I fall. My hands go to him, but they don't work. The black comes in at the edges of my vision, like I'm playing with the vignette setting on my own personal image filter.

My eyes flicker, I grit the molars, and when I try to get a fix on him, he's gone. He's a ghost of crap strip light, wafting through a doorway into a tiny disco.

Before I know it, I'm on my back, and there's three young lads around me. But they can't touch me. They're still bound.

One of them rests his head on my chest. I don't know who it is, but they gasp into my jacket, 'Thank you. Thank you.' My arms come up around the child's back, and before I know it I'm holding all three of them.

'Jake?' I say.

One of them says, 'Ben?'

'Yeah.'

He buries his head into me. 'I want to go home for Christmas.'

That hurts, and it's not thanks to the physical injuries. 'Ok buddy, let's do it.'

This beautiful kid is going to get his Christmas.

I pull myself up, bash the darkness away, and reach for the nearest kid's blindfold. It's not Jake, but he could be. In terms of where my heart is, they're all kids of mine now. His mucky blonde hair is matted with sweat, and the blindfold comes away easy.

'What's your name, my mate?' I ask.

'Logan.'

'OK Logan, when I get your hands free, can you help your mates?'

'Yeah,' he says through a brave sniffle.

I get his hands free - his hands and wrists being so small I find it alto-gether shocking. 'Alright buddy, let's do this.'

'OK, Ben.'

I grab the kid I've now worked out is Jake, while Logan helps the other one. 'It's me,' I tell him. 'I've got you, mate. It's all finished now.' He cries into my shoulder, and when I remove his blindfold, there's a sudden salty squirt down his shepherd costume.

I manage to undo all their restraints, Logan helping the last boy who tells us tearfully his name is Shahid. We walk out of the sensory room, which will now occupy the stuff of nightmares, and head to the entrance, past the twinkling Christmas tree, the sense of the surreal fully realised. Through the front door, out into the swirl of breeze and icy flakes, to the assembled forces at the gate. My legs are hammering thanks to the fall, and my heart is almost too full. Halfway up the path,

Blake runs through the gate to assist us. Logan and Shahid, on seeing a female face offering calm and safety, run to her and grip her like they may never let go.

Jake is doing the same - but to me. I lower so we're eye to eye, man to man.

'You're a brave one, you,' I say.

His brow splits and his mouth stretches to form a sob, and he hugs me around the neck. I stroke his hair as he chokes a couple of times into my throat.

'Easy, mate. Easy,' I whisper to him. 'I need to pop back in, and get your mum and your brother and sister, OK? Then we'll have that Christmas, alright?'

'Promise?' I feel snot on my cheek, but I don't care.

'Promise.' I stand and address Blake, who's looking at me like her own maternal sense is firing on all cylinders. 'You've got Jake, Shahid and Logan here. They need a little TLC, can you get them somewhere that'll have that?'

'Of course. They can sit in the big van, would you like that lads?'

They are in too much shock to reply, they just huddle into each other.

'I need to go back in,' I whisper to Blake, leaning in.

'You need medical attention immediately. I mean, have you seen yourself?'

'Can't say I have.' My neck falls, exhausted, and my eyes dip lower. I'm shocked to see I've left a pool of blood at my feet. Something is open, and it's not stopping.

'Okpara's gone to the north-east corridor. He's not checked in yet.'

'Get him on the phone, and tell him to hold fast. We'll pincer them. And tell them to accept whatever they want. Lie to them. Tell them their mates are getting released, and the chopper's on the way.'

'OK. What are you going to do now?'

I pull Mac's pistol from inside my jacket. 'I'm going to…'

I literally can't think of what to say, because I don't know.

'Insert witty Christmas-themed action movie one-liner here?' Blake says.

'Yeah. When you think of something, let me know what it was.'

I turn, gun raised, and shamble back into the building.

Chapter Forty-Six

Head down, back into the warmth, hobbling past that sodding Christmas tree again, and I'm getting into one of those moods. One of those frames of mind where I'll stop at nothing and no course of action is improbable - although I still need to make myself keep it together. Keep fighting smart. The end is in sight.

Santa's coming.

Arriving at the double doors to the assembly hall, I crouch with difficulty and look inside. Same story in there. Winks and Nicolas, now both wearing the SGP colours as masks, are stood on the stage, watching over the forced congregation. Nicolas is on the phone. I hope he's receiving the good news, and that Blake has convinced those in charge to tell them what they want. At the back of the stage, so far removed I almost missed them, are two kids, tear-streaked. I only need one half-decent glance to make the connection, and it's not through anything as obvious as bone structure or hair colour. It's all in their eyes. The fire and fervour, like they begrudgingly accept that they're too young and small to alter the course of these events themselves. They're Bennett's kids. Sam and Gwen. They found them.

They obviously still think, on some level, their objective can be achieved.

But why a chopper? Where would they take a helicopter? They're notoriously short-range vehicles, albeit quick with it. It obviously means they've given up on escaping via the back road, now the Dog has scarpered.

So where are they headed? The two of them, sitting there, they'll be listening out for it.

Listening.

They'll be listening.

Bingo.

I run back to the headmaster's office, which is situated directly opposite the tree in the hall. There. The door plaque reads Headmaster Bill Clay, and I push through. Luckily, it's not locked, and I check the desk.

It's something Jake had said, wasn't it? Or was it Grace? About Clay being a bit full on, always interrupting lessons with his voice for pointless announcements. He's got one of those microphones hooked up to a PA, through which you can speak to the whole school.

There, right between his computer monitor and the phone. A microphone unit. I pick it up, and check it out. Two buttons, and a plastic stalk with the receiver on the top. One button has a little alarm symbol, and the other has the universal mic symbol.

I take my phone and do a YouTube search for helicopter sounds. Immediately, I'm offered loads, so I pick the top one and listen. The juddering of rotors rings through the tiny speakers. It's perfect, so I hold the phone to the mic and press button number two.

I hear the muffled thud of rotors echoing throughout the school.

I wish I could see what's going on in the hall. With any luck, they're looking up at the ceiling, thinking that their ride is here. And with a bit further luck, I'm hoping they're abandoning their post. I keep it there for a full thirty seconds, before letting go of the mic's transmit button. I run back down the hall to check, and whatever this Christmas has to offer, for me, Santa has been.

They're both gone.

Chapter Forty-Seven

It's time to get these people out of here and bring this fiasco to an end. I throw open the hall door, pistol raised, and start waving towards myself, whispering as loud as I can, 'Come on, go, *GO*! Now!' Before the mass exodus, I manage to slip inside the hall, and push a small chair in front of the door, wedging it open. The tide of people goes one way, and I go the other, gun up covering them, heading towards the north-east corridor where the door is still swinging slowly shut after Winks and Nicolas' exit. As I get closer, I check back to see how all the hostages are getting on.

The room is emptying. They're going to make it.

All except for the man in the Christmas jumper, whose blood I can see leaking under the other door into the hall.

Can't think of that now. Got to finish this.

I stay low, and push the door open gingerly. Listening for anything. Any signs of life. They must be looking for the roof access. When they showed me the schematic in the car, when we were going through the final plans, I remember that this particular corridor had a rear exit that leads out onto a small play area that has a locked service cage, which houses the boilers and associated pipework - and roof access.

But as soon as I'm about to start turning the corner to head down into the corridor, and hopefully find my family, I hear them start to return.

The left-hand wall has a door marked *boys*, so I duck inside and leave it ajar, my right eye and the pistol barrel the only things looking through. I can smell urinal cakes and briefly check the space around me, but only find a selection of small porcelain thrones.

Surprise is going to be the big one here. I think I can get off two shots if I'm quick.

Suddenly, they are crossing my vantage point, masks still on, and I immediately step through, releasing the first shot - which hits Winks cleanly in the shaven side of his head, right where the military bare blade meets the longer blond on top. A puff of almost-purple splatters the coats on the racks opposite the toilet door, and before his body's down I'm out fixing on the second man, Nicolas Raine - except he's stood there holding the hands of a couple of small children, one either side, who now look at me with incomprehension so dense and blank there's almost no other emotion at all.

I just executed a man in front of them. In front of some children - no older than ten. And they're not just any children, they're Michael Bennett's children.

All I can do is save my horror at myself for another time, as Nicolas lets go of the children, and his hands dart to his jacket. I rush at him, but he's too fast, the old battle-readiness still never very far away.

I'd been softened by the sight of the children. Becoming a family man, and a father, has robbed me of my edge. I truly hope it doesn't rob them of their lives too.

His Glock is out just as I reach him, and I have to hold back. I'm holding my gun, but I don't want to point it anywhere near these children, so all I can do is stand there impotent.

'You fucking idiot,' snarls Nicolas, his breath fluttering the modified St George over his mouth and nose. 'We weren't sure whether to trust you, so Mac kept an eye on you. Too good to be true, you were. So we kept tabs on you, from the minute you left Helen's flat with the H.'

'Mac's dead,' I say.

Nicolas' eyes blink twice, then drift to Winks on the floor. 'These boys. These brilliant boys were with me every step of the way. And to think they survived all the hellholes of Helmand Province, only to come home to bleed out on the floor of a primary school.'

'I went to those same hellholes… but I never came back to make my country worse.'

'Your country…' He takes off the mask, and I can see the anguish across his features. He's flushed with exertion and the stress of the occasion, and

226

his mouth is curled in a grimace of pure distaste. He spits into the mask, and throws it to the ground. 'Your country is a joke. It's a sovereign-less state of mayhem and impurity. If I'd have known this is what I was coming back to, I'd have walked into one of those filthy Afghan villages and taken out as many as I could. You don't even believe in *this*, do you?'

'Your ideology makes me sick,' I say. 'Everything about you and your politics turns my stomach.'

'I knew it.'

'Broadshott is finished.'

He smiles. 'She'll never be finished. She's too good that one.'

'Her apartment was raided today by GMP and the NCA. She's done, she just doesn't know it yet.'

There it is. The first crack. He'd been flying on bravado and self-important purpose, bolstered by his believe in the righteousness of his crusade.

'We're going to undo everything you've been working for,' I say.

'I don't know why you're so bothered. You're a disgraced soldier. Your record is worse than ours.'

'The difference is, I've been trying to atone. I'm been trying to make up for my mistakes. You haven't.'

He actually smiles. 'Then maybe we're not that dissimilar. We've both been trying to save the country, in our own separate ways.'

It's my turn to grimace. 'I'm nothing like you.'

'He's right - he's not. Hands up.' The words are out but Nicolas didn't say them. It's only when I see Okpara move around the corner behind Nicolas with the semi-auto rifle raised, that I realise it was him - and I couldn't be happier to see him. Twice now, he's appeared just when I needed him. I owe him a couple of rounds in Mulligan's, that's for sure.

Nicolas smiles weakly, and begins to turn. His gun begins to rise with it. I pick up my own and beckon the kids over.

'Come on, you two.' They walk towards me, still blank with shock. The boy, eyes saucered, with a thatch of light brown, poker-straight hair, can't stop looking at Winks' grey matter all up those bright coats. As soon as he's near enough, I grab him and pull him to me. 'In the hall, now.' I push them through the door. 'Ollie, I have no powers of arrest - can you place this man into custody?'

'With pleasure,' he says. 'Fancy that, hey, Nicolas Raine - arrested by a brown man. Who'd have thought it?'

Nicolas tenses - and that's when I see it in his hand. It's tiny, silver, nothing more than an attendance clicker at a carnival entrance way.

'You've got me,' he says. And his arms begin to lift in surrender.

I see wire snake down his wrist. It's a detonator. I don't know what he's got it linked to, but I've got no doubt he's gonna pull the trigger and send us all to hell.

I'm thinking. It can't be a big explosive. He has no bag and there's no obvious huge weight attached to his body. It won't take the school down with it. It must be C4 designed for close proximity to target, given that anything more would require more size than I can see. Yet there's literally no other reason he'd have a detonator, other than to light himself up.

It strikes me that, for all the ideologies he has fallen into fighting, he's adopted similar methods of entering the afterlife. Approaching martyrdom with as many people as he can take with him.

'You're prepared, are you? To die for this cause?' I say.

He knows I've caught his plan.

'What was it you said? About the people that used concealed suicide bombs? Worthless, godless rats?'

I've hit a nerve there, from the way his back has straightened. He knows I've punctured his rationale. I wave my hands to Okpara, and mouth the word 'BOMB' has vividly as I can. He gets it immediately, and takes three steps back. And I take three steps forward, using Nicolas' indecision to my advantage. That wire, down his wrist. It's slack. I think it has length.

I take that left hand, and pray it's not pressure activated to a release circuit, drag his right shoulder and pull him back. As soon as I move, Okpara turns and runs. I swing Nicolas behind me and throw him backwards, straight through the door of the kiddies' toilet. He crashes backwards through the opening, as I slip the detonator from his finger hoping there's enough wire. The split second the little door shuts, I push the clicker.

The explosion is huge in the small space, even though it's muffled by the toilet walls - all of which blow outwards in a burst of chipboard, porcelain and urinal cakes. I'm blown back several feet, landing hard into the brain-covered coats, and end up in a heap on top of Winks' body.

Everything is fuzzy for a couple of moments, then I see the welcome sight of Okpara over me, pulling away a huge chunk of what I realise now is a blue cubicle door. 'My friend, are you OK?'

'My friend, I believe I am. Just about.'

'Raine?'

'Martyrdom.'

'It's over?'

'Over.'

But it's not. My family.

Where are they?

I start to drag myself to my feet. It's bloody hard, and Okpara helps me. 'My family,' I say. 'My *family*.' I start to run but again it's more of a hobble.

'West, West!' he says, as I run around the corner to the only classroom I can't see. 'Stop!'

He's trying to stop me from seeing. He's trying to stop me from seeing a sight that will destroy me forever, the last thing I see before I go to bed, and the first thing I see when I wake up, for the rest of time.

Please, no…

'*Wait!*' he shouts, as I run into the classroom, my heart fit to burst. Whatever it is I have to see, I'm going to take it like a man.

The classroom is dim, but I can see them. Grace, slumped against Carolyn, herself up against the classroom wall, dinosaur pictures all around her. Ben Bracken Jr is in her arms.

He's burbling softly. *They* are smiling. Grace jumps up when she sees me.

'You came!' she throws her arms around me, as I fall to my knees.

'I did. Wouldn't miss it for the world,' I say. I'm sobbing, and I pull myself over to Carolyn. 'Are you OK?' I ask.

'Yes,' she says, the tears coming for her now too. 'We're all fine. Your friend untied us.' She points to a bunch of cut cable ties at her feet.

I look behind me to see Okpara standing in the doorway, smiling. 'I was trying to tell you there's no rush.'

I try to say thank you, but no sound comes out. I take my boy, and cuddle him like it's the first time I've held him. I'm not sure I'll ever let him go.

Five minutes later, we are walking out into evening air, the stench of explosives and charred flesh blown away in an instant, as the swirling snowfall catches the twirling reds and blues of the police lights, lending the scene the air of a festive winter disco. As NCA officers and tactical aid operatives swarm in the opposite direction to enter the building, I walk to the gates, holding my son. On my right, is Carolyn, with Grace and the two Bennett kids under her wings. Okpara walks behind me.

Blake is the first through the school gate, running down towards us with Jake, who runs to his mother. Blake grabs Okpara, and kisses him, any professional pretenses forgotten. Michael Bennett and his wife Henrietta run down to their own kids. And as we get to the gate itself, there sits Jeremiah. The snow lights in his hair, and the scarf around his neck blows wildly behind him like a wartime aviator.

'You mad, useful bastard,' he says to me, with a smile on cheeks rosy as St Nick's.

All I can do, is hug him.

EPILOGUE

As I came to learn in the days after, the SGP security team all died in Moorehill Primary School, following their ill-gotten and ill-advised ideology. Helen Broadshott was arrested, her deeds quickly becoming seasonal tabloid fodder, and the St George Patriots disbanded in a full disintegration following the loss of its leader and her enforcers. The Dog of the Moors, however, was never found, the only trace left being the scars, wounds and holes the doctors are trying to heal. I try not to think of him, but it's not easy.

And as for me, Christmas wasn't cancelled, but when I try to recall it in years to come, there won't be much of it I remember. It passes me by as a morphine-induced swirl, a sickly palette of images I can barely focus on, yet somehow see that they mean a lot to me.

All I know is there's people around me I love. Santa clearly made it because there's wrapping paper and toys, I'm in a hospital, Carolyn, Jam, Gracie and Jake are here, and I'm smiling.

The two older children take turns holding my hand, as if I might evaporate without human touch. Carolyn keeps kissing my forehead, and whispering in my ear, all things naughty and nice, and everything in between. And Jam holds my thumb with his entire chubby fist.

They're alive.

And that's good enough for me.

Merry Christmas to all, and to all a good, opiated night.

THE END

Acknowledgements

Huge thanks to all at Lume Books who support me in every way imaginable. Thank you to all the amazing bloggers who read my work, encourage me endlessly and share their thoughts - and special thanks to Dan Stubbings for beta-reading like a true wingman.

Immense gratitude to Mike Craven, Trevor Wood and Rob Scragg for their words, with a special mention to Heleen Kist for both her endorsement and amazing suggestions, all of which made this book so much better - and thanks to all the authors who have lent their support and encouragement. And to my family and friends, on all sides and distances - true, unending thanks and love to you all.

Lastly, you there, holding this book - thank YOU.

Lightning Source UK Ltd.
Milton Keynes UK
UKHW041619230821
389329UK00004B/639